Nomaswazi

BUSISEKILE KHUMALO

NOMASWAZI

This book is a work of fiction. Names, characters, businesses, organizations, places, events and incidents either are the product of the author's imagination or are used fictitiously. Any resemblance to actual persons, living or dead, events, or locales is entirely coincidental.

For information contact : **http://www.busisekilekhumalo.com**

Book Cover and layout design by West Park Design

(**www.westparkdesign.co.za** | 066 223 0319)

ISBN: 9780620797320

First Edition : May 2019

Dear Reader

As corny as it may sound, first of all I'd like to thank you for entrusting your imagination to my hands. I hope I do justice to your expectations. Now before you read, I want to apologize for my language, I try hard not to swear but it's like that drunk uncle who's always swearing lives in my mind. Also you'll come along quite a handful of Swati terms, don't panic I'm also learning siSwati. The dilemma starts with Swati words which are spelt like English words for instance *Babe* which is a constant throughout the story is not the English term of endearment but siSwati for father. This is the same for *Make* which is Swati for mother. You will notice I put the words in Italics, as I have done throughout the book to differentiate them from English. Now to avoid the monotony of brackets, I created a translation page which you'll find at the end of the book should you not understand the phrases or the context in which they are used.

That's all for housekeeping. Please feel free to post your reviews online. You can freely interact with me via social media on the following handles:

I'm on Facebook my account is Busisekile Khumalo, on Instagram my handle is busiee_nichol and on Twitter my handle is Busisekile Khumalo @khumalo_busie. My e-mail address is ***nicholkhumalo@gmail.com***

Dear Death

I have had many encounters with you
All the times you have left me hanging
Almost like teaching me a lesson...
Who is Boss?
Fuck you ... I am not your friend
You have stripped me of my loved ones ... Granted
You are even ahead
But know that I am not going down without a fight
Your awareness of my strength and power, has caused you to send your cousins
Sure I have met them... namely sickness, anxiety, stress, fear even mild depression
They won their battles
I must admit at times I have felt so defeated I wanted to give up
I got news for you ... the war is not over
Dearest death I do not walk alone
I walk among the shoulder of giants, angels you can't fuck with
So there .... Death .... In your face!!!
Don't call me ... I will call you when I am damn ready.

"In order to win in life, you have to stop fighting and surrender to your enemy"

- Khosi Nkanyezi Buthelezi

Chapter One

I've never been strapped to the rails in the path of a moving train. I imagine, your life passes through your eyes in a flash and you excrete body fluids as the rails rattle from the weight of the oncoming train. You look at it wide-eyed and try to scream through your gag. With a racing pulse you pray for some miracle that the train stops before it hits you but in your heart of hearts you know it's too late. That's exactly how I've been feeling all morning like I'm stuck in a horror movie and my oncoming train is that beautiful monster.

My day starts on a well enough note, my alarm jarring me awake from a deep dreamless sleep. I stretch, wiping the drool from the corner of my mouth. Jo'burg City is already up and buzzing at 5am. I can hear the blaring sounds of taxi horns from our two-bedroom flat. The only thing that can successfully wipe away sleep fog from my mind is a cold shower. *Babe*, my father, always teased me about how deep of a sleeper I am.

Just thinking about him pierces my heart but the pain has lessened over the years to a constant dull ache in my heart. Like a zombie, I mechanically strip off my Minnie Mouse pajamas, which my roommate always makes fun of. According to Akhona, they are the sole reason I am single at twenty-four. If only she knew, but of course no one knows the reason that had me running to the City of Gold.

I've been running away from my past life and after six years, I am finally settling into my new life. My past life locked and buried or so I thought but I'm getting ahead of myself. There I am shimmying out of my full cotton panties. Don't judge; they are the most comfortable panties in the world. I get under the shower and abruptly open the tap. I yelp as the icy shards of water hits my body and only then am I fully conscious.

I squeeze a generous portion of sheer butter organic shampoo in my hand before I roughly massage it into my coarse afro. I make a mental note to book an appointment with Ochiame, my hairdresser. I need to get my unruly mass of coarse hair under the lock of cornrows at least. Braids would last longer but they cost a whooping R500 that I can't afford to spare. More so now that I am saving for college.

After a quick scrub down, I rinse my body careful not to let any soapy suds into my ever-sensitive eyes.

As I vigorously rub down my body to get some warmth into my limbs, I catch sight of my body on the vanity mirror. As always, I stare distastefully at my flat stomach. In my mind all I see are the bulges and rolls of fat that used to constitute my midsection. You would too, if at grade seven you were already wearing size forty jeans and gained weight with each year after that until you were eighteen. I shut down my mind before I go down the name calling memory lane but not fast enough to shut out "*nkhomo*".

You'd think that now as a size thirty-two I love my body more but no, I still hate these curves and these jugs with everything in me. My stretch marks are fading thanks to the five oils that I religiously smear all over my body twice daily. They are greasy and leave my clothes oily, but they get the job done. With the towel snug around me I brush my teeth frowning over my dark gums. They are almost black, sharply contrasting my pearl white teeth.

I always make it a point to make my bed and leave my bedroom spotless. Unlike Akhona, her room is always messy, and things get swallowed in the piles around her bed. It's a miracle she even finds her bed every night, although she sleeps out most nights. Thank God her man friends never come back with her. Beautiful, yellow and skinny Akhona with legs for days. Model Akhona. Soul of the party

Akhona, is such a pig. Vivacious and loving to a fault, but still a pig. I used to clean for her but gave up along the way. She enjoys her "organized chaos". I'm grateful for her though because without her I wouldn't be able to afford the R3400 Trentbridge flat in Berea. She insists on me only paying R1400 because I have the smaller room even though I would swear our rooms are basically the same size.

I met Akhona when I was 20 and working at an up market nightclub in Sandton. Some guy slipped something in her drink and I saw him. When she was about to drink, I hurriedly knocked off the drink from her, effectively drenching her and her companions. She threw a fit, I apologized and explained myself. I have never seen a girl as tiny as her executing such a mean right hook and the poor guy was probably emasculated for life. I lost my first real paying gig that day and gained a friend for life.

I make breakfast like I always do: poached eggs, toast, pork sausages and a glass of orange juice. I put Akhona's breakfast in the microwave making sure it's twice the size of mine. I know she will start off with a bowl of Muesli before wolfing down the breakfast as well, yet she never gains an ounce of fat. Life! I take out my bag, the Gucci one which is my absolute favorite, perks of having a model friend. Sadly, I can't fit into most of the clothes she gets from her gigs, so I get the bags, shoes, scarves and sunglasses. Akhona has taught me to dress tastefully even though my clothes aren't designer labels like hers. I am still uncomfortable wearing pants so this morning I am wearing my high waist skirt. Akhona says it accentuates my waistline and that black is slimming. I pair it with the light peach almost cream Armani blouse that she bought me for Christmas and the nude pencil heels she discarded after her last fashion show. I feel confident enough to face the world. As always, I peek into her room.

"Good morning buttercup. I left your breakfast in the microwave and the milk is in the fridge. I'm off to work love you mwaaaah!" my voice chirpy as always.

"Go away!" she mumbles her groggy morning voice deep. Another daily ritual.

I grin as I let myself out and go to queue for the taxi at the bus stop. Nothing out of the ordinary during my ride in the local taxi which drops me off as usual at the MTN Noord taxi rank where I queue again for the connecting taxi to Germiston. In the taxi I have to drown out this man next to me who is trying to make advances on me. Forget that I'm sworn off from men, his nicotine stinking breath and stained large teeth are a huge turnoff. Worse; he makes it a point to talk all up in my face while his saliva rains out of his mouth. I cringe inwardly. Fortunately, I got the window seat, so I face the window blocking him out then listen to Sands' husky gravelly voice blasting in my ears:

□

Udlala kabi um' udlala ngenhlitiyo
Ung'tsintsa kabi, um' utsints' imizwa yami
Udlala kabi uma uts' uyangtsandza
Keph' uts' angkhulume ng'tsini
Uma song'tsintsa le nalena"

As always listening to Sands makes me homesick but I shrug the broody feeling away. I am the face of the company, as Ms. Kobus is always quick to remind me, and I can't afford to look sour. How I even managed to get the reception job at Van Gogh Attorneys, one of *Thee* best law firms in Jozi was nothing short of a miracle. It probably had a lot to do with them fulfilling their B-BBEE obligations so what better way than to get the darkest female to man the front desk and answer their calls? Most of the white male clientele are fascinated by me while their female counterparts mostly address the top of my head. The annoying man thankfully disembarks at the first stop and the rest of my journey is in perfect peace.

My morning is still perfect when I greet Bab' Dlomo at the door of the tall and imposing building where I work. He smiles his full toothy smile, only reserved for me in the building and grunts "NaDlamini," in response. I settle in way before 8am when Ms. Kobus comes in and critically assesses my big black gummed smile then harrumphs her response to my greeting. She asks me to be extra sharp today as they are expecting dignitaries. My smile remains in place even though my facial muscles protest at the forced muscle movement. She leaves me in peace and I work swiftly smiling and greeting as the lawyers file in. Most of the partners are elderly and courteous enough. There are also the younger attorneys with a spring to their stride, ambition coating their faces and an unhealthy dose of their own self-importance. Only Ashton insists I call him by his first name and is all chatty, too chatty if you ask me. I am here only to make money and finally continue with my studies not to make buddies. He is also a little touchy feely but he is like that with everyone so I guess it's his way but that doesn't make me any less uncomfortable with it.

I've just finished connecting a call to Mr. Van Halen when I feel a prickling sensation on the hairs of my neck. I look up into charcoal pools of fire. This is when my train wreck starts, and it has been spiraling since. Inwardly I cry out to the earth to open and swallow me up, but the treacherous ceramic tiles remain pristine and intact. Even though I have seen those sinister eyes only once for under five minutes, six years ago, I have never forgotten them. They haunt me in my nightmares where I wake up drenched in my sweat and a sobbing mess. Those eyes haunt me whenever I want to indulge in Akhona's black forest cake.

Those charcoal eyes are responsible for my insecurities with my weight and I choose to blame them for my separation from my family. I loathe those scornful arrogant eyes.

My stunned eyes take in the smooth planes of the bastard's face. Leaving nothing out from his pinkish full lips which have thinned as he studies me with the disdainful drop of the corners of his mouth. His warm chocolate skin is two shades lighter than mine, if he used face powder he would be a 3. His skin stretches without a wrinkle or a crease across his surprisingly straight nose all the way to his tiny ears. He hasn't aged a bit but there is something sinister in his classic good looks, something dangerous and closed off. He has a Maps Maponyane beard going on now and I grudgingly admit to myself that he looks handsome. A beautiful monster is what he is. After the stare down which I break off, I wish and pray that he doesn't recognize me after my drastic weight loss. Yes, I've changed a lot from that fresh-faced double-chinned teenager, that he discarded so carelessly. All hope I have of him not recognizing me is blown to ashes seconds after it crosses my mind as if he can hear my thoughts.

"Nomaswazi."

My name from his lips sounds like a warm caress but his stare is arctic cold. I panic and all I can do is stare at him, my mouth slightly hanging open like the idiot that I am. I don't know how much time passes before Ms. Kobus comes briskly to my rescue.

"Mr. Hlongwane you're here. I hope you haven't been kept long? And the rest of your party?"

Ms. Kobus' crisp tone holds a bit of reproach as she glances at my near comatose stance.

"I have been waiting for a long time to be right here at this very moment and your receptionist has been very helpful. The rest of my party will join us at a later stage."

All the time he is talking to her, he keeps his eyes trained on me. Like a moth drawn to a fire I can't look away.

"Ok please follow me this way," Ms. Kobus' breathless voice catches my attention and I break off contact with the two scorching coal pupils and properly focus on my senior. Her leathery skin is flushed, and poor Ms. Kobus even has two red patches on her cheeks. She is also not immune to the devil's charm.

......

Oh, I was charmed once too, but in my defense, I was young and naïve. I was devastated when my father told me he was marrying me off to his friend's son, but I got slightly mollified when he explained that he was getting old and he wanted to die knowing that his little princess was taken care of. I was actually looking forward to the wedding when *Babe* showed me my intended's picture. Love at first sight?

□

Believe you me, it's real. I fell head over heels in love with him, not knowing that in future I wouldn't be able to bear even the thought of his name. In my childish thoughts I saw him as my hero, he would love me like my darling father did and he would treasure me, serenade me and kiss me endlessly. I forgot to mention I am an avid romantic reader and I binge watch movies like The Notebook.

So, in my teenage mind, he became The One.

I'm ashamed now to admit that he soon became a constant in my racy dreams that left me drenched. The lobola negotiations went smoothly even though he wasn't there, this should have been the first red flag. I was crushed but comforted myself in the knowledge that he was busy building an empire for me and our family. I was so infatuated I even didn't feel bad for not proceeding to college with my peers. I scoff now at my stupidity but back then school wasn't my favorite place, what with being bullied and the name calling.

My marriage was supposed to be my saving grace. My new start at happily ever after. Boy was I in for a rude awakening.

The day before the wedding, my father had booked out Royal Swazi Spa in Ezulwini Valley and as the name suggests it was paradise on earth. I didn't have any friends and my siblings loathed me, story for another day, so I went around investigating on my own. *Babe* said I shouldn't explore the grounds on my own, so I settled for snooping around the luxurious hotel. I started with the spa and I got the pampering of my life. There I was all relaxed then headed to the casino. In all my sheltered life I had never been to a casino and my curiosity resulted in me getting the shock of my life. I heard raised voices and instead of retracing my footsteps I chose to eavesdrop.

"I wouldn't marry that fat cow! Mswati himself wouldn't marry her if she was the only dancer during *Umhlanga*," the words so carelessly uttered and scornfully at that, thrust a knife deep in my heart and shattered my glass castle. I vividly remember clutching at my chest and stuffing my chubby fist in my mouth to stop the sob from reaching their ears.

"Look that fat cow you are talking about, cost me a large portion of my own head of cattle. Her sister is pretty but *lesibumbu sakhe sati wonke emapipi aseMbabane.* Besides the old man's weak spot is his youngest daughter. I heard that he will be leaving all his mines to her not his brat of a son or slut of a daughter."

I remember recoiling at the brashness of that voice and I didn't stay to hear more. I creeped out until I was out of earshot then I broke into a run and didn't stop until I threw myself on my bed.

I cried myself to sleep that day. I even threw up and

woke up with a migraine. That wasn't even the worst part. Gasp all you want but it gets worse. See I was torn because I didn't want to disappoint my father, he was the center of my world. There was also a little part of me that hoped by some miracle that the loathing and disdain I heard in his voice would disappear.

I vowed to lose all the weight after the wedding then maybe he would love me and maybe even touch me. I needed someone else who wasn't my father to love me. Young, stupid, gullible me woke up the next day with resolve.

I won't depress you with the sordid details of how I wished my mother was there fussing over me. Maybe if I hadn't been so big she wouldn't have died giving birth to me. I was a girl on a mission. I let the lady from the spa do my makeup and then I was sucked into a body shaper; the corset wound so tightly to give me that perfect hourglass figure in my princess ball gown with diamonds embellished on the sweetheart neckline with the lace covering my chubby arms gracefully.

When Makhulu, the lady who raised me from birth, my nanny and mother rolled in one, put that delicate cathedral veil on my coiffured and curled extensions, she had tears in her eyes.

"*Umhle NaDlamini ngkufitela inhlanhla lenhle...*", it

turned out no amount of luck could prevent my heartbreak that day, but I was hopeful, and I squeezed her hand with misty eyes of my own.

My wedding was well organized and the golf course at Royal Swazi Spa looked breathtakingly beautiful.

The lofty greens rolling seamlessly merging with the tall lush trees. The podium was set against a small pond and there were flowers on the sides of the makeshift aisle and on either side of the aisle the Windsor chairs covered with white material and secured with peach bows were filled with guests of the highest social standing in Swaziland. Even King Mswati, The Third was there with his then youngest wife. My father squeezed my cheeks before tucking my hand in the crook of his tuxedo draped arm and the music started. Funny how I still remember the lyrics.

"Angisafuni kucabanga
Kutsi kukhona lo k'ngcono kunawe
Angisafuni kucabanga baby
Kutsi kukhona lo mhle kunawe
Ngiti khandza ng'guce ngemadvolo
Nale ndandatho ye daymani esandleni sami
Ngicela kunye nje kuphela baby
Kuts' uvume k'ba ngumkami
Ohh

Lo mhla ngidibanisa ilanga nenyanga

Ngitsi asibe kunye, kukhanye phakadze
Lo mhla ngidibanisa mina nawe
Ngitsi asibe munye ngonaphakadze
Ngicel' uvume baby, lo mhla
Vuma vuma..."

Now whenever I hear the song I cringe but, on that day, it was perfect. As was the groom waiting for me at the end of the aisle, molten coal pupils trained only on me. It was like his charcoal eyes could see right through my soul and silly me was blushing. Oh, to be young and drunk in love! He stepped forward and clasped my father's hand then took my hand in his. I felt a rush of electricity course through me at his touch and I sneaked a peek at him under my elongated eyelashes and he seemed unmoved. While the preacher was saying a few words, the groom pierced me with his eyes and everything else faded into oblivion until I saw him raise a hand and stopped the preacher mid-sentence. An expectant silence fell over us, not even a baby cried, or a pin dropped and yet he was still looking into my eyes.

"I'm sorry I can't go through with this," those eight words of rejection elicited gasps from our guests, but they also buried what little self-esteem I had. The bitter taste of rejection almost drove me to an early grave and a part of me did die on that alter. He finally broke eye contact and without a backward glance walked away leaving me gaping after him at the altar.

......

"Hey, aren't you going for lunch?" Ashton's casually asked question startles me from my walk down memory lane and I jump a bit. He puts his hand on my arm caressing it, placating. "Sorry I didn't mean to startle you."

I smile nervously at him and shrug off his hand.

"It's ok," my voice is hesitant.

"So, there's this new pizza place around the corner can I take you there for lunch?" his voice sounds hopeful and certain at the same time.

"No thanks, I have a packed lunch," I respond quietly while shutting down my computer for lunch and taking care to turn on the automated voice prompt before picking up my purse. All this while Ashton is watching me.

"Come on I'm not taking no for an answer," he says while clasping my hand forcefully. I wince in pain and try to shrug out of his painful grip. Where is everyone?

"No Ashton let me go," I try to muster as much confidence into my voice as possible but then he turns and kisses me. At first, I'm startled but then my reflexes kick in and I sink my sharp teeth into his thin pink lips. Could today get any worse? He yelps and lets me go anger and disgust blatant in his face as he lifts his hand to slap me. I recoil as I prepare for the impact of that slap but when it doesn't come I find Ashton angrily held up while his neck is being squeezed.

"Get your filthy hands off my wife, you scum!" the words are slung at Ashton in a roar by the devil himself and poor Ashton looks red in the face from lack of oxygen. Ms. Kobus comes running from God knows where, probably at sound of the roar and she is shocked at the scene in her foyer.

"Mr. Hlongwane what on earth!" Now is probably not the right time to laugh at how she pronounces the devil's surname. Only then does the devil let go of Ashton and he falls into a wheezing heap on the floor and Ms. Kobus rushes over to him shouting for me to get some water and I stay rooted in shock.

I don't know whether to hate the devil for what he did to me all those years ago or thank him for saving me from being manhandled. His hands feel soft and I find myself leaning into his touch. I feel safe. Wait a minute what did he mean wife? And what's with this sudden concern? He's holding my face gently but now his hold burns with his rejection. I shrug off his touch and I see the confusion and hurt flirt through his eyes. The nerve! I just want to die, and it doesn't help that Ms. Kobus is throwing murderous glares at me. Welcome to my life.

CHAPTER TWO

I have never lost my cool before, ever! I am my father's son and from an early age, my father drilled in me, as the eldest son, that emotions make a man weak. My enemies would use my emotions against me. Whatever situation I have faced, I somehow manage to go through life with a certain level of detachment, bordering on cold.

Seeing this sleaze-ball with his tongue down her throat, I see red. I am livid! I fail to keep my emotions in check and I am pleased when she bites into his sorry lip. My girl, I feel proud, but quickly discard that thought before I can fully analyze its significance. It is when he lifts his hand to strike her, that I tip over the edge. I find my hands around his scrawny neck squeezing all the breath out of him. Watching in satisfaction as the rat's face turns purple from the lack of oxygen. I hear Shelly's shrill cry, I want to kill him with my bare hands. She rushes to help his pathetic arse while I look at Swazi, I mean really look at her.

Swazi has lost all the baby fat, she's left with flesh in all the right places. Her skirt wraps around her like a bandage and leaves little to the imagination, moulding her generous curves. That waist, I can just span my hands around it, that's how tiny it is. In the struggle, the top button of her blouse has come undone, blessing me with a view of her ample bust. Is that lace I peek? I feel myself growing hard, just from the thought of my face buried deep in her cleavage. The things I want to do to those boobs. My erection tightens at the sudden image of me fucking her cleavage. Get a grip Zikode! I chasten my errant member.

Swazi looks frozen and her large eyes swimming in tears become my undoing. I feel an unfamiliar warmth in my chest area and use the pad of my thumb to wipe away the stray tear that falls from these hypnotic eyes. She looks far away, conflicted and I want to kiss her. Electrical current flows between us jerking her from shock and then disdain fills her eyes as she shrugs my hand off. Her glare could kill an elephant.

“What in God's name is happening here?” The skinny

white woman splutters in anger ticking off my own anger.

"I will tell you what's happening. That imbecile was busy sexually harassing my wife and..." the emotion in my voice deepens into a growl.

"No!" Swazi cuts into my growl her eyes wide, Shelly and I turn and look at her.

"So, he wasn't sexually harassing you?" Shelly is as perplexed as I am, and I hope that I haven't made a fool of myself only to find that they have a thing going on.

"No. I mean yes, he was harassing me but no I am not Mr. Hlongwane's wife." There is quite a resolve in Swazi's voice and that makes me mad.

"She's my *wife*," I stress the word wife with a growl and narrow my eyes at her daring Swazi to contradict me. Even I am surprised by how possessive I sound but I keep my emotions in check. My boardroom glare works because I see her gulp, but she doesn't say anything to contradict my statement and I continue addressing Shelly. "And my *wife* was being manhandled by this man and he would have hit her too had I not intervened." Just the thought alone is enough to infuriate me further.

The older woman let's go of the scumbag so quickly his head crashes to the floor and he winces, she rushes over to my Swazi and fusses over her.

"Are you fine dear? Did he hurt you?" The concern in her voice seems genuine and Swazi doesn't shrug her concern away. It stings, but I push that thought away.

"I'm fine Ms. Kobus just a little shaken." Even her voice sounds shaky.

"You know what, take the rest of the day off. We will make a formal complaint on Monday and Mr. Hlongwane will be your witness, ok?" Shelly speaks gently and it's unlike the brisk lawyer I spent the whole morning discussing my affairs with.

Swazi nods fighting back the tears and shakily takes her bag and walks past me. Her hips swaying provocatively, without so much as a look in my direction. I stay a few moments while Ms. Kobus asks if I will manage to come on Monday and I agree. I quickly exit and see Swazi's hastily retreating back almost at the car park. In five long strides I catch up with her and grab her arm careful not to exert too much force. She tenses up and looks at me with dark emotion in her brown eyes. Is that hate I see in her eyes?

"Let go of me!" The hostility in her voice answers my question.

"I'm taking you home Swazi." I'm not taking no for an answer.

"Go to hell! Now because I'm no longer a fat cow, you deem me fit enough to be taken home? You're the devil, and I want nothing to do with you! I am not your *wife,* you left your wife at the altar! That girl died that day. I don't need your protection or your help, I've been doing fine without you. Now fuck off, back to whatever hell hole you sprung from!" She's not really shouting because she didn't even raise her voice but the vehemence in her voice is loud and she accompanies each sentence with a poke on my chest. Her words floor me, and she easily detangles her arm from my grip and marches away from me all fired up and I watch in disbelief as she flags down a taxi and gets in. Damn it, this is going to be harder than I thought.

......

I'm in my hotel room now at the Sandton Sun Hotel, deep in thought, her words keep ringing in my ears. The thought that she hates me doesn't sit well with me and for the first time I'm perplexed. My hands are aimlessly circling my forgotten glass of whiskey. The hate in her eyes keeps flashing in my mind. I deserve that after humiliating her in front of the whole of Swaziland, but I thought I was doing her a favour.

I couldn't go through with that sham of a marriage not when her innocent brown eyes were shining with so much love for me. Maybe if she hadn't looked so adorable with her double shallow dimples on her chin and that one deep dimple on her cheek. I couldn't bring myself to crush her innocence plus back then I had Ramona. Ramona my beautiful, foxy Ramona. I met her in Oxford university where I was studying my Architectural degree.

□

You know how rich Africans send their children to universities overseas as a sign of their affluence? Well my father was no exception and he makes it a point to remind me how fortunate I am, and how much I owe him. Most times I want to remind him that I didn't ask for his funding, and that on my results alone I would have secured my own funding. Unfortunately, I don't have the guts to stand up to that old beast yet. As for the burning need I felt earlier to mark her as mine, I have no idea where it comes from, but I just need everyone to know that Swazi is mine.

I was twenty-four, rebelling against my father's tyranny and raging with lust. I couldn't accept that my marriage to a seventeen-year-old, turning eighteen on our wedding day, had already been arranged for me. The lobola was paid while I was vacationing in Europe with Ramona, fucking like rabbits just across the Place de la Concorde. There was no space for emotions in my life and Ramona understood that and she worshipped my cock. In retrospect, I was trying to fight off the demons of my childhood. I was trying to erase the picture of me and my brother standing over our first dead body at the age of fourteen. While he turned to drugs, I stuck my penis into any available hole. That's exactly how my father found me and Ramona, with me balls deep in her mouth. To say I was pissed is an understatement. My old man couldn't give two fucks. He said my wedding was in two days and I should get dressed as the rented jet was waiting for us. I was fuming!

I was dragged back home under threats and duress. It didn't help that my brother kept laughing at me saying they chose the blackest and fattest spoilt brat for me, I was enraged. Things got heated, voices were raised but as always, my father won. To get through everything I had to remind myself that the arrangement was simply a business transaction and no feelings would be involved.

All my resolve crumbled when I saw her coming towards me, her face and eyes alight with happiness. It was like there was a bulb stuck inside her, the whites in her eyes were milky white just like her teeth. Her honey brown irises were twinkling with hope and love. A love I didn't want and certainly didn't deserve. I couldn't take my eyes off her dimples, her smooth ebony skin, I wanted to touch it and determine for myself if it was as soft as a baby's skin. When our hands touched, I felt an underlying current that I had never felt before and I quickly let her hand go. When she smiled, I knew I was screwed and my first instinct was to run.

I knew that I couldn't reciprocate the love that was shining through her eyes and she deserved better than a jaded me. She deserved the chance to go into the world and live her life, maybe fall in love with a decent block who was nothing like me. I would have crushed her spirit, so I walked away leaving her shocked at the altar. I saw disbelief mixed with pain on her face, my chest tightened painfully. It took all the strength in me, to look away from her eyes. To walk away and never look back.

My ringtone cuts into my thoughts and I felt my throat constricting as I stare at the caller ID. He won't stop calling so I clear my throat and accept the call.

Ndvodzana." The voice is cold and impersonal, he doesn't even wait for me to respond. "How did the meeting go? *Umbonile umakoti wakami*?"

"They were eager to take on managing the South African side of our portfolio, and I have another meeting set up with the rest of the shareholders for next week Friday." My tone is as clipped as his and I ignore his last question.

"Hmm so are you coming back home until your next meeting?" I know he noticed that I avoided his question, but he doesn't push the matter.

"I have some business to attend to on Monday. I will see afterwards." I just want this conversation to be over.

"What about the shareholders meeting this side on Monday?" His question sounds rhetorical.

"I won't be there, the matter this side is more pressing. I'm sure you and Ntsikelelo can manage the Board without me." I grit my teeth at the mention of my brother's name.

"Fine. *Umakoti wakami yena?*"

"Father, there's an incoming call that I've been waiting for, I will call you." I hang up before he can even protest. I don't want to discuss her with him or anyone for that matter until I have sorted out my feelings about her. I down the whiskey in one go and shudder at its bitter taste but it warms me up after the chilly conversation I had with my father.

Coming to Johannesburg was no coincidence and choosing Van Gogh Attorneys was also part of the plan. I have known where Nomaswazi is for the past 5 years. After she ran away from home, her distraught father begged me to look for her. After almost a year the PI I hired found her in Johannesburg, but her father said we should let her live her own life. We have people always tailing her. Her father obviously dotes on her. He says she's stubborn like her mother. I send him the report from the PI every month, but I never open the reports. My phone goes off again, speak of the devil.

"*Skoni sawubona, unjani*?" There is warmth in his voice and I find myself smiling in response.

"*Ngikhona babe*, how are you feeling today?" The concern in my voice is genuine.

"These old bones are failing me, but I will live. More importantly how is my baby?" his voice is wistful.

"She is fine and feisty, she wants nothing to do with me." He laughs on the other end of the line until the laughter turns into a raspy cough. He coughs for a while and I hear his nurse telling him to drink up.

"She has always been stubborn-willed like her mother, kind and an introvert but stubborn as a mule." There's a smile in his voice even though his breath is wheezing. "You have to bring her back home now, I'm not getting any younger. I can't die without making things right by her."

"You won't die, you have the best medical care that money can buy." I'm reassuring myself as much as I'm reassuring him.

"When your time is up son, not even the best medical care can keep you here. Bring her home, I need Maswazi."

Our conversation plays in my head long after I hang up. How will I convince Swazi to go back with me, when she obviously hates my guts? When did she grow into such a temptress? Unbidden, an image of her naked on my hotel bed springs to mind. It's so vivid, I can almost touch her sweaty skin.

"Bend for me baby, arch that back." My voice is hoarse and raspy, and her moans fill up the whole room. I can see her treasure in all its glory and I dip one finger inside and she whimpers. I add another finger and she tenses up. The sounds she is making make Zikode pulse. I can't stand the torture anymore, I thrust into her and her heat almost pushes me over the edge. She arches her back even more, her breasts flattening,

and she takes me even deeper. The sound of my balls slapping against that marvelous arse, drives me insane. I drive all the way into her snug haven and I'm like a beast unleashed. Her moans and cries fueling me on, her muscles tightening around me are the last straw as I grunt my release.

I feel wet warmth on my thigh, crap I just came from indulging in a fantasy. What is wrong with me? I'm not even having a wet dream; a simple fantasy has thrown me over the edge. Great! I just ruined my favourite suit pants. That's it I need to get laid! It's been too long, five nights without sex are too many in my books, but first let me go shower. Swazi haunts me in the shower as well and I jerk off to the memory of her boobs before washing off the evidence of my weakness. It's funny that I haven't even seen her naked yet and she has already reduced me to a horny teenager.

......

Twenty minutes later, I feel fresh in jeans and a biker jacket, as I make my way to a club that my friends once took me too. I liked it so much I bought shares in that place. I have already called them, Mpho is away on business and Melusi can't get away from his wife. So, it's just me and since I don't plan to get too wasted I drive my rental metallic grey Audi Q7. It purrs softly as I pull out and I enjoy its smooth strength. The valet is also impressed with my ride as he takes my keys like a fat child receiving candy.

It's Friday so there's one of their famous events at The

Sands. There's a long queue but I just get in without so much as a check. Perks of being a part owner. I make a beeline for the champagne bar, Marko smiles widely as he sees me and makes my usual poison. While I wait, this petite lady "bumps" into me and I catch her before she falls. She's smiling all flustered, getting laid tonight is going to be easier than I thought.

"I'm so sorry, I didn't see you there." *Of course you didn't because it's hard to miss a 6 foot man standing alone at a bar*, but I still give her a half smile.

"It's ok, I got to be a hero for the night." She leans in to hear what I'm saying above the music also giving me a glimpse of her girls. They are not as full and as perky as Swazi's, but they will do for the night.

"I'm Tiisetso by the way." She half shouts and I really couldn't care less but I take her hand in mine all the same.

"So what drink can I get for you Tiisetso?" My charm is kicking in and she flutters her fake eyelashes at me.

"I wouldn't mind a flavoured Mojito." I can tell she wants to know my name but I'm not going to volunteer it, not for a one-night stand anyway. I motion for Marko and tell him what the lady wants, and he shoots me with a grin and a "Sho bhoza". All this time Tiisetso is looking at me like I'm meat on a stake.

"What do you do?" Her squeaky voice rises above the

music. I will not fall for that trap, she has calculated the cost of my clothes and watch, in her mind already and wants our hook up to turn into more. This isn't a date and I have to shut down any false expectations from her.

"I can give you a magical night." I lower myself to whisper in her ear.

"Just one night?" She pouts prettily and flutters those fake lashes again. Just as I'm about to respond, a familiar figure catches the corner of my eye and I look at her in disbelief. Is that Swazi? What the hell is she wearing? I feel my blood boiling as she furtively tries to pull down the little material of her short black leather dress.

"Excuse me." My voice comes out harsh as I address Miss Petite and I don't wait for her to respond. I make my way to the pool deck, where Swazi is seated with a group of others. She doesn't see me coming, but her skinny friend who looks coloured sees me and is batting her eyes at me seductively. Swazi downs a glass of vodka as if it's water and her face screws up at the taste. What on earth, is that paint on her face? I stand behind her and she still hasn't seen me, and she reaches for her friend's glass and is about to down it too, but I hold her hand. She looks up with fire in her eyes and I stare back trying to get my fury under control.

"You!" She says trying to stand up and she's unsteady on those demonic heels that have spikes and look like pure torture. I hold her steady and she swats my hand away.

□

"Don't touch me *wena* Devil, I hate you!" The finger poking again. It's really cute because her fingers are so tiny, and I barely feel anything on my chest.

"Nomaswazi, you are a drunkard now?" My voice is controlled masking my fury.

"What gives you, the right to come here and judge me? I'm living my life, now let me pass I need to get laid tonight." It must be the alcohol talking, and I came for the same thing but hearing those words from her mouth, makes me see red. Her gang is watching us in amusement and Swazi pushes her way past me. Just her butt, brushing against me, makes me hiss in frustration. This woman is either going to drive me to an early grave or a mental institution.

I don't want to cause a scene, so I watch as she walks to the dance floor swaying dangerously on those heels. She's not pissed drunk, just tipsy and she starts swaying to the music. Her dress is hitching up as she twerks, making my teeth clench. I'm mad as hell and turned on at the same time. It's bloody frustrating! She twirls and goes down crossing her feet and coming back up all in one smooth move and all I can do is stare. Her hips and butt are toned and firm, her every move is graceful. I'm enjoying watching her when this guy comes from behind her and starts grinding her arse.

I don't even try to stop myself as I march to the dance floor. He turns her around, then the swine has the nerve to put his lips on her neck and she doesn't stop him. I'm beside myself with anger and I don't even think before I wrench her from him and smash my fist on his face. The impact gratifyingly lands on his nose and a spurt of blood comes out of his nose. My hand hurts like hell but I ignore it when he comes back up to throw a punch, I land another one this time on his jaw and this one decks him. I hear Nomaswazi's screams and the bouncers come but when they see it's me, they make no move to stop me or intervene. The music has stopped and those trying to take video footage have their phones taken by security.

"Next time your hands come even an inch towards my woman, I will cut them off do I make myself clear?" I'm hissing in anger and the poor bloke is nodding and his friends help him up as I turn angrily to my little vixen.

"It's either you walk out of here on your own or I drag you out of here. Which is it going to be?" I bark at her and even though fear flirts through her eyes momentarily, she angles her chin defiantly at me. She must not test me! But I have a feeling that Nomaswazi would try the patience of a saint.

CHAPTER THREE

Great! Just my luck, on my first night out in like forever, drama has found me. All I wanted was to curl up on the couch with a tub of ice cream, a glass of wine and listen to all three of Adele's albums. Yes, I'm obsessed with Adele, her songs speak to me. I was ready for a 'cry me a river' pity party but Akhona was having none of that. It took all my strength to walk away from the devil and get into that taxi while feeling his eyes scorching my back. Luckily no one bothered me in the taxi and I kept blinking away the tears.

Seeing him there brought it all back, the shame filled whispers and the pitiful stares from the guests and more so my sister's evil smirk. I felt the rejection all over again. Then he had the nerve to come to my work place, acting like a hero and telling everyone that I am his wife, yet he is the one who rejected me. My emotions were all over the place so instead of queueing for the local taxi, I took a meter taxi that dropped me at my flat.

The moment I got inside the flat, I dropped my bag on the floor and sobbed my heart out. I missed my father so much, but I couldn't stand being ridiculed anymore and to save him from the shame of having me for a daughter, I ran away. In hindsight, it was very selfish of me, but had I stayed, I probably would have succeeded in committing suicide, that's how depressed I was then. I slumped on the floor as wave after wave of pain washed over me. I sobbed until Akhona helped me up and made me sit on the couch and made me drink sugar water.

After I calmed down, I told her that the husband I was set to get married to and the reason why I ran away from home, had somehow tracked me down and that Ashton had tried to force himself on me. Of course, it wasn't necessarily the Bible version of what happened, but I didn't want her pity. When I called him Hlongwane, she assumed it was a man old enough to be my father and I didn't correct her. Akhona's way of dealing with problems is glamming up and partying in exclusive clubs. That's how I ended up being painted and prodded by her glam squad, which also happen to be her closest friends Thulane and Teboho.

Thulane is the make-up and hair god, though he prefers goddess, while Teboho knows all the latest fashion trends like the back of her hand. No amount of resistance on my part helped and, in the end, I was squeezed into Akhona's leather dress, which is a size smaller on me, but I was assured that it made me look like Nicki Minaj, in her latest video. I was then dragged to The Sands night club under duress I might add.

The first round of virgin cocktails, didn't help to lift me out of my funk, so the next round I asked Akhona to get us some vodka. She raised her perfectly arched eyebrow but complied. My mistake was gulping it down like water and the bitter taste and heat of the vodka hit me hard, instantly numbing my pain. So, I was reaching for Akhona's glass when a huge hand yanked my glass from me. I felt anger rising when I saw that it belonged to my so-called husband, and the Dutch-courage from the vodka made me bold enough to tell him where to get off. One thing you should know about me, is that when sober, I have two left feet but get me drunk and I can do the Vosho all night.

I was enjoying myself, dancing to Midnight Starring. I could feel the devil's coals on my every move. Usually I don't allow guys at night clubs to grind my arse but today I just wanted to get back at that bastard. Show him that even though he rejected me there were still some men who found me attractive. What I didn't expect was for him to floor the poor guy. I think he broke his nose and that makes me feel bad. I have never been in the spotlight before and its uncomfortable.

Why isn't security throwing him out? Who exactly is this guy? I wonder but maybe they are just scared of this hulk of a man. Without a suit, his physique is even more intimidating. Angry Hlongwane is scary but I have had enough of his bullying, he can't just waltz back into my life and act like he owns me! I tilt my head up and narrow my eyes at him, just as I am about to respond to his demand a shrill voice interrupts me.

"Baby there you are, come let's finish our drinks." The Devil doesn't look pleased by this statement.

I turn and look at the owner of the shrill voice. At a glance, her small frame would fool you into thinking that she's young but the wrinkles around her mouth and the strained veins on her neck show that she has seen many Christmases. So, he has the nerve to deck a guy for dancing with me while he is here with this *Makhulu*? I need to get out of here, my night has been ruined. I go back to my table and get my purse.

Akhona looks like she has a lot of questions but I'm not in the mood to indulge her or anyone for that matter. At least I have enough money to Uber home. The other guys seem like they just started having fun. I say my goodbyes and request for an Uber. I decide to go and wait for my Uber downstairs. There's no sign of the Devil and his granny anywhere, they must have gone to finish their drinks in private. I don't know why that thought hurts, but I won't dwell much on it.

I wish I had brought a jacket, it's now chilly outside. Thank God, my Uber didn't take forever, I can't wait to go home and curl in my bed. Just as I'm about to step into the car my arm is yanked back. Gosh this guy is like a very bad case of Herpes!

"Can you just stay out of my life?" I address him irritation evident in my voice, but he doesn't even pay me any attention. He addresses the Uber driver.

"How much was the drive supposed to be?"

The driver looks from me to the devil uncertain of what's happening, no doubt.

"The lady is the one who requested my services *mfondini.*" Finally, someone to stand up to this bully.

"It's either you tell me your fare, or I take my wife and leave without paying. What's it going to be?" The control in his voice is scary! I see the driver swallow a lump before telling him the amount while I fume silently. *I am going to rate him low on my Uber app.* I think to myself, yet part of me doesn't blame him because he did try to stand up for me.

I watch in despair as my ride pulls away from the curb. All I want is for this day to be over already! I'm startled by the devil draping his leather jacket over my skimpy dress. The jacket feels warm from his body heat and smells of his cologne scent. I would shrug it off, but I am feeling cold, so I opt for a silent sulk.

"Let's go Swazi." I ignore the authority in his voice and stare at him blankly not moving an inch.

I don't know where I'm getting the strength to look him in the eye, must be the vodka. He grits his teeth obviously fighting to reign in his temper. I'm even more convinced that I am not going anywhere with him. His anger scares me and all I've seen him do today is manhandle and punch people. If those aren't red flags, I don't know what is. He is a controlling, violent prick.

"Nomaswazi, I hate repeating myself, I said let's go." His hiss is frustrated.

"I don't go to strange men's homes." I try to muster all my courage and act unfazed.

"I'm not a stranger, I'm your husband." He deliberately enunciates each word and I scoff.

"I've only ever seen you once before today and that was the day when you left me hanging at the altar before the priest officiated us. That in my books makes you a stranger not a husband."

"We can debate about this in my hotel room not outside

a club close to midnight." His calmness is ticking me off.

"I'm not going to your hotel room, I'm going to my flat," I've had enough of this meaningless conversation, I take out my phone to request another Uber. He grabs my phone and when I try to get it back he holds it up. Even when I try to jump I can't reach it. He's taking me back to my school days of being bullied. The bullies would hold up my schoolbag and chant, "Jump *nkhomo*, jump!". I feel tears of frustration fill my eyes, but I won't give him the satisfaction.

I start walking in the direction that the Uber took, my shoes the only sound in the almost deserted carpark. I don't know where I'm going but I want to be as far from him as possible. I hear him let out a string of curses behind me in Swati, not the pretty ones. I continue walking, the tears I've been holding back clouding my eyes and tipping over my cheeks. I hear his footfall behind me and I quicken my strides. Who am I kidding though because in three long strides he has caught up with me. I screech when he scoops me up and flings me over his shoulder like a sack of potatoes.

"Put me down!" I scream as my fists pummel his back, but he only spanks my arse and pulls down my dress. The part where he spanked me stings and I stop struggling and allow my tears to fall freely.

We pass the guards at the door and they just look on,

none of them steps in to rescue me. I'm feeling dizzy from the alcohol and being held upside down.

"I want to puke." I warn him even my voice has become faint.

He stops to put me down but he's too late. I vomit all over his jeans and shoes. He curses softly but holds me as I continue vomiting on the tarmac road. When I'm done I can barely stand my knee joints are weak. He scoops me up but this time carries me like a baby. I must stink, but I don't care I cling on to his neck. I don't protest when he opens the door of a big flashy car and bundles me into the front seat and takes care to buckle my seat belt. Being sick has left me vulnerable and this seat is so cushy, I curl up as he starts the car and drift off to sleep.

……

I wake up in a strange bed, naked as the day I was born. My mouth tastes bitter and my head is slightly pounding. I reek of alcohol and vomit. Memories of last night flood me and I burrow my face in the fluffy pillow. That means that he took off my clothes and saw all my stretch marks and my two-fold belly. I feel sick just at the thought. I slightly lift my head and scan the room, it's beautiful with earth tones and blessedly empty. My eyes land on the glass of juice next to the bed on the stand there and pills placed on a tissue. I gulp down the pills with the orange juice and I feel slightly alive.

There's a hotel gown at the foot of the bed, its huge and smells masculine.

I paddle my way to the shower and indulge in my icy cold wake-up shower. Today I need it even more than usual. There's no dryer in the cabinet, so I tie another towel on my hair turban style. When I'm done, I almost feel alive, but I still need to brush my teeth and be rid of the lingering bitter taste in my mouth. There's only one toothbrush in sight. Oh well, this ought to teach him not to bully me in future. I use his toothbrush and round off with his mouthwash. There are circles and bags under my eyes which are never there, I wonder how Akhona does this almost every night. Akhona! Gosh she must be worried sick about me! I left to go home yesterday or was it this morning, the memories are fuzzy. Not fuzzy enough to dispel the memory of me throwing up all over my supposed husband. I don't know why but I find joy in the thought and my giggles echo throughout the huge airy bathroom.

"Share the joke *nkosatana.*" I stop mid-giggle and turn towards the direction of the lazy drawl. My eyes find him leaning on the doorway like a huge panther, amend that to a huge black panther. Suddenly I'm nervous, what must he think of me?

"Since you have suddenly become mute, come let me dry your hair." He's laughing at me, the brute! Laughter laces his words and I'm not sure whether to be relieved or mad.

He moves towards me and my reflex is to back away from him until I'm pressed against the basin and he's towering in front of me. His look is intense like he wants to dig into my soul.

"You know it's funny that yesterday you had a lot to say and you were ready to defy me at every chance." He is trailing his finger across my cheek, beneath my chin to my collarbone and I find his actions highly distracting. My breathing patterns have become hitched and shallow. Abruptly he stops and pulls the towel from my head, my afro is still wet. He leans over me and I almost melt into a puddle right there on the floor. I should be mad at him, he ruined my life dammit but strangely I'm attracted to him. He's taking out a comb inside the cabinet and in his other hand he's holding a hair dryer.

"Where did you get that?" I ask frowning up at him.

"I bought it now when I bought you clothes to wear," he says dismissively.

"Oh." Is the only response I can muster. He switches on the dryer cutting short any conversation. Surprisingly his hands are nimble as he puts the comb through my hair while waving the dryer around. I relax for the first time since he invaded my space in the bathroom. Surprisingly, he's pretty good at this.

"Done, all dry," he states eventually. I tentatively touch

my hair and it's all dry and soft. I smile my gratitude at him and his eyes twinkle down at me momentarily. And almost as if I imagined the twinkle it's quickly gone and replaced with a scowl.

"Follow me to the bedroom. Now." Oh brother, we are back to grumpy Mr. Bossy Pants. I roll my eyes at his retreating back and follow him.

I find him pacing and he's already made the bed, so I sit gingerly on the bed.

"Nomaswazi, I do not like what I saw yesterday. You were drunk and half-naked allowing any random guy to touch you. If I hadn't been there, would you have woken up naked in his bed? Last night I could have had my way with you and you wouldn't have stopped me because you were too out of it." His words make me cold and unwittingly I look at my nana worried. "Relax, had I done anything to you, you would have felt it the moment you woke up." My shoulders sag in relief, I trust him. Anyway there's no way I would know I have never done it before.

"Is this the life you live here? Getting drunk and getting random hook ups?!" He's angry now but so am I.

"Don't you dare judge me as I recall you also had a hook up with that old skinny hag last night Mr. 'Baby there you are, come let's finish our drinks'." I mimic the shrill voice from last night. I see humour light up his eyes, then it's quickly replaced by his signature stony expression.

"That's different, I wasn't the one vomiting and passed out last night and your so-called friends haven't even called to check if you got home safe," he barks at me and I cringe. I feel like a kid being berated for being naughty. I remember that he still has my phone and that makes me even more rebellious.

"Well I've been doing fine without you and just because you didn't want me doesn't mean other men don't want me. I am bloody twenty-four years old, I can get drunk and fuck whomever I want!"

"Don't fucken raise your voice at me! If it's dick that you want so bad, then I'm going to give it to you. No need for you to prowl clubs just to get laid." I gulp at his proximity.

He doesn't give me a chance to respond as his lips latch on to mine. The kiss is angry, punishing and oddly passionate. I'm not that experienced in this department, but I follow his lead, tongue for tongue, suck for suck. I feel a foreign heat in my lady parts when he bites into my lower lip and I swoon. He's an expert at this, drawing pleasure from my lips if his groans are any testimony. He unties the belt of the gown and his warm hands are all over me like a rash, while his lips are unyielding on mine. I find my hands underneath his t-shirt exploring the hard planes of his abs. Both of us are greedy in our exploration of the other's body.

Fortunately, he's wearing sweat pants and the daring side of me tugs once at his waistband and the pants slide down. There's a siren at the back of my mind telling me to stop. That I will regret this after the cherry has been popped. However, the horny part of me is fired up and not willing to back down. I've never been desired in this manner before, the feeling is dizzying. I want him to go all the way. I want to know how it feels like to have a man inside me.

He lowers me on the bed and swiftly grabs a pack of condoms on the table stand. I gulp as I see a penis for the first time in my life. I have no idea what size he's supposed to be, but he looks huge and he keeps swelling. How is all that going to fit into my tiny hole? I want to chicken out, but I keep giving myself the pep talk, at this rate girl, you will end up a 40-year-old virgin. You want this. No, you need this. So what if he didn't want to marry you? The thing is he wants you!

My head and heart are at war, I watch in fascination as he peels off the foil in the condom and rolls the rubber on his intimidating length. He does it all in smooth and precise movements. I can't help wondering how many times he's done this before while a pretty lady lies waiting for him or was I supposed to roll it onto him? I ignore the pang I feel at the thought of him with other women. I'm so lost it isn't even funny.

I feel relief when he swoops in and captures my lips again shutting down all my warring thoughts. The heat is back in full force, worsened by the friction of our naked bodies grinding against each other. He rubs his penis against my folds, massaging my clitoris and I lose all sense. I'm consumed by the pleasure he's bringing me.

"Baby you don't know how much I've wanted to do this." His voice has deepened and has a rough texture to it as he dips his long finger inside me. The invasion is uncomfortable at first but when he deepens, I find myself arching my back. "Yes baby, arch that back for me."

His whispered words just drive me crazier and I want more than his finger now. He flicks my clit with his member again and I purr in pleasure. He braces his arms on either side of me and eases himself into me. I try to relax as much as I can, but I wince as he brushes against my barrier, with a frown he tries again to push in, but the barrier is intact. He pales as he looks at me in disbelief.

"Swazi?" I can't bring myself to respond so I turn and look the other side.

He removes himself from me, leaving me feeling empty. He takes off the condom and goes to the bathroom and I stubbornly face the other side. The moment the bathroom door closes behind him, I let the tears of rejection flow. What was I thinking offering him my most precious gift? It's obvious he doesn't want me, and he never will. I must really disgust him. I am laying bare and entrusting him with my womanhood, but for the second time he has rejected me and I feel like filth.

Now is not the time to feel sorry for myself. He can't see me so shattered once again. I get up quickly and spot the shopping bags he placed on the armchair by the window. I put on the underwear, not bothering to wear the bra. I shrug into the pencil dress he bought not taking any time to admire it. He also bought me shoes that I hurriedly put on.

I'm dressed in under five minutes, my hair seriously needs to be combed but a run through my fingers should do for now. I take my purse and leave his penthouse suite as quietly as I can. The elderly couple in the elevator look at me pityingly but I ignore them. What is so wrong with me that he couldn't bring himself to sleep with me even when I offered myself in a silver platter? I blink the tears back as I enter the first meter taxi I spot outside the hotel. I need to be as far from him as possible. The devil never changes but I'm not sure if I will ever be able to bounce back from his rejection this time around.

CHAPTER FOUR

"Fuck!" I hiss as I slam my fist on the bathroom wall.

Why do I keep royally screwing up when it comes to Nomaswazi? What did I miss? The way she was grinding her arse at that bastard last night did not suggest her purity. Neither did her responsiveness to my touch. I'm still hard from her fevered kisses, her soft hands wantonly exploring every inch of my body. I try to shut off the flames that licked my whole body while she was grinding against me.

The little moans which kept escaping her slightly opened lips are still ringing in my ears and they are giving me chills. At one point when I was teasing her folds with Zikode, she purred like a cat presented with a bowl of fresh cream. That sound was my undoing and all I wanted at that moment was to bury myself deep in her heat. I have never wanted a woman this desperately. How could I have misread her so completely?

I curse again as I take off the condom and wrap it in tissue before throwing it into the dustbin. I have never been so out of my element before. Ever! How do I face her after basically accusing her of prostituting herself? I don't know where I got the strength to stop before the damage was done. It could have been her trusting eyes on me even as pain flashed across her face. I couldn't bring myself to take her innocence, not in that manner anyway.

She deserves so much better. After the life I have lived, the demons I carry with me: I do not deserve her innocence. I'm awed that she chose to make me her first, my throat tightens at how trusting she is. I don't deserve her. I probably never will. But I want her so bad, now more than ever. I want to be her one and only and protect her. Virginity does not have that much significance to me. In fact, I've always preferred my women experienced and eager.

Yet here I am right now, hiding in the bathroom. Afraid to face the hurt in her eyes. Shit! She's probably overthinking everything. I quickly leave my hiding place and am met by an empty hotel suite. The bed is rumpled where our bodies were just minutes ago. I catch myself at the door when I realize that I'm butt naked. I hop around the hotel suite throwing on different pieces of clothing. I can't let her go. I made that mistake once and I'm not going to make the same mistake again.

The lift is taking too long, and I opt to take the 20 flight of stairs downstairs. I'm practically leaping down, three stairs at a go, my feet barely touching the floor. I'm so fucken stupid. Why did I leave her like that? If anything happens to her, her father will have my balls for breakfast. I pass the foyer running, but she's nowhere in sight. I'm panting as I turn to the doorman standing discretely near the door.

"Did you see a black beauty come out of the hotel right now? About this tall and she has natural hair." I'm still catching my breath and he looks at me calmly.

"Yes sir, the lady got into a cab and left just now." Something in his tone is accusatory or is it just my guilt.

I curse under my breath, I go back and get my car keys. I don't even know where she stays. I will have to ask the private investigator we have tailing her. I doubt he will be very cooperative after the earful I gave him last night. I was so incensed watching Swazi sleeping in that drunken state. If I hadn't been there at that club, any fool could have had his way with her. Her stupid friends didn't even check if she was home safe. The private investigator's one mistake was to state that he hadn't seen her coming out of the apartment and that she never went out after coming from work. I didn't believe him then but after what just happened, I'm beginning to think I was the fool in all this.

He's unimpressed with me but he still sends me her address and confirms that she just came out of a cab. I decide to shower first to get my bearings. She left her phone behind, I call my IT guy to come with a tracker. He arrives as I'm coming out of the shower and gets to work as I dress. He's done by the time I finish dressing. I hate invading her privacy like this but from now on, her safety is top priority. And I do not like where their apartment is situated.

……

I'm nervous as I drive to Berea. Nomaswazi is something of a spitfire and she says what's on her mind. Her nose flares when she's pissed, and her eyes become narrow slits. I smirk at the memory of her little finger poking my chest. Her passion and fire turn me on big time. She's nothing and yet everything like I expected. Confusing I know, but that's the only coherent way I can describe her. She reminds me of my mother.

I pull up at the curb of her apartment block and grit my teeth at the sight before me. This place is worn out, the paint is peeling off and it seems like it's barely maintained. Khumalo, the private investigator walks towards me as I get off my rental. He must have seen me as I pulled up. He stays in the flat opposite Trentbridge, in an apartment directly opposite Nomaswazi's apartment.

"Is she still inside?" I don't have time for pleasantries.

"She hasn't left her room ever since she came out of the cab crying," from his tone I can tell that I am not Khumalo's favourite person. I feel a stab of guilt when he mentions that she was crying.

The guard at the door gives me a hustle at first until I produce a R200 note then he lets me in. That's it, I am moving Nomaswazi from this dump. She needs a more secure place. Ideally, if all works out, I will convince her to go back home to Swaziland for good. I have to knock three times before the thin friend comes to open the door. The door looks like it will fold in if I kicked it down and the window is broken, closed by a huge black plastic. Her attitude when she opened the door was hostile but now she is batting her eyelashes at me and all smiles.

"Can I help you?" she asks in an alluring tone but I don't have time to entertain her.

"I'm here for Swazi." Her face drops for a moment then she plasters her smile back in place.

"She's not here," she lies with a bold face.

My patience has run its course; I push my way in while she tries to close the door in my face. The first door I open leads to a room with clothes everywhere. On the floor, on top of the bed, on the chair next to the bed and on every available surface.

"Hey! You can't just come budging into my room like that!" the twig screeches behind me.

I ignore her and move to the next door. Thankfully it yields when I turn the door knob, but the sight that meets me breaks my heart. My Swazi is curled up in the middle of the double bed, sobbing her eyes out. I feel shitty and close the door in her annoying roommate's face. I take off my shoes and climb on the bed. At first, she resists my touch but somehow, I manage to pull her onto my chest. She pummels my chest and I let her. I hold on until she relents and sobs into my chest. Her sobs are muffled now but each sob cuts across my heart. I'm not good with emotions and I don't know how to comfort her.

At first, I'm patting her awkwardly at her back. Then instinctively I start rubbing her back and making soothing noises. I give in to temptation and lift her face. She's an ugly crier. Her eyes are puffy red, tears are hanging from her naturally long eyelashes, she has snort and I wipe it off with my t-shirt. Her lower lip is trembling as more tears spill over. I tug at her lower lip with my teeth and taste the salty tears resting on her lips. She tastes so good; a groan leaves my throat unbidden.

This is the only way I know how to communicate my

feelings. I pour in all my frustration, confusion and love into her lips. Her eyes are closed and she's also whimpering into my lips, her body shivering. I don't know how she ended on top of me, her breasts feel heavenly squashed against my chest. My hands are squeezing her generous arse, bringing our core into closer contact. The friction generated by our bodies has Zikode straining against my jeans.

I gather all my strength to resist the urge, to bang the living daylights out of Swazi. It's not an easy feat, Zikode is not used to being left hanging and he's raving for action. I ignore my carnal desires and drag my lips from Swazi's juicy lips to kiss her forehead instead. I can't resist nibbling her ear and sucking on her neck and she shudders uncontrollably. I smile against her neck; I have found her Achilles heel. My baby looks sinful with her lips swollen from my kisses, her crazy hair a jungle and her eyes tiny slits of arousal. Indulging in one last short drink of her lips, I can't keep my hands away from her.

She is snuggled against me; we are a perfect fit. Her swollen eyes are still red and her skin is flushed. I cradle her cheek in my hand and look into her eyes. I want to make things right so bad. Take away her tears and pain.

"*Ngiyacolisa naNkosi.*" She's eyeing me warily not responding. I still have a lot of grovelling to do.

"Say something baby, please." Her silence is freaking me

out.

"You rejected me." Her voice is low and flat. She doesn't take her eyes off me. She doesn't say the word Again but it's there, loud and accusing.

My lungs drag in some air as I'm conflicted. What can I say to make up for my screw up? My first instinct is flight and I'm also tempted to make her forget with my lips on her neck. I am not the kind of guy who pours out his heart to a woman. I don't even know where to start or what to say. Maybe lying would be better but I opt for honesty.

"I didn't expect you to be pure, the way you were grinding at that guy and when you kept taunting me I got so angry. When I made that discovery I couldn't bring myself to take that away from you in anger. You deserve so much better than me." Her eyes widen with each sentence I utter. She searches my eyes and I see the disbelief in her eyes.

Silence stretches over us, both of us don't know what to say. I can hear her heartbeat strumming wildly in perfect pitch with mine.

"Why did you wait?" the question propels itself out of my mouth making her uncomfortable. Her skin is flushed again, and she breaks eye contact with me to play with her fingers. She's blushing! The realization makes me proud. I tilt her face up and my eyes linger at her lower lip, which she is nervously chewing. She sighs, releasing her full lower lip and I fight the urge to ensnare it with my own teeth.

□

"This is going to sound stupid, but I was saving myself for my husband. I've always dreamed of finding a kind husband, who will love me and worship my body. And I wanted him to be my one and only lover." The quiet conviction in her voice burns my chest, mostly because she is describing everything I am not.

"But this morning you were so eager and willing to give yourself to me...?" I'm bewildered and overwhelmed. She's also uncomfortable and tries looking down but I hold her face in place. I want to see what goes through her mind, each emotion is honest and telling as it passes through her eyes.

"I was fighting with myself, I thought if I don't give my virginity to you, no one else will ever want me. You made me feel wanted and then you just stopped and got off me. Am I that repulsive?" a tear falls onto her cheek as she utters her last question. Shit, I am an even worse shithead than I thought.

"Nomaswazi listen to me. Any man will be lucky to have you, but I don't think any man is deserving to have you. Least of all me," I'm so desperate for her to believe me. I take her hand and put it over Zikode who's still raving for some action.

"Feel this. Feel how much my body is longing for you. Feel how insane your lips are driving me. Feel how much I yearn to bury myself in you, to mark you as mine." My words are a hiss as her hand is doing inexplicable things to my body. Zikode is straining against my boxers, bearded with pre-cum. Her eyes are wide and innocent, as she grazes my tortured manhood with the sole of her palm.

"Baby stop..." my voice is pleading and needy. What is this woman doing to me? I am weak around her and I hate feeling weak or needy.

"But you called me a cow." I can hear the hurt under the sullen tone and I frown trying to remember a time I had ever uttered such a cruel remark. As hard as I wrack my brain, I couldn't remember ever calling her a cow. It sounded like something Ntsikelelo would say. I learnt from a young age that saying that made me look deceitful, they all believed Ntsikelelo over me.

"I'm sorry naNkosi, I was young and stupid. Please, forgive me?" I rest my forehead on hers and I feel her breath hitching. To seal the deal, I subject her to the rare treat of my genuine smile.

"I forgive you," her voice is raspy and she's out of breath like she was running a marathon.

"Now don't ever cry again. You are so ugly when you cry, I thought..." I don't even get to finish my statement; she hits me with a pillow. I see a small smile and I tickle her until she laughs. Seeing her laugh, I want to blurt out that I love her but I'm so shocked with the revelation myself. I stop tickling her and look at her beaming face.

Her tear-streaked face doesn't have a drop of make-up, her hair is uncombed, but she is the most beautiful thing I have ever laid my eyes on. She surprises me by giving me a short smooch before she gets up and heads to the bathroom.

I look around her room for the first time. Everything is in its proper place, tidy without a hint of dust. There are pictures of her father next to her bed. I feel a pang of regret. Had I not stood her up on the altar, she would still be at home under the doting protection of her father. I was young, foolish but mostly selfish. My only fear is that I haven't changed much from the person that I was.

She comes back with a fresh face and has combed hair, looking more like the lady who has turned my world inside-out.

"Hlongwane, what is this? This thing between us," I feel warmth at the way she calls me. It's respectful yet sexy as hell. I can't wait to hear her chant my clan names.

"I want you NaDlamini. I want you to be my woman, my friend and my wife, but I realize I screw up a lot where you are concerned. So, I'm willing to get to know you. Court you until you can trust me again," I don't know where all these sentimental words keep coming from but today it seems like my heart is doing all the talking.

"Won't you leave me for the next skinny woman to

come along? Don't sell me dreams then break my heart again." Swazi means business, she's looking me straight in the eye.

I swallow as I think of her words. Right at this moment no woman comes close to her, she is all I think and fantasize about. She evokes these emotions which I have been running away from all my life. Am I ready to put down my bachelor card and commit to one woman? What if she's just a phase?

"I make no promises baby but please let me get to know you so that my heart can function again. Right now, you have taken full possession of my heart. Give me a chance to be the man that you need. I know we started off on the wrong foot but please allow me to redeem myself." Hee! If only Ntsikelelo could hear me now or my friends, I would be a laughing stock. I have never been one for hearts and flowers but for Swazi I am willing to be the man she desires. I just hope I won't fail her.

"Another chance I can give you. But don't expect me to give you my heart. I gave it to you too quickly once and I am still living with those scars today." Her words are measured and careful. I hurt her more than I imagined. How could I ever make this right? And the funny part is that now I'm the one baring my heart to her and she is keeping hers from me.

CHAPTER FIVE

I wipe my hands on my dress to get rid of the sticky sweat. I'm nervous, it's the day of the hearing and I am waiting to be called into the conference room. All the partners are inside and so is Ashton. Hlongwane just got here and its awkward, I lean in for a handshake and he engulfs me in a lingering hug. He smells of home. I don't know how to explain it, but I find myself longing for home in his arms.

The weekend was a revelation. After I told him that I won't be giving him my heart, I lied and said I needed to do my hair. A bad lie, instead of throwing him off; he insisted on accompanying me and I was subjected to the speculative looks from the ladies in the saloon. The truth is, I wanted to lock myself in the bathroom and cut my inner thighs. Something I haven't done in a while, when I was younger I used to try to cut away the fat. It didn't work but the physical pain took my mind away from my inner turmoil. So the cutting stuck with me.

I've discovered that Hlongwane is easy to talk to and his dry humour gets me laughing in spite of myself. Underneath his standoffishness, he is sweet, funny and blunt but I am still wary around him. One does not get over that kind of hurt overnight, but I meant it when I said I forgave him. I'm just wary to give him my heart again so soon. Between you and I though, this traitorous heart flutters whenever he is around me. I'm falling for him no matter how hard I try to fight it.

"You're going to do great baby," his voice is gruff but warm as he squeezes my moist hand. I offer him a small smile.

"You can come in now Ms. Dlamini and you too Mr. Hlongwane," Ms. Kobus instructs, showing us into the conference room.

My nerves come back in full force. What if they don't believe me? I'm not sure how I'm going to feel about being labelled the black woman who tried to frame her white senior. Sexual harassment is such a sore accusation to make, you end up on the firing line and your morals are called to question. At least that's what I've been led to believe by the news and crime series that I watch.

Hlongwane takes my hand and my nerves settle down a bit. He smiles at me for the second time since I've known him and instead of nerves I feel butterflies in my belly. His smile! It is not a full on toothy smile, no. His lips stretch and reveal a glimpse of his beautifully aligned teeth. But his whole face changes, lights up and transforms him into a boyish, carefree daredevil.

The panel of the Disciplinary committee is assembled in the front of the conference room. Only Ms. Kobus smiles reassuringly at me while Ashton is scowling at Hlongwane. My devil really did a number on him, or maybe he's just pale pink that's why the red marks around his neck are glaringly visible.

Just as we are about to start, a long legged young lady strides in. her complexion and the way she carries herself reminds me of my father's first-born, Zamaswazi. Her pantsuit is obviously Armani and her dreadlocks are swept up in one of those complex styles revealing her chiselled cheekbones and diamond drop earrings.

"Ms. Molope this is a private disciplinary action; you cannot just budge in here uninvited." Mr. Schoon, one of the first partners' states, obviously irritated by the arrival of the interloper. She smiles at him and it's not a friendly smile.

"I am here to represent my client, Ms. Dlamini." What? I don't remember hiring any legal representation. I turn to this rogue sitting next to me and he squeezes my hand, his eyes pleading with me, not to make a scene. Laawd, why me?

While the interloper and the angry looking white man argue about whether or not I require legal representation, I find myself thinking about my elder sister. Zamaswazi. A beautiful name for a beautiful girl, well woman now. I could never understand why she hated me so much and carried such bitterness in her heart. Even when we were young, she'd constantly remind me that no one wants an ugly, fat thing like me.

Zamaswazi usually led the people bullying me at school. It went on for a long time until *Babe* had them transferred to a school in Mbabane, her and my brother. Her mean words still ring in my mind, no matter how hard I try to bury them. Someone squeezes my hand and I look up into the worried eyes of Hlongwane. I don't understand how he can be cold and angry one moment then caring the next. I focus instead on my hearing.

A heated, almost whispered argument ensues among the disciplinary panel. After a while a red Mr. Schoon allows my legal representative to sit in on the hearing. Am I wrong to be angry that she decides to sit next to my supposed husband? Isn't she my representative not his.

The hearing continues, I'm asked to narrate what took place and I do so calmly. The disciplinary panel askes me questions which make me feel like they are accusing me of throwing myself at Ashton. The new black woman thirsty for male attention. I become grateful for Miss Legs, because she rebuts and shuts down any attempt to shred my reputation or inference of any sexual relationship between me and Ashton. No wonder most women don't come out and report sexual harassment, the victim is made to feel like the perpetrator.

Hlongwane also gives an account of how he came down and saw Ashton shoving his tongue down my throat, how I bit his tongue and how Ashton wanted to strike me. I notice pride in his voice when he mentions that I bit Ashton's tongue and he's incensed that Ashton almost struck me. He doesn't leave out that he strangled Ashton and he doesn't sound apologetic about it.

Ashton is also given a chance to defend his action. What pisses me off the most is when he dares open his thin lips and say,

"I thought Ms. Dlamini was also coming onto me, she always laughs at my jokes, never complained when I brushed my hand on her and she's always wearing those tight skirts. Leaving very little to the imagination."

"Is there anything wrong with wearing tight skirts to work Mr. Roberts? Do you realize that she might have been uncomfortable with your earlier inappropriate unwelcome gestures? Which incidentally qualifies as non-verbal form of sexual harassment in accordance with article 4 (1) (c) of the Code on Sexual Harassment in the Work place of the Labour Guide." Ms. Molope states in her crisp notes. Take that you perverted pig! My inner goddess is wildly doing the Gwara-Gwara as Ashton squirms.

The hearing drags on until the presiding officers release us so that they can make their deliberations in private. We trek outside and Miss Legs offers Hlongwane a hug, he's smiling till he meets my narrowed gaze and then he squirms and moves out of her embrace. Then she has a nerve to offer me her hand for a handshake.

"We formally meet, I'm Omphetse your lawyer," a petty side of me wants to yank her by her stupid dreadlocks. But the lady in me smiles and takes her hand.

"Nomaswazi, his wife," don't ask me where that came from, I also don't know.

Maybe I just want to get back at Hlongwane, it's obvious these two have something going on. Her confident smile falters as she frowns at Hlongwane.

"Oh, I didn't know you were married." I also narrow my gaze at him anticipating his response. He clears his throat and looks from me to Miss Legs.

"Umm yes Omphetse, meet my wife Swazi." I smile in victory and mark my territory with a brief kiss.

"We've been married six years. I wonder why he's never introduced us." I hear a gasp from Miss skinny Legs next to me and Hlongwane chokes on his saliva. I smile serenely and add, "I will leave you two to catch up, I need the ladies."

I make sure to sway my generous hips, the hips that Miss Legs is sadly lacking as I show them my glorious behind. I hear a hissed exchange behind me and I smile to myself when heavy footfalls echo behind me. I'm about to step into the ladies when Hlongwane holds my arm and turns me to face him. I school my features into innocent nonchalance.

"NaDlamini..." his voice is rushed, I interrupt him.

"Did you sleep with her?" I'm proud at how even my voice is.

"It's not what it seems..." I've never heard him sound so flustered before.

"Hlongwane, a simple yes or no will suffice."

"Yes, I slept with her baby, but it was a long time ago. Before I..." he sounds earnest while his confirmation does funny things to my chest. I know it's unreasonable to hope that he also waited for me, but it still hurts.

"Ok. Please excuse me I need to use the ladies," my voice

quivers lightly betraying my turmoil, but I hope he doesn't notice.

I quickly get into the bathroom and close the door behind me. This is the man who was declaring his love for me and begging me to give him a second chance with my heart just two days ago. Not only am I going to guard my heart but I'm going to lock it in a cell and throw away the keys, even if he makes it flutter every time he smiles.

......

"After much deliberation, we have concluded that Mr. Roberts acted in a deplorable manner towards Ms. Dlamini. Therefore, we have undertaken to suspend him for a month in which he will receive no pay. Ms. Dlamini we are pleased to inform you that you have been selected to be part of our Accounting internship program. We will pay your tuition with ACCA while you work under our accountants and you will also get a basic salary. It however only starts two months from now." My heart thumps in excitement as Mr. Schoon utters those words. My dream of going back to school is being realized! With the Association of Chartered Certified Accountants, no less.

Hlongwane utters a mirthless laugh next to me and I look at him with a frown.

"Is this some kind of a sick joke? My wife was violated by that man and you think a little slap on the wrist and a bursary will make this right? If he isn't dismissed with immediate effect, I am taking my portfolio elsewhere. I can afford to send her to any institution of her choice and make no mistake after this I am going to pursue a criminal and civil suit against that thing that thinks, he can go around violating my wife!" his voice is vibrating with anger and we all look at him in shock. He can't mess this opportunity up for me.

"Can I please have a word with my husband outside?" I ask already standing and I drag him outside.

"What the hell was that?" I hiss as soon as the door closes behind us.

"Can't you see that they are trying to buy your silence for their precious prestige? They think you need their stupid internship? I can afford sending my own wife to school!"

Nkhosi!

"Hlongwane, this isn't about you. This is about me. Now if you want to come here and start controlling my life, I think whatever it is you think we have got going on must come to an end. I left home to make it on my own and I have been making it so far. *Angilufuni lolusito lwakho*!" he looks at me like I've committed the biggest crime. Without saying a word, he goes back inside and I'm left pulling my braids. He's so frustrating! I follow him back inside.

The partners seem nervous as they look from the devil

to me. I hate being in the spotlight like this, I clear my throat uncomfortably.

"Thank you I will gladly take your offer," through the corner of my eye I see him scowling darkly at me. He better not ruin this for me.

"Our only condition is that Ashton is transferred to another city, if he so much as breathes in my wife's direction everyone in this room will suffer the consequences." Hlongwane says pointing a menacing finger at Ashton. As long as I get my internship, I really don't care about where Ashton works.

A few details are hashed out and I sign a nondisclosure contract and a few forms, only after Miss Legs has read through them. Sigh. But she is more subdued now and she won't meet my eye. I'm given the two months off, to prepare for school. Accounting has always been my dream, I love numbers. Most women don't get any justice when they are sexually harassed, but I got an internship out of it. They might be trying to get me to keep quiet for their reputation, but I don't care. A blessing is a blessing no matter how it came about, that's what my *makhulu* always told me growing up.

……

The ride back home is fraught with tension. I can tell from the way he is clutching the steering wheel that he is

□

mad as hell. Well so am I, instead of driving me back to my apartment, he drives to his hotel. Choose your battles girl, the little voice in my head tells me and I agree. He holds the door open for me without a word and I get off silent as well.

In the elevator, my bravado is fast evaporating and all I want to do is run away. It has everything to do with the way he keeps popping his knuckles and flexing his hands. I try looking into his eyes and I regret it immediately. His eyes are back to a fiery whirlpool of burning coals, his lips are set in a thin line. His whole aura is intimidating. My anger is quickly replaced by fear. Too quickly, the elevator pings at the top floor of his penthouse suite and I follow him like a sacrificial lamb.

"Sit," his voice brooks no argument as he points me to the sofa in the middle of the room. I comply, sitting on the edge of the sofa, my back ram-rod straight.

I watch with wary as he takes off his jacket and tosses it neatly on the back of an armchair. He rolls his sleeves and heads over to the bar. My eyes follow his every movement as he pours himself a double shot of whisky and downs it in one go. I want to ask for some vodka as well, to lend me some Dutch courage, but I decide I still want to live a few more years on this earth.

"We are only going to have this conversation once. Clear?" controlled anger underlies his words and I nod my head repeatedly. Even though at the back of my mind I know, this isn't the only time we are going to have this conversation.

He comes to sit in front of me on the coffee table, his knees gripping the sides of mine, effectively prisoning me. His jawline is squared, no hint of a smile and his eyes are narrowed at me. A part of me wants to reach over and cradle his chin, but like the vodka idea I dismiss this thought as well.

"You do not talk to me in that tone, ever. You do not raise your voice at me. You do not question my authority, especially in public..." he sounds really angry but some of my anger is also coming back.

"But then I..." I try to interject but he talks over me easily.

"And you do not disturb me when I am talking. You listen first." He says this part with narrowed eyes and pauses to see if I want to continue talking. I gulp down some saliva and decide to keep my mouth shut.

"I don't care if you don't want my help, you will get it. Everything I have is yours by virtue of you being my wife. Your father told me you are stubborn, and I see that, but you will respect me Nomaswazi. You will give me my place as your man or so help me God, I will make you respect me."

"I'm not your wife!" I say in exasperation earning myself a fierce scowl.

"You were introduced to the Hlongwane ancestors as my wife, it doesn't matter that a piece of paper doesn't proclaim you as mine." His arrogance sets my teeth on edge, but I decide this is one argument that I won't win with him. My mind goes all over the place at his speech. Does this mean he would hit me? Do I have to fear my own husband?

"I would never hit you Nomaswazi but there are other ways to punish you and get you in line," the way he is able to read my emotions is creepy. I wonder what other ways is he talking about?

"There was no need to be bitchy to Omphetse," I snort my derision at that statement and he raises his eyebrows in a manner that says, talk.

"You decked a guy for simply dancing with me and you go around marking me as your wife. Yet you bring one of your sleeping partners to represent me without my consent. How did you expect me to feel when she was all over you like a bad case of herpes? I need my respect too as your woman." He has to know I am not the timid teenager I used to be anymore. I have my demons, but I know how I want to be treated by my man.

"I told you we hooked up a couple of times a long time ago, it didn't mean anything." How can such a smart man be so dense at the same time?

"Oh, so I can also bring my ex-boyfriends who used to

pleasure me and do things with their tongues to..." he hisses like a wounded animal and shuts me up with a rough kiss. His lips are punishing and demanding.

I'm glad he didn't call my bluff, I have no exes who pleasured me, except if you count the yummy characters in my erotica books. I got to put my point across. I accept that he has a history, I just don't want him rubbing it in my face.

"Be very glad I can't punish you yet," the way he says this as he stares at me with his smouldering gaze makes my breath hitch. I feel an icy hand squeezing my spine.

CHAPTER SIX

"I've never felt more alive man, even though most times she makes me behave like an angry bull inside a china shop." Saying that out loud sounds weird even to me.

I take a swig of my beer and find Melusi looking at me like I'm some lab rat. I couldn't stay another minute around Nomaswazi, I would have strapped her to my bedpost and denied her an orgasm until she was in tears and begging me to take her. So, I dropped her off at her apartment. I called Melusi because he's the married one, maybe he can make me understand what that witch is doing to me. The only time she gave me hope was when she marked me as her husband with Omphetse.

"Balance me real quick here. So, this is the same girl you were arranged to marry six years ago, you didn't pitch for your traditional wedding to the same girl and you ditched her at the altar because you didn't want to marry her. She ran away from home and you've been keeping an eye on her, out of obligation to her father. The old man feels like he's dying so he asked you to persuade her to come back home, but instead the moment you saw her, your caveman habits came to the surface. You've been shoving down her throat, that she's your wife and now you want to ask her to marry you after spending a weekend with her. But you are afraid she is going to reject you and tell you that you are out of your damn mind?"

The scepticism in Melusi's voice makes me sweat a little. When he puts it like that my attraction to Swazi sounds insane bordering on delusional. Still I nod my head sheepishly. He throws back his head and laughs. A full deep throat laugh that rankles me and sets my teeth on edge.

"How good is her cunt man?" he manages to ask after a while but he's still chortling in mirth. Maybe asking Melusi wasn't such a good idea. I see the barman leaning closer, obviously enjoying the free show.

"That's the thing, I haven't slept with her yet," I manage to say that through my teeth. Melusi stops laughing and looks at me in shock.

"Whoa you mean the Zee-terminator hasn't tapped that

yet?" the use of my college nickname for Zikode maddens me further.

I met Melusi and Mpho overseas, we were studying the same program. You know when you are all foreigners you immediately click as *umkhaya.* Over the years our friendship had solidified into brotherhood. Melusi knows me better than my own brother and I know he will put things into perspective for me after he's done being an idiot.

"Man, you really love this girl, don't you?" I sigh in frustration and try to put what I feel for Nomaswazi in words.

"The moment I looked into her eyes man something in me changed. Those eyes have been haunting me for six years, but I chose to shut them out. Bury them in the deepest dungeon of my brain and throw away the key. Back then I wasn't ready to be tied down. I still wanted to explore and sample what other women had to offer. Now I feel like I was just looking for her and it all made sense when I saw her again. Yes, I want to fuck her smart mouth into submission, but most importantly, I want to protect her, shield her from any harm. I don't want to see tears in her big owl eyes. I want to mark her so that everybody knows she's mine. The thought of her barefoot and pregnant in my kitchen gives me a boner. She makes me want to be the man of her dreams. I knew from the moment I walked into that foyer and watched her busy on the phone, smiling as she brushed her hand against the keyboard. I knew I was done running from her. I haven't had a single nightmare since I saw her again. I need her and I want to go the whole nine yards with her."

Understanding dawns in his eyes and his fist lands playfully on my shoulder. Melusi knows part of my demons, I would wake up drenched in sweat and tears; he kept me grounded. Even when I blacked out and thrashed our apartment, he and Mpho helped me clean up. They tried getting me to see a therapist. I did for a while then I stopped.

"I never thought I would live to see this day, but she's got you by the balls. The same way Nokwanda owns mine," affection laces his voice as he speaks of his wife.

They have been married for four years and he hasn't looked at another skirt since. We always made fun of how whipped he is, what Nokwanda wants, Nokwanda gets. Now I get it, I want to give Nomaswazi the world too, but she doesn't trust my intentions anymore. I can't say I blame her.

"You are going about this the wrong way. Women love to be dominated but hate to be controlled." Huh? I look at Melusi with confusion.

"Don't give me that look, you should be jotting this down son. I'm about to impart some wisdom. Barman give us two glasses of Armagnac on the rocks please! Mr. Lovesick Puppy here is footing the bill tonight." This fool!

□

......

I'm nervous as I park in front of Nomaswazi's dingy apartment building. Melusi's words are ringing in my ears.

"You need to woo her properly. Some grand romantic gesture will melt her heart as well..."

Operation woo-her-panties-off was on. I am a man of action, once I get the wheels turning and put the plan in motion, I feel more at ease. I didn't waste any time preparing everything, I just by lifted my phone. Yet all this hangs on Swazi's response, that's why I'm nervous. I knock and this time she opens the door, looking flushed. Her eyes are cautious as she looks at me suspiciously. I hope I don't smell like a brewery, I came straight from the bar and its now a little after 8pm.

"May I come in?" I eventually ask when a full minute passes and she's just standing at the doorway eyeing me warily.

"Of course, come in," she's blushing and that warms me to no end.

The tantalizing aroma of *sitambu nemabhotjisi* hits me square in the face, the moment I step into her apartment. My mouth is watering, and my stomach timeously growls. Nomaswazi looks at me like she's trying hard to contain her laughter but fails dismally. She has a deep belly laughter, the type which makes you join in even when the joke is on you.

She points me to the lounge while she heads to the kitchen. I marvel at how homely the place feels, with its two mismatched couches and the sizeable flat screen. She was watching Telemundo and I can't stand those soapy telenovelas, so I change the channel to M-net Action and settle for a Denzel Washington thriller.

She comes back with a basin with warm water and a cloth to wipe my hands dry. I'm suitably impressed, more-so when she brings a steaming plate in a tray and places the tray in front of me. She paired the classic samp and beans with beef curry and grilled vegetables. There's a side plate of chakalaka on the tray.

"I wasn't sure if you liked chakalaka or not, it's hot," she explains almost apologetically.

"It's perfect NaDlamini, everything looks perfect." She brightens up at my compliment and laughs freely.

"Hold the compliments until you have tasted the food, it might taste like cardboard and sandpaper," I love how at ease she is right now. She isn't avoiding my eyes and she's even teasing me.

"Maybe I should make you taste the food first, in case you poisoned me," I tease her back and she laughs again. I think I'm getting addicted to her laughter.

"Well you left me at the altar that's a good enough reason to poison you," she's still teasing but I can see the hurt just beneath the humour.

"I shouldn't have left you, I was stupid and afraid of how you made me feel. Please forgive me Swazi." There's no teasing in my voice, I mean every single word. She smiles sadly at me.

"Forgiving you is easy, it's the forgetting which will take a while." She never sugar-coats her words.

"Then please allow me to help you forget," she raises her eyebrow and I rush to ask her before I lose my nerve. "Please go away with me, just the two of us. We'll go tomorrow and come back after a week on Sunday. I just want to get to know you and make up for my past sins."

I'm pleading with my eyes and I can see the doubt and mistrust in her eyes. I can tell she's at war with herself.

"I don't know Hlongwane, we just met Friday and we've been butting heads since. I think we're rushing things." I panic and the ruthless business man in me wants to close this deal so badly.

"I promise I won't do anything you are uncomfortable with baby, and if you feel the slightest discomfort, the jet will be at your disposal at all times to bring you back home."

"Why should I trust you? Won't I wake up tomorrow all excited and you stand me up again?" I deserve that but I won't let that deter me.

"One last chance NaDlamini. If I let you down I promise

to walk away from your life and never look back. I messed up but please let me redeem myself and prove I am the man for you." I'm not taking no for an answer I add silently. She sighs like she knows how relentless I can be in my pursuit.

"Where are we going?" I smile in victory and pure pleasure.

"It's a surprise baby. All you need is to be ready tomorrow morning by 9am and you don't need to carry any luggage not even your toothbrush." I have been a very busy man in the last two hours and I know everything will be in place. Those working under me know I always require no less than precision.

"What about my underwear?" she blurts out then blushes furiously. It's my turn to laugh heartily, I can't remember the last time I laughed so hard.

"Don't worry *nkosatana,* I got you covered." I bite my lower lip as I remember the pleasure I felt choosing her lingerie in the catalogue my PA sent. No more cotton panties like the one she was wearing on Saturday. I made sure I ordered loads of lace, some garters, bikinis and flimsy thongs. I can't wait to see her face as she goes through my purchases. Pure romance is pure haven of all things fantasy.

She frowns at me like she can see right through me. Now I'm worried that she won't agree to wear any of it. I've come to learn that Swazi is very opinionated, and she doesn't hold back on anything.

□

"Should I dish you more food?" her voice is back to teasing.

I look at my plate and realize I have polished off the food. I can't remember the last time I ate so much. Wait I do, it was when I ate my mother's food and I tell Swazi as much.

"Your food reminds me of my mother's food but thank you I'm full." I belch my appreciation and her smile brightens her face again.

"How is she? She was so kind to me," her innocent question opens a wound that hasn't really healed yet.

"She passed away last year." My voice is flat not portraying my inner turmoil. Her one regret was that she left me before I settled down and before she held her first grandchild.

Swazi looks shocked and hurt. Instead of uttering those lame words of comfort, she crawls onto my lap. She's hugging me fiercely as she cries for my mother and for me. I draw comfort and strength from her tears.

"She had leukaemia and she hid it from us until it was too late. Not that there was anything that could have been done for her except to undergo many tests and procedures. She knew that but maybe if I had known I would have been there for her. I wouldn't have travelled so much. Maybe my memories of her would be more than seeing her on her deathbed." My voice is gruff with unshed tears. It feels good to offload on someone. No one asked me how my mother's death had affected me.

My father and I don't see eye to eye, but my mother was my rock, I never could say no to her. She was warmth and hugs personified. I never understood how such a loving person could end up with such a cold and calculating man as my father. Theirs had been an arranged marriage too but there was no doubt that the old man dotted on her. What little heart he had beat for her that's why he always forgave me because she always interceded on my behalf. I missed her kind eyes so badly.

Nomaswazi has cried herself to sleep and I smile at how her breasts heave and fall as she sleeps. Her tearstained face is peaceful. Getting up with her in my arms isn't an easy feat, I must hit the gym harder since I'm going to be carrying this one around. Without waking up she hooks her arms around my neck, her generous breasts cushioned against my chest. My arms are underneath her lush curves, holding her in place. She feels perfect against me. Zikode vehemently agrees and it takes all my willpower not to wake her up and have my wicked way with her.

For the second time I strip her down to her cotton panties and tuck her in her bed. She grumbles, turns and sleeps flat on her tummy. I kiss her lips gently and let myself out of her bedroom, after switching off the lights. I take the plates and wash them before leaving them on the sink. I tidy up before letting myself out of her flat. At least the door locks itself the moment you close it and I also locked the burglar gate. I'm still not fully satisfied with where she stays but it will do for now.

I make a few calls, confirming that everything is in place. The beach house was cleaned and the clothes will be delivered and hung up tomorrow morning. The fridge has been stocked up and the jet is ready. The necessary documents have been drawn up. Siphiwe, my PA, is nothing short of a miracle worker and I make a mental note to give her an early bonus. It's only March but she earned it.

……

My breath hitches as I look at Swazi waiting for me in front of her apartment. She's wearing a wrap dress, it's deep red almost maroon in colour with splashes of orange and yellow. It's artistic and fun with her orange dangling earrings and brown wedge shoes which match the beads on her braids. It artistically molds her generous hips making her bum look sinful and the dip in her bosom presenting a wicked cleavage.

The colour in her dress makes her ebony skin shine with good health and highlights her unmade-up face. She looks youthful in the half-cornrows half-braids hairstyle I chose for her. She listened to instructions and she's only carrying a small purse which is as tribal and festive as her whole outfit.

Her teeth shine brightly in the sunlight when she smiles her welcome, as I step out of the rental Phantom. It seems out of place in these Berea streets but I'm going all out to woo her. A few busybodies are now almost hanging out of their windows ogling the Phantom, but I only have eyes for my princess.

"You're bright and early today *nkosatana*," I murmur as I kiss her chastely on the lips.

"I had a deep and refreshing sleep." She responds equally as quietly. "A Phantom huh?" her eye quirks up in barely concealed humour.

"A ride fit for a princess, just a glimpse of the week ahead." I can't keep the cockiness out of my voice, at least she grins back at me.

"I'll be the judge of that."

She gets in before I can even hold the door for her, but I close it after her and get in the other side. Her dress has hitched up showcasing her healthy shiny legs which are sturdy and smooth. The sight does things to me and to distract myself, I get busy pouring champagne for us. I hand her, a flute and propose a toast,

"To an amazing time ahead of us," she clinks her glass with mine without saying a word and sips from her flute.

She's quiet all the way to the airport yet the silence isn't oppressive. It's calm and serene as her yet bristling with so many unsaid things. She smiles her wide smile at the cabin crew and settles in gracefully. I'm watching her every move like a hawk. I wonder why I have never noticed this before but Nomaswazi has a comeliness to her, a nurturing and soothing side which draws you in without her saying a word. Her taste and style, understated yet elegant.

"Staring is rude you know," her voice brings me back from my thoughts.

"You're beautiful." The words just tumble out of my mouth and she looks at me in disbelief and embarrassment.

"How long is the flight going to be?" she changes the conversations whenever I compliment her. It's one of the most annoying traits about her but I don't push it. If she doesn't believe my words, then maybe I had to make her see and feel for herself how truly beautiful she is.

The flight isn't long; neither is the drive from King Shaka International Airport to Ballito. The first thing that hits me after we disembark is the crispy fresh, salty air. Coming from a dry, landlocked country makes me appreciate the moisture in Durban. Driving along the ocean side lifts my spirits and it gives me so much pleasure to see the same serenity plastered on Swazi's face. I see her taking pictures on her phone of the mountain slopes peppered with greenery.

I own property there as well as in Cape Town, Manzini, Italy and the Caribbean. That was one of the reasons I didn't feel ready for marriage then. I was still wholly dependent on my father and he had no qualms reminding me of this. He tried to control me the way he controls Ntsikelelo to do his dirty work. Now I am my own man with my own properties and investments, I can give Swazi the life that she deserves.

I open for us at the gate and we go up the winding driveway of Perissa No: 8. Swazi is looking around in excitement at the beautiful white villas in the Apartment Set. Our villa is nestled at the top and I take my time driving towards it. Giving her ample time to gawk at the beautiful white buildings. This time I rented a Range Rover Sport I love the power of big cars. She's still mesmerized by her surroundings; this time I get to open the car door for her. I can't help sneaking a picture of her childlike wonder.

"This place is so pretty," she breathes out with a wonderful smile on her face. I want to tell her that it's not as pretty as her but because I don't want to make her uncomfortable, I smile back at her. Clasping her hand in mine I move up the staircase and open the door for us.

The smell of a freshly cleaned villa mixed with the salty ocean breeze is welcoming. The place is spotless, and I just stand enjoying watching Swazi explore. She goes to the kitchen first, sweeping her hands gently over the island counters. She marvels at the grey granite counter tops and beams at the mirror fridge. She seems smitten by the whole kitchen, I can it's her favourite room in the whole house.

Then she heads into the lounge. The lounge and main bedroom open up into a large and very private patio with breathtakingly beautiful coastal views of the Santorini semi-private beach and the Ocean. One of the things which sold the villa to me. The scenic view is beautiful and the whoosh sound of the ocean calming. The neighbourhood is also very quiet and private, my kind of place. I don't even know who my neighbour is.

"You rented this whole place for us?!" her squealing voice is cute and childish; it makes me loosen up as well.

"No, it's ours *nkosatana.* I bought it for us and the children we are going to have." Her skin is flushed at the mention of children.

It pleases me that the thought of having our children makes her happy. I hadn't thought about it at the time when I bought it but now I can picture Swazi and our children in future running amok in this place. Maybe I'm getting ahead of myself but the picture in my mind's eye is splendid. I'm tempted to start making babies with her right now, the ocean is reflected in her eyes making them shimmer beautifully.

She moves from the rails and goes back inside to continue her exploration. I take a minute to appreciate the humidity in the air and enjoy the blueness of the ocean. I barely ever take time off to actually enjoy this place, I'm always too busy working hard to acquire more property. Maybe it's time I started taking more time off, work from my MacBook every now and then. I don't want to end up old and senile like my father without enjoying the fruits of my labour.

My tranquil introspection is disturbed by a shrill scream coming from the master bedroom. Swazi is hollering my name in full and it can only mean one thing; she has found the lingerie I handpicked for her. This promises to be fun.

CHAPTER SEVEN

I'm being tested! *Breathe Swazi, count to ten*. All these calming mechanisms aren't working. Whatever little calm I have is blown away when he comes sauntering into the bedroom. One hand is in his pocket, looking laidback with a smirk plastered on his devilishly handsome face. I throw the offensive piece of negligee in his face. He holds it close, rubbing it against his face, feeling it and even sniffing it. I hate to admit it but it's kind of turning me on watching him, dammit why did he have to be so hot? Those twin pools of coal are looking at me, taking in my reaction and scorching me at the same time.

"*What the hell is that?*" my voice is shrill as I point accusingly at the little scrap of material he has between his fingers.

"Your underwear," he thinks he's so smooth, gaaarr!

"I'm not wearing that!" The certainty in my voice bellies the nerves that hit me just at the thought of my stretchmarks and cellulite in full display.

I pick another more risqué piece; this one has holes in the butt-seats. An unbelieving laugh escapes my mouth and it quickly escalates into hysteria. His corky expression changes into a look of confusion then when the waterworks start, alarm and panic are plastered on his face.

"Baby what's wrong? I didn't mean any harm. You don't have to wear it if you don't want to. I will get you brand new underwear." He is blubbering as he tries to comfort me and hide the offensive pieces at the same time.

The truth is, the underwear isn't the cause of my tears. It's beautiful and the lace feels heavenly on my skin. It just showed me how far removed I am from the sophisticated women he is used to. I'm sure Ms. Skinny legs can rock these outrageous items of lingerie because she doesn't have a single drop of cellulite or stretchmarks in her blasted long legs. This underwear screams seductress and I'm anything but if I'm lucky he would want to do it in the cover of darkness.

"Talk to me baby, what should I do to make this right?"

□

shame he looks dead scared and that calms me down. I'm tempted to make up some lie, but his eyes see right through me. So, I settle for the evasion.

"Nothing I'm just being silly," my giggle sounds shrill and off to my ears I hope he doesn't pick it up.

"Try again princess." His voice demands that I cut the crap and level with him. I sigh and wiggle out of his arms and sit on the bed, pushing the shopping bags away to make room for us. He sits next to me, his gaze earnest.

"All this," I point at the bags of lingerie, "just showed me how out of your league I am. I have stretchmarks Hlongwane, not just the average on the surface stretchmarks. Deep ugly stretchmarks which look like scars and these would leave me exposed. I'm not as sophisticated as your former women. My tummy might have shrunk and flattened out, but it has rolls of flesh. I don't want you seeing all that."

I bow my head, I feel vulnerable and exposed. I'm afraid that he will burst into laughter. The silence stretches, and I risk a peek at him. He looks pained. That's the best description I can give for the expression on his face right now.

"I only bought this to make you feel sexy and confident, because you, my princess, deserve to be draped in lace and pearls. I'm new at all this Nomaswazi, you're the first woman I've ever bought lingerie for and maybe I was so selfish because thoughts of you in this made me hard. All this is just embellishment; my ultimate fantasy is you sprawled completely naked on my bed. I don't care about the stretchmarks all I care about are your glorious curves. You have reduced me to a raging hormonal teenager NaDlamini, can't you see that?" his every word warms my cheeks until I feel like they will explode from overheating. I look into his eyes to see if he means what he's saying and all I find is the raw truth in his eyes.

I'm glad we had this talk and that at least in this aspect I'm also his first.

"Give me time to get used to all this, please." I'm begging him for patience and understanding. He cups my face and places a chaste kiss on my lips.

"You don't have to wear it if it makes you feel uncomfortable. We'll go to the mall and get you what you need baby." I can't respond with the lump in my throat. He's turned me into a cry baby. Before last Friday I had not cried for years since I got to Jo'burg, but now all I seem to be doing is crying.

"What's this?" my curiosity is genuine as I lift the lingerie with the holes on the butt-seats. He grins at me and I admire how truly beautiful he is.

"This is part of the Love Thyself set. This is the high waist brief, it comes with this suspender and this half cup bra. It's actually my favourite." The name is pretty apt; I just don't love my body. Yet maybe I can try for him with time, I can see the fire in his eyes as he holds it up for me to see.

We're now laying on the bed facing each other. He insists on me keeping the lights on, he says he wants to see me. I'm looking into his charcoal eyes; they have a tender look that warms them.

"How come your mother had grey eyes?" he got his eyes from her.

"They say her grandmother was the concubine of a white man and all her children including grandchildren took his eyes. My mother also passed them to me and my brother." I could listen to his deep throaty voice all day long.

"Who's older between you and your brother?" He flinches at my question and it strikes me how little I know of him and the family I was to marry into.

"I'm older." His answer is abrupt and cold.

I want to ask what's the deal between him and his brother, I have never met his brother. He's become closed off so I opt to pleat my hands instead. He curses and then lifts my chin using the pad of his thumb. Shivers run up and down my spine. No matter how hard I try, I can't deny this chemistry that is between us. I want to go back to hating him, at least that feeling is familiar and comfortable. This awareness of him is unsettling.

"I'm sorry *nkosatana*, Ntsikelelo is just a sore subject for me. That doesn't mean I should have talked to you the way I did." He doesn't strike me as the apologetic type and him making an effort for me is heart-warming.

"It's ok. My siblings hate me and they blame me for our mother's death." I regret the words as soon as they leave my mouth. This isn't something I've ever told anyone and it might throw him off. He looks deeply into my eyes like he's stripping me bare before leaning over and brushing his lips against my forehead.

"You remind me so much of my mother."

I want to argue that I look nothing like her. She was beautiful, with her straight nose and pinkish lips. I remember how soft-spoken she was and so fair-skinned I was afraid the scorching Swati sun would melt her. He pulls me into his embrace and my heart literally stops before running a marathon in my chest. None of my books prepared me for this feeling of serenity brought by the sound of our hearts thudding as one.

……

"Wake up sleeping beauty," the annoying voice breaks into wonderful dreams of the devil and I skinny dipping in the ocean.

I don't want to wake up! I feel the blankets being tugged away from me but I'm still in my comatose half zombie state. I'm being lifted into sturdy arms and I snuggle into a broad chest. This feels nice, my sleep fogged brain registers. I'm being stripped, and my arms are lifted, and I comply, I even shimmy from my panties. A shower-cap is carefully put on my head and my braids secured under the shower-cap. Without warning icy shards of water tumble down my body and I yelp into full consciousness. I scowl at the devil who is laughing at my reaction.

He has learnt that only cold water makes me fully awake. Our first morning here, he made the mistake of putting me in a warm scented bath. I promptly drifted back to sleep, almost drowning in the process. Waking up has never been my strong point and for some strange reason he has taken it upon himself to wash me every morning. I gave up complaining yesterday and now I just enjoy being pampered. No, we haven't done the hanky panky yet. I watch as he applies a generous amount of shower gel onto the sponge and then proceed to scrub my back thoroughly.

He has a thing for my breasts. He takes longer soaping them and I watch in amusement as Zikode stands to attention. I laughed so hard the day he told me that he calls his penis by his clan name, now it's kind of grown on me too. The way he gives attention to my breasts, my arse and my nana while washing me makes me feel, wanted. I don't see the fat girl I was anymore when I look in the mirror, I see a desirable woman; stretchmarks and all. He worships my body and I love that about him.

In the three days we have been here, I have found a lot of things that I love about Hlongwane. I love that he listens. I could be telling him about the weather, what I like or what I dream about and he will pay me the same undivided attention. His shrewd business mind is also a huge turn-on. His eyes sparkle whenever he talks of his business plans and the projects he is involved in all through SADC and the global market at large.

His father's company specializes in logistics, but he wants to branch out and start his own property company. He studied architecture. He has the same sparkle when he's talking about his friends and what they used to get up to back in their college days and even now. However, he's closed off when it comes to his family, he barely says anything about them. Like the first night when I mentioned his brother, he also clams up when there's mention of his father.

Not that he's a chatterbox like me. I must draw him into conversations and he's happy to let me lead. He's also a man of his word, as promised on our first afternoon we went to the nearby mall and bought more underwear. Still in lace but it wasn't as risqué and covered enough of my flesh to make me comfortable.

"Open wider," I open my mouth as instructed and he

brushes my teeth.

I rinse off at his instruction and watch him brushing his own teeth. Such a simple act yet it fascinates me how in control he is. His square jaw has a rubble of growth and I watch him trim it to his normal meticulous beard. We don't talk much during our morning ritual, but it feels so intimate and normal like he has been washing me all my life.

"Good morning *nkosatana*," his voice does things to my stomach.

"What's good about it?" I retort earning myself one of his rare panty dropping smiles.

"So grumpy baby and you haven't even had your morning run yet." I groan at the reminder.

We've been running every morning at the crack of dawn on the stretch of the private beach. His words were if I don't like the way my body is, I should do something about it. So, he dragged me along to his morning runs. I think he just enjoys torturing me.

"But it's Friday today," I whine trying to get myself out of the torturous run.

"Good try baby but it's not going to work. If you're not dressed in ten minutes I'm adding another 2kms." I don't bother arguing because I know he means it. As I leave the bathroom he spanks my arse and I yelp, "Hey!". He winks at me with that smug look on his face.

......

"Where are we going today?" I ask as I smear butter on my croissants.

Every day since we got here he has been choosing activities for us to do. On Tuesday after shopping we watched a movie at the mall. I wanted to watch a romantic movie, but he bullied me into watching Black Panther and I hate that I loved it so much. From the yummy men to the Xhosa they used and their detailed traditional wear, I was hooked. It felt nice to share popcorn with him and randomly kiss like teenagers under the protection of the darkness in the cinema house.

Not that Hlongwane needs the cover of the darkness. He stopped in the middle of the busy mall corridors and kiss me until I was out of breath. He's big on PDA and I love every smooch, every hug and that he holds my hand the entire time.

"We're going to Umfolozi National Park." He doesn't elaborate further he just stuffs toast into his mouth. Some crumbs fall onto his beard and I reach over and swipe them off with my index finger without even thinking twice.

My hand stills when I notice that he's stopped chewing and is looking at me with such intensity. Before I get a chance to snatch my hand away he nibbles the pad of my finger. Electricity shoots down my whole arm. It's so intense

I close my eyes for a second and when I open them I find him staring at me.

"You're so beautiful Swazi," his voice is gruff, and I let it wash over me. I'm getting used to his random compliments, but they still make me uneasy. I snatch my hand away and busy myself with my serviette and I hear him chuckling softly. He is also an idiot from time to time. Charming but an idiot still.

Like on Wednesday when we went whale watching at ScubaXcursion all the way in Scottsburg, he picked me up threatening to throw me into the water with the whales. I clung onto him in fright while he kept making those weird whale sounds. When he's in his goofy mood, the years fall off his face and he looks like a 20-year-old. I must work on maintaining his goofy moments, I love them more than his control freak moments.

This place is nothing short of breath-taking! There's a peaceful stillness in the air that isn't broken even by the droning of the rickety safari van we are on. The van drones on the reddish dust road as the guide points out the rhino studiously feasting on its patch of grass ignoring us nosy humans. I lean as far as I can, looking at the herd of zebras not that far from the feasting rhino. The guide goes on and on about rhinos being endangered, how the poachers don't even bother killing them first before ripping out their horns.

My blood curdles at such inhumanity while Hlongwane is more interested in taking pictures with his camera.

I almost scream out of my mind when a giraffe pokes its head into the van just close to me. I can even see the hair up its snort.

"Don't freak out baby, just pet his head gently." Hlongwane's voice is calm and soft, I feed off his energy and place my shaking hand on the giraffe's jawline. It nuzzles against my hand and this is the most perfect moment. I wish Akhona was here to see all this. Thinking of her just brings back our last heated talk.

"Swazi you don't even know this guy, he's rude and controlling yet you just agreed to go out with him to God knows where. What if he kills you and uses your body parts for muti? I don't trust these businessmen and something about this guy is just off nje."

"Don't patronize me Akhona. I know him ok, his family and mine are close and my father trusts him. My family married me off to him for crying out loud! I'm not stupid." Akhona had looked at me in exasperation, her whole stance condescending.

"You're stupid if you think a guy like that is into you. I mean he barely looked at me and I'm glamorous. All he wants is to get in between those huge thighs then he'll discard you like everybody else." To say those words had hurt is an understatement, they cut deep and opened up all my

insecurities. It's funny how she had been ok with Hlongwane being my husband when she assumed he was an old man with two wives and a potbelly.

What if she's right? Yes, he's been nothing but a gentleman and hasn't made any move to have sex with me, even though the sight of his boner is a constant morning fixture. I mean, I'm nothing like that fancy lawyer he used to shag. She's thin, has long endless legs, a light beautiful complexion without even a hint of a blackhead and she has a freaking law degree. Seeing them standing next to each other then, I was struck by how formidable they looked together as a couple.

I'm just a mere receptionist for crying out loud, I don't even have a diploma to my name, high school doesn't count. All I have going for me is my family name and maybe my father disowned me while I was away all these years. I haven't even called home in all the six years I've spent in South Africa. At the back of my mind I can't help but question if I'm going too fast, entrusting him with my heart for him to break again.

"Hey princess, what's in that pretty head of yours?" the devil's voice brings me back to the safari. I hadn't even noticed that we are now viewing a lioness licking one of its cubs clean.

"Brains," I retort to his question, sticking out my tongue

at him. I'm trying to take away the concern I see in his eyes. He doesn't smile or respond but just stares at me like he can see right into my soul.

Without saying a word, he puts aside his camera and brings me closer to him, laying my head on his chest. I snuggle into him the same way I used to snuggle into *Babe* when I was little and there was a thunderstorm. He kisses my forehead and then rests his chin on top of my head and we go through the rest of the safari like this; me clinging onto him for dear life.

……

He's restless and cagey tonight. He has been like this since we came back from Mozambik, an intimate afro-porta restaurant not far from here and just next to the beach. Come to think of it, he was unusually subdued even when he opened the chair for me to sit. I watched him covertly as he ordered a bottle of Boschendal 1685 Cabernet Sauvignon, his commanding aura drawing in the bubbly waitress she was literally swooning over my man. I felt like yanking her perky boobs and screaming Mine! He's all mine!

As if he feels my jealousy he holds my hand and caresses it asking me what I want for a starter. I settle for steak trinchado fillet while he orders the Portuguese chorizo sausage. I keep the conversation afloat, telling him about my first day in Johannesburg. Looking back, it was hell but funny and it is strange that he's barely cracking a smile.

He doesn't eat much of his calamari espetada while I devour my chicken and prawn combo, stealing some of his calamari as well. The mild peri-peri sauce is to die for! All he does is watch me eat and I enjoy his attention. I do regret allowing him to make me have the chocolate lava cake, I'm so full all I want to do now is crawl inside my blankets and sleep.

His pensive mood is rubbing off on me and I'm also feeling edgy now. Did I do something wrong during dinner? Granted I had two and a half glasses of the intense black fruit and spice, red wine, but I am not that tipsy. I made sure to drink a glass of still water in between and another after desert. I can safely say I'm clear headed. His restlessness is suffocating me. I need some air. Taking off the Louboutin heels he gifted me with, I move outside to the patio and lean against the balcony ledge staring out into the ocean.

The moon is reflected on the water, dancing beautifully on the peaceful tide. The crisp air drives away all the lethargy I have been feeling, making me more aware. The hairs at the back of my neck stand up, informing me of the devil's proximity even before his woody scent tingles my nose. I don't turn to face him; I'm tired of his moods. I'm the one who's allowed to be moody, he has testosterones for crying out loud!

He places his arms on either side of me, caging me in against the rails and he rests his chin on top of my head. I marvel at how perfectly we fit, there's no awkwardness our bodies just sync. Silence stretches between us, but it isn't offensive, I can taste his nerves in the salty air.

"Nomaswazi,"

Yeeeerrr he never calls me by my full name unless he's mad at me. I don't respond, I let him continue.

"I know that we didn't start off on the right foot and it's my fault I was a coward and selfish. I know what I am about to ask of you is very selfish of me, but I just can't live without you anymore. This might feel rushed or too soon, but my soul tells me it's been long coming. I tried to rationalize it, but I just can't, and I know that you will also try to rationalize it, but I just want you to answer me with your soul. Don't think about it, let your heart and soul decide for you. Nomaswazi Dlamini *ngicela ube wami*?"

CHAPTER EIGHT

Nerves are killing me; I'm even sweating a little. I wanted to court her properly in the restaurant, make it romantic and all that. I want this time around to be perfect for her but then she told me about how lost she had been the first day in Park station. How she sat on those cold steel chairs watching others being collected while she knew nobody.

She sat there until an old lady she was on the same bus with, asked who she was waiting for and she made up some story. Fortunately, when the old lady's children had come to get her, she refused to leave Swazi behind. Guilt consumed me, had I not humiliated her at the altar, she wouldn't have run away from home.

She hasn't said anything to me and I'm scared. She is still facing the ocean and she hasn't turned to look at me but I'm comforted by her not shrugging away from my touch. The fear of rejection tastes bitter on my lips and for once I understand a fraction of what she must have felt when I rejected her all those years ago. I want to beg her to say yes, but I think I will understand if she says no. My heart is beating so rapidly, and I know she can hear it, it's too loud to be missed.

"Say something *nkosatana*, please." I hope my desperation isn't as loud to her as it is to my own ears.

I have never asked a woman out before and I feel like a teenager right now. Even in high school, girls had a tendency of throwing themselves at me and my brother, heck at times we even exchanged girls. The past days in Durban have been great, she has been letting me in but at times she just zones out and shuts me out. After our Safari drive, she closed herself in the bathroom for two straight hours and I was worried sick.

"There was a time when I would have jumped to be your anything. I fell in love with you by just looking at you from a photo. You were so handsome. I thought you would love me the way my father loved me." Her voice is soft, whimsical.

I hold my breath as she turns around and faces me, with my arms still caging her in. The moon is reflected in her eyes, it makes them shine brilliantly and I can't read the emotion illuminating her beautiful eyes.

"I realize now I wanted a fairy-tale and I built you up to be my prince charming and my saviour. Do you know what I've come to learn Hlongwane?" I shake my head even though I know she isn't really looking for an answer.

"I've learnt that fairy-tales aren't for people like me. I've learnt that I have to be my own saviour. Yes, on good days I feel fabulous but most days I'm still that fat kid waiting for someone, anyone to pick her to be in their team. I'm struggling to love the woman I am and I don't think I can be the woman for you."

Her voice breaks and her eyes which haven't wavered from mine are swimming in unshed tears. I would do anything to remove the jaded pain in them. To replace these tears with the blinding trust that shone in her eyes, the first time I looked into them. It hits me just how much I damaged her confidence and self-worth. I've gone on with my life, with her just at the back of my mind while she has been second guessing her worth. I'm an arse.

"Swazi I *know* you are the woman for me. I'm so sorry

that I ever made you doubt that. I'm sorry I made you see yourself as anything less than the amazing soul you are. I just need a chance to try to be a man worthy of you. I know you also feel this pull between us, please *nkosatana*, give me one last chance with your heart. *Ngicela umukele lutsandvo lwami.*" I think I'm holding her too tightly, I'm just afraid of letting her go.

Something deep in my soul is afraid of being with her but I don't think I can live without her. I don't want to live without Swazi. I've never put myself out there, laid myself bare for anyone this way. This is the weakness my father always talked about, the thought of losing her or any harm befalling her literally makes me weak in the knees.

"Talk is cheap Hlongwane. I'm sorry but I'm not convinced yet that you love me and you won't leave me hanging again." My heart drops to my shoes. I know I said I will understand if she rejects me but I'm crushed.

"But I'm willing to get to know you and see where this attraction between us will lead us..." I'm so happy I don't let her finish before I twirl her around. She squeals and the sound fills the still night.

Don't mess this up again, I think to myself as I cling to her soft, warm embrace. I have to remind myself that I am stronger than my demons and I have paid enough for my sins as I look into the moonlight dancing in her eyes. To quieten the voices in my head that are screaming that a demon like me doesn't deserve an angel like her; I crush my lips into hers. Wrong move because Zikode almost combusts at the sound of her moans.

......

I know this is a bad idea, the minute she twirls shyly for me yet her luscious curves are just screaming to be touched. This high waist bikini was made with her body in mind, the top hugs her girls lovingly and brings out her cleavage. While the bottom emphasises her tiny waist and teases you with the fullness of her hips. Damn, I had no idea her butt would stick out so temptingly. The neon colour makes her melanin dripping skin pop and shimmer with good health.

I can't help but stare at her unblinkingly. The saliva has been drained out of my mouth and words have deserted me. I've been so focused on her body that I frown when I see the distaste marring her beautiful face.

"This is a bad idea, let me just take this off." The bitterness in her voice makes me sick to my stomach. I hold her arm as she turns to go to the bathroom, probably to change.

"Why? You look perfect *nkosatana.*" Too perfect in fact.

"My stomach and thighs are exposed Hlongwane, look at all these stretchmarks. I can't show people these!" she's agitated and she keeps trying to pull the material of the bikini to cover herself.

"Hey, look at me," she bites her bottom lip as she looks up at me and it takes all my self-control to focus on what I'm saying. "You are beautiful. I love your body. I even love your stretchmarks. You've grown and it shows. I want to lock you in this house so that no man looks at those curves. But you want to go to UShaka Marine World and what my woman wants, my woman gets."

She's still doubtful but I swear I just saw a glimmer of the same look she gave me on our wedding day. We might be getting somewhere after all. I pick up the crocheted see-through black throw that is on top of the bed.

"Look, if you're still uncomfortable you can put this over your swim wear."

She takes it and gives me a grateful smile before sliding it over her head. It covers nothing really but she seems satisfied and a tad bit more comfortable. I bite back a sigh, I made her into this woman who's so self-conscious. Unwittingly I poured some of my demons into her. I shrug off the despondency threatening to engulf me and wait for her to take her bag so that we can leave.

As I stare at the unhappy looking shark in the large wooden plaque at the gate of Ushaka Marine, I can't believe it's the first time and that I'm even in an aquarium theme park. The deep blue water is reflected in Swazi's eyes and she doesn't try to hide her excitement. She loves the Sea world and she wants a picture with a shark. My heart squeezes when she slips her hand into mine as we walk through a wooden plaque written African Penguins. She's pointing at the dolphins standing on their tails and I'm taking pictures of her. The lenses love her and she isn't even aware of her captivating beauty.

She's letting loose, the throw came off at the Village walk and Swazi isn't tugging at her bikini anymore. I'm about to snap another picture of her leaning over to touch a dolphin when I see two boys, almost the same age chasing each other with water guns. Their laughs are carefree and their shouts loud, their father is shouting at them to stop but they are undeterred and also shoot him with water. He laughs as he also starts chasing them. A yearning so strong grips my heart and I brush it aside, I am a grown-arse man.

The older boy trips and falls, he cries and the father rushes to him and picks him up rocking him like a baby. He says something to the boy and his tears dry up, his face lighting up instantly. He sets him down and the boy is back to shooting water at his brother. They run out of my sight yet I can't look away.

"Mabhuqa are you ok?" Swazi calling me using my clans name snaps me out of the trance I'm in. I try to muter a smile for her.

"I'm fine *nkosatana*. Let's go to the Drop Zone now." She

looks like she wants to say something but then she changes her mind.

"Okay." I can see her closing herself off and I want to kick myself but I'm not sure I want her to come face to face with my demons just yet.

I hate how crowded the slides are. I take Swazi's hand and I'm relieved when she doesn't pull it away even though it's now limp in my hand. She's no longer curling her fingers around mine. Her anger I can stand rather than her revulsion.

"No. There is no way I'm going down that slide." She's already turning back down the wooden steps but I hold her waist. We've been in a queue to go down the Drop Zone for thirty minutes now and there's no way I'm going back without trying it.

"Nothing will happen. I promise I'll be with you the entire time." I've seen some men leering at Swazi and I am not letting her out of my sight.

After some coaxing she's sitting between my thighs and I can feel her shaking. She needs something to distract her from the height. I suck her neck and she shivers while snuggling into me. Instead of continuing with my sensory attack, I launch us down the slippery red slide and she's screaming as the water splashes us. The endorphin rush of going down between showers of water is exhilarating and by the time we reach the bottom, we are a tangle of limbs.

□

She's laughing and carefree again, ensnaring my heart deeper into her small hands.

"What's the one thing you regret the most?" she asks as she sips some wine.

We are now having dinner and the mood is ambient. I don't want to spoil it by mentioning leaving her at the altar so I think of something else. She's looking at me expectantly; I swear those big eyes can see right through my soul.

"I regret letting my father control my life for so long and letting my frustration and anger with him affect the people I care most about. Like my mother and Ntsikelelo." *And you*, I add silently.

She narrows her eyes at me over her wine glass, contemplating my words or just savouring the wine. I'm not sure which. She even tilts her head and I think she's tipsy. I've noticed she grows bolder once she has alcohol in her system.

"It's not too late for you and your father as well as brother. You need to get along for your mother's sake."

I wish it was that simple. I cannot even begin to try to break down to her my family's dynamics. How twisted and broken we all are. My mother was the glue holding us together and now she's no more. I don't know how to paint our toxic relationship without chasing her away.

"When are you going back home?"

"You're doing it again. Evading a topic that makes you feel uncomfortable Hlongwane."

She's getting too intuitive for comfort. I've managed to evade intimacy in relationships by just having sex and I can't even have that with her. It's frustrating. I've suddenly lost my appetite and I push my plate away.

"I'm tired. I'm going to sleep now." I look away from the hurt in her eyes. She clears her throat and gives me a half-smile.

"Go ahead, I have this movie I've been wanting to watch."

I hate this distance which is suddenly between us but maybe it's for the best. I kiss her chastely on the lips and I head out to the bedroom. The bed feels so huge and lonely without her. I toss and turn. Sleep is evading me. She finally comes to bed after about two hours and I feign sleep. She slips into the bed snuggles against me. I wrap my hands around her and I find myself drifting to sleep soon after.

......

"Hold her down!" the gravel voice snarls as always.

I see us standing there watching him in trepidation. The fear palpable in the darkening forest with its scary shadows. The thorns impaling themselves in our bare feet.

We're huddled in a group and there are stifled sniffs, no one dares voice their fear or pain. There are big red ants moving along and not minding us except for the occasional sting.

"Why are you staring at me as if I'm your mother's vagina? I said hold her down!" his breath stinks of opaque beer and raw eggs. The pus on the scar over his eye is fresh and I focus on it trying to block out the screams of the girl he wants us to hold down.

"Imbeciles! How do you expect to be men if you can't handle a woman?" Only she's not a woman, she could be fifteen or sixteen years old.

The rest of the men stand over us in a circle, their cold eyes piercing us from their balaclava masks. It's dusk, we can all see the girl clearly held down and trying to break free. Her lips are burst, her face bruised and her eyes swollen from all the crying.

"You go first!" the gravel voice again and they kick Ntsikelelo towards the girl.

Ntsikelelo looks at me with begging eyes, the fear stark naked in those eyes which are just like mine and I stare at him helplessly. The girl screams again and Ntsikelelo runs, breaking through the circle of men. He doesn't go far, one of the men grabs him and drags him back kicking and screaming. One of the men raises a rifle to strike him and without thinking I throw myself over my brother.

"I'll do it. I'll go first, I'm older. Please don't hurt him." I'm pleading, my voice vibrating and cracking with emotion and they laugh at my desperation.

"This one seems eager." The leader says and the men snicker and jeer. "Fine, you can go first. Be quick so that you all take your turns."

My heart is leaping out of my chest and beating so loudly, I'm roughly pushed towards the girl while the others are made to hold her down. As long as I live I will never forget the stark fear in her eyes, her screams and the way she's thrashing around even as they hold her down.

The tears in her eyes turn into blood and her tears are flowing so heavily I feel myself drowning in the red sea of her tears. Ntsikelelo's eyes have changed from grey to a blood-chilling red and I'm shrinking until I'm the boy with the water gun. I'm choking on the bloody tears; my little lungs are filling up. I see my father standing there watching me with a blank look on his face.

"Help me! Help!" the more I scream the more water that goes inside me, filling my lungs.

He can hear me. I know he can. He doesn't move just stares at me unblinkingly and now the pus oozing scar is on his eye.

"Hlongwane! Wake up, you're hurting me!"

Swazi's voice jars me from the nightmare I'm having

and her scared eyes are so round they almost swallow her face. I'm breathing heavily as if I've been sprinting a 5km marathon and I'm clasping her arm with a death grip. I let go of her arm as if it burnt me, ashamed of having been caught in the throes of a nightmare.

I haven't had one of these in ages and today it was so vivid, it felt like it was happening again. My body is filled with goose bumps and I would give everything to erase the memory from my mind. The worst part is that Nomaswazi looks freaked out, her body is shaking like a leaf. I reach out to hold her and she recoils from my touch.

I won't lie that stings, my worst fear is playing out before my very eyes. This is why I walked away in the first place. I didn't want to be vulnerable to how she thinks of me. I didn't want to expose her to my demons. I don't know how much of the nightmare she saw or heard and I can't come out and just ask her. My blood ices over at her next question.

"Who is it? Who did you rape Hlongwane?"

BUSISEKILE KHUMALO

CHAPTER NINE

"Baby," he sounds nervous. So many emotions are passing through his face but I can't keep count of them because I have a myriad of emotions of my own.

His thrashing, his mumblings and scream are still fresh in my mind. My hand hurts from his grip but I'm way too horrified to give my hand too much thought.

"Help me! Help!" his cry is still ringing in my ears breaking my heart. What horrified me was what he said just before his cry.

"I'm sorry, I won't rape you again. I won't do it. They can't make me do it."

He's quiet now, not answering my question. I can't stop my shivering, what kind of monster am I falling for? I'm so confused because while he was having the nightmare, he seemed scared and yet his words chilled me.

"Hlongwane what did you mean? Who did you rape?" I ask again hoping to get some clarity.

"It's just a dream Swazi, let it go." He sounds tired and the carefree devil I've grown to love is slowly fading in front of my very eyes.

"That wasn't just a dream Hlongwane, stop patronizing me. You said you raped her, who was it? Who did you rape?"

He looks at me long and hard. I try to act like I'm not intimidated and scared of him right now. He clicks his tongue before getting out of the bed. I watch as he roughly puts on his sweat pants. He doesn't say a word until he's fully dressed and he's taking the car keys.

"Hlongwane, you can't leave in this state. Please talk to me." I hate how nagging I sound right now.

He plain ignores me and I quickly get out of the bed and hold on to his arm. He really isn't in the right state of mind and no matter how shitty he is, a small part, ok a large part of me cares about him.

"*Ng'yakuncenga* Zikode, talk to me."

He looks at my hand for the longest time before looking at me. There's darkness in his eyes, his stare sends chills up and down my spine. I wish I just stayed in bed.

"I raped her, a 16-year-old girl while they held her down. Then I also held her down as others took their turns and she fought until all she could do was whimper. I've talked, happy now?"

I let go of his arm as if someone just electrocuted me. Regret flirts through his eyes before the dark look comes back shutting me out and he turns on his heel, banging the door behind him. I don't know what I expected, but it wasn't how cold and clinically he just spoke of gang-raping a teenage girl, no show of remorse or any emotion for that matter.

I slide on the floor as I wonder how everything has gone so horribly wrong. We were happy, scratch that, I was happy. I was beginning to think he loves me. Maybe he does, I don't know anything about the man clearly. The thing is I have stupidly fallen in love with him all over again. Since we've been here he's shown me his soft side, his playful and loving side. I forgot he was the devil.

I don't know how long I've been sitting here with my thoughts, its light outside when I hear the door open. I don't even bother looking up. My mind is clearer than it's ever been. The stench of alcohol hits me as he slides down next to me.

"Take me home Hlongwane." I don't wait for him to talk

first because my treacherous heart may just betray me again.

"*Nkosatana*, I'm sorry about my reaction earlier. I shouldn't have..." his voice is low and filled with regret but I don't want to hear what he has to say anymore. I put my hand over his mouth.

He looks a mess. His eyes are bloodshot and swollen. His sweatpants are rumpled and wet around his ankles. His knuckles are bloodied and yet he keeps cracking them nervously. He is far from the devil who stood me up at the altar and the polished devil who saved me from Ashton. He looks lost and drained. I stand up on shaky legs and head to the bathroom.

"Nomaswazi." His voice halts me as I reach the bathroom door but I don't turn. "I love you. I know I disgust you right now, but please never doubt what I feel for you."

I open the door without turning back because I don't want to break down and cry in front of him. I know what he confessed to me is vile but it's taking everything in me not to throw myself in his arms and tell him I love him too. How do I be with him and love him and not see the sixteen year-old they gang-raped?

My chest is tightening and I feel like I can't breathe. I want to hit something, anything to make this heaviness and tightness around my chest go away. I spot Hlongwane's razor and a battle within me ensures. I haven't felt the urge to cut myself in so long but now I feel like it's the only escape I will get from this conflict raging inside of me.

Maybe love wasn't made for me and him. Maybe him walking away from me that day at the altar was the best thing to happen to me. Now that I know that when his lips tilt a bit upwards he's biting back his laugh, now that I've seen him throw his head back in uninhibited laughter; I can't help but fall in love with the man beneath the devil. How is it possible that someone who is so possessively protective of me and deep down even of his brother, how is it possible that he would do something so heinous?

The sight of my blood somehow calms me down and I don't even feel any pain. I'm careful not to cut too deep. The tightening around my chest is loosening and I open the tape. When I come out of the bathroom Hlongwane is nowhere in sight. He made the bed, laid out a blue summer dress out for me and of course lace panties. There are also suitcases with a matching handbag next to the bed. The sight breaks my heart even more, why does he have to be so perfect?

The dress is long, with a synched drop waist and the front is two scraps of material held together by crisscross tiny straps while the back is just two crisscrossing straps. It's something I wouldn't have been comfortable with wearing before, but the past week with Hlongwane has let me be at ease with my body. The dress doesn't allow room for a bra and my girls feel dangerously liberated.

Hlongwane comes in as I am bending over to wear my sandals, he's showered and no longer smells like a brewery. I guess he used the other bathroom. He's just standing there gawking at me. His eyes have cleared, they are no longer bloodshot.

"Are we going now?" My question is met with silence.

I look up from strapping on my thong sandals and he is distracted by the sight of my breasts. I stare at him blankly. He clears his throat looking cute and hot under the collar. He's wearing a simple t-shirt and cargo shorts, dazzling me with his muscled slightly bowed legs.

"We have to go back eSwatini tomorrow. You need to see your father baby, he's not well and the doctors don't know how much longer he has left."

I feel the energy leaving my body and I'm grateful that I'm sitting down.

"What? How? Why?" I sound like a lost child right now, how could I have been so stupid? I turned my back on the one person who has loved me unconditionally all my life.

"His diabetes is getting worse; they have to amputate his left leg, but he has been refusing. He's also been having a nasty cough and the doctors suspect TB or worse lung cancer but he refuses to take the tests."

No! Not *Babe*, I can't imagine the man who raised me without a leg. He was always so strong. My whole world is crushing around me. The tears fall hot and steady, I find myself plastered against Hlongwane's chest as I sob.

"Why didn't you tell me?" I hiccup between my sobs and he's hushing me until I'm a bit calm.

"He didn't want you to know but he asked me to bring you home and I know after last night you won't agree just to go with me. I had to tell you now. I think you have to go and see him before it's too late." No, he won't die, not my father! I should have gone home sooner.

I find myself locked in the bathroom again with Hlongwane's razor. I don't want to believe what he just dropped on me. He's been knocking ever since I locked myself in but thankfully he's given up. I've spoiled the blue dress with drops of my blood, it's not really noticeable and I hope Hlongwane won't notice it.

He's not in the bedroom when I come out again and the suitcases are also gone. I take my phone and dial Akhona's number. I need someone to talk to right now, I feel like I'm drowning in my own emotions. Everything is just so overwhelming. The phone rings for the longest time before Akhona's cranky voice comes on the line.

"Swazi are you aware what time it is? I just got back from a rough night out man!" she clicks her tongue in annoyance.

"It's my father. I just heard that he's sick and he might have to have his leg amputated and the doctors don't know how long he's got," it all comes out in a rush and saying it out

loud just feels like someone thrust a knife in my chest. Her exasperated sigh makes the line crackle.

"He will be fine, take him to a doctor or something. Now can I go back to sleep?" She doesn't wait for me to respond, she drops the line. Wow! Just wow. I stare at the phone in shock.

A throat clears and I turn to see Hlongwane leaning at the doorway. He's so tall. His head nearly touches the door frame. He moves towards me hesitantly until he's standing right in front of me and staring down into my eyes. I should hate his touch but I lean into his palm as he cups my face.

"Listen to me, this is not your fault. You were young and hurt. Trust me your father forgave you a long time ago because he loves you. And you can't change the past so don't dwell too much on it. We are going to go and see your father and he will be so happy to see you. He misses you and talks about you all the time." I nod repeatedly while biting my tongue to stop the sobs in my chest from coming out.

The only other time I was this scared, was when my sister made me climb down a dried up well when I was six. There were rats down there and she left me alone there until my father and some of the village men came looking for me. I had even soiled myself by the time they found me. Hlongwane's hug calms down my nerves.

"What is this?" He asks while looking at the fresh cut on my arm. I quickly snatch my arm from him and move away from his embrace.

"It's nothing. I had a small accident while I was bathing. Can we go now?" He looks at me like he wants to say something but then he changes his mind and allows me to pass.

I look at the beautiful villa with the backdrop of the ocean as we drive away. The white looks dazzling against the deep blueness of the ocean and I wish I could stay here forever. I wish I could stay forever near the serene droning of the ocean waves far away from my sister's hatred. I wish I could stay and watch the sun dancing on the water bed and not have to face the possibility that my only parent can possibly die any minute now.

......

The dry heat is the first thing that hits my face when I disembark from the plane, its stark contrast from the moisture in Durban air confirming that I'm really home. Last night we slept at his hotel in Jo'burg, I did the sleeping while he disappeared to where only God knows. He only came back this morning to bath, I swear he reeked of female perfume. I didn't have the strength to confront him, we've gone back to being strangers.

I wipe my sweaty hands nervously on my skirt, staring blankly ahead. The flight here was awkward with me and

Hlongwane not saying a word to each other. I can't stop thinking of *Babe* all alone in a hospital bed. I also can't stop the guilt that has been consuming me for abandoning the only man who has ever loved me whole heartedly. There's an elderly man waiting for us at Arrivals with a wide smile wrinkling his leathery face.

I can see their lips moving but my anxiety is zoning me out from their conversation. They seem very close. The only thing is that the elder is Bab' Mlandeli and that he is Hlongwane's driver. Somehow I manage to smile at him and greet but that's as far as I can bring myself out of the turmoil in my head. This is the first time back home after six years and the thoughts of my departure leave my stomach queasy.

I'm not even enjoying the cushiness of the backseat of the Range Rover that is Hlongwane's pride and joy. I could see it from the way his hands caressed it lovingly once we got off the Matsapha airport. The pride in his voice as he mentions that it's the first car he bought for himself using his own money not his father's money. He takes my hand and intertwines our fingers and electricity shoots through my body jolting me from my thoughts and making my body yearn for his.

I don't understand how even after knowing what I know about him, my body is still so aware of him and this chemistry between us seems to be strengthening. The car swerves to avoid a rut and I use the opportunity to slide closer to the window and look at the passing trees. The country may have changed its name during the six years when I wasn't around but nothing much has changed. After getting used to the hustle and bustle of Jo'burg being back home is like stepping back in time.

We've left the tarred road and are now on the dust road and cattle just come out of the bushes and the car stops. The boys herding the cattle are admiring the car and wave at us. Bab' Mlandeli honks at them and they excitedly wave again. I'm grateful for the darkened windows when everybody stops and stares as we drive past. The children star struck with the car and the adults with their nosy curiosity.

I've never really been part of the community or felt accepted. As a child I usually played alone within the walls of my father's yard. Then I had to attend school with the other children and there I was snubbed and I couldn't make any friends. Then the whispered ridicule after my monumental rejection at the altar. To be honest I didn't miss much about this place except for my father and makhulu.

I'm not keen on being seen and being the talk of the village again. I can just imagine the headlines around the water holes and shops; the prodigal daughter has returned without even a dog or cat to her name.

CHAPTER TEN

I wish there is some reset button I can use to erase the last two nights of my monumental fuck ups. I'm tittering on the brink of the deep dark hole I spent most of my adolescence and half of my adulthood in. I can't even call Melusi and tell him any of this in detail. Melusi and Mpho may have an inkling of my demons, the occasional nightmares and how they drove me to women and drink back then but they don't know the specifics or how deeply tormented I am. Only Ntsikelelo is fully aware of all the demons that plague me because he was there with me and he feels what I feel.

He called me last night, he could sense my destructive state but even he couldn't pull me out of the darkness. We used to be close growing up but as we grew and dealt with our demons separately, that brought us apart. It became worse when I left to study abroad and he remained behind and became my father's right hand man. My mother was the one holding us together but ever since her death, all we seem to do is constantly tear each other apart.

I fell back into my old ways of dealing with the guilt, I picked up some random whore at a club. She was more than willing to take the party to her place. No matter how hard I pound into her it couldn't exorcise my demons. It only made me feel shitty about myself when I saw Swazi sleeping so peacefully on my bed. I wish I talked to her when she was begging me to stop, but I'm not sure I would have managed to explain my jadedness to her.

I keep stealing glances at her and she seems lost in her thoughts. She hasn't said more than five sentences to me since we left South Africa. I can tell that coming back here is taking a serious toll on her but I can't even reach out and take her hand. She's too good for me, my mind knows this but my heart is failing to accept it. After all I've done in my life I don't deserve a good woman like her, I'd only hurt her. Being in Durban made me think I could change, that I could try to be half the man she needs but now I'm just consumed by my own darkness.

Mlandeli smoothly swerves into the imposing gates of the Dlamini homestead. *Indvuna* Sobhuza Dlamini had done well for himself. One can tell not only from his sprawling homestead but also the homesteads around his *Inkhundla* (Constituency). All of them are well kept and some have electricity while others have solar panels on their grass-thatched roofs.

He built sturdy traditional beehive huts, around an impressively large cattle byre. The byre is made of steady oak which is perfectly filed and staked so closely together that nothing could possibly escape. The architect in me has always appreciated the perfect symmetry of the concave buildings around his homestead which are perfectly thatched with premium dry grass.

They are a true relic of Swati homesteads of old but on the inside are surprisingly modern with heated ceramic flooring and air conditioning. Underneath the grass are study tiled walls. The windows are large and made of shatterproof glass. I love the merging of tradition and modern architecture and I always wonder which building materials would be more sustainable on a bigger scale.

Nomaswazi still hasn't said a word to me and she's made no move to leave the car. She seems rooted in the seat almost fearful of leaving. I want to hug her and tell her that everything will be fine but I've forfeited that right by sleeping with some random whore while she slept alone in my bed. I get out of the car first and wave off Mlandeli, this is one job I rather do on my own. She holds on to my hand, more like clings to it as I help her out of *Inathi*. My car is too much of a beauty not to have a beautiful name.

I've been here a couple of times, so I know my way around. Swazi looks lost and nervous and I guide her gently towards the main entrance. A crushing sound startles us and an older lady with tiny moles over her leathery cheeks stands by the doorway, the scattered pieces of the tea set barely registering to her. She looks like she's seen a ghost, her hands visibly shaking. Swazi has also tensed next to me, her grip on my hand unyielding and painful. Damn, this woman has one hell of a death grip!

"Maswazi?" the elder's voice carries shock and disbelief. Finally, Swazi let's go of my hand and I try hard not to wince or stretch it out in pain, being a man is tough.

"Makhulu!" she half runs and half strolls towards the elderly lady who is still an ice sculpture by the door.

Once Swazi reaches her makhulu, the elder breaks down and starts wailing. Not quite the happy reunion I was anticipating, one would mistake it for a funeral wake. I'm standing here uncomfortably not sure what to do as the woman wails and Swazi sobs in her arms. I catch Mlandeli's discreet smile at my predicament and obvious discomfort. He's lucky he has been my driver since I was a child and I can't exactly fire him.

Indvuna is wheeled out by his nurse, probably to investigate the ruckus in his doorway or look for his tea, which by now is probably being enjoyed by the ancestors. Not sure if the ancestors drink chamomile tea. He's also shocked and emotional at seeing his long-lost daughter but like a true man he only allows one tear to trickle down his aged cheek. He looks worse than the last time I saw him, thinner and gaunter. A husk of the giant man he was in his prime. Yet he still commands respect even from a wheelchair.

The wailing has subdued somewhat, thank God. The chief catches my eye and mouths the words 'thank you' and I nod imperceptibly back at him. Swazi finally notices her father, she rushes to him and curls up on his lap bawling like a baby. Ah my cry-baby! I feel for the chief; my girl has such a generous behind and packs some weight there. I should know, I've been carrying her every morning for the past week. He doesn't seem to mind, he's just happy to have his baby back. I'm a bit jealous as it is obvious who holds first place in her heart. She keeps saying I'm sorry like some mantra and her father kisses her all over her face, snort and all.

I feel a pang watching their obvious unconditional love in their bittersweet reunion. Even as a child, our father never embraced us. I remember coming home with a bloodied nose and a torn toe because I had tripped over a rock and fallen while playing soccer in the field. I was told men don't cry and if I was so weak my enemies would crush me. I was bloody five years old. He wouldn't even allow my mother to 'baby' me. My teeth always clench at the memory, so I push the memory back into the box with my other unwanted memories.

The reunion is over, and we are ushered into the lounge in the main house. Just as I'm walking in I receive a call from my father.

"Where are you?" well hello to you too, I don't dare say that out loud.

"Just landed will be there in an hour or two." The line goes dead after that and I feel cold after that call.

My eyes land on a picture of Swazi during the *Umhlanga* dance in her *Indlamu* (traditional Swati wear). Her colorful attire looks youthful and fresh. Her beautiful perky breasts are full, her dark skin glistening. Drawing me to her tiny waist, expanding to her barely covered curves, making Zikode twitch painfully. She is barefooted, her head thrown back laughing, a sight leaving me breathless. I choke on my saliva. Swazi immediately focuses on me and tries rubbing my back, before rushing off. The chief knows better he laughs, belly deep laughter, resembling Swazi's and I'm glad it doesn't turn into a coughing spree. He must be getting better.

"You can take that picture and keep it. It is my thank you for bring her back home and looking out for her all these years."

I don't wait to be told twice, I quickly snatch the picture from the display that has other pictures. I see a headshot from the same day and eye my father-in-law. His eyes are twinkling, he nods at me, and I take it as well placing both pictures into my inner pockets. Just as I sit down Swazi comes rushing back with a glass of cool water. I'm touched that she's showing some signs of care after what I've put her through the past two days.

"I am ready to bring the rest of your cows now." I say boldly even though Swazi's stare makes me want to choke on the water she brought me.

Her father on the other hand is beaming from ear to ear and I can tell this makes him happy.

"It's not necessary Skoni, your family already paid the lobola in full and Swazi left here with her *lusiba*, she's your wife." *Lusiba* refers to the gall bladder which is squeezed on the bride's mouth and other parts of her body, then the inflated bladder is tied with a string above her forehead. The *lusiba* is the sign that she left her parental home with her father's consent

"*Akulotjolwa intfombi kulotjolwa umfati.* Besides my father paid for everything and now I want to pay for my wife myself and in full." If looks could kill, the looks I'm getting from Swazi would have strangled me by now.

"Spoken like a true man *ndvodzana* you will let me know the dates and we will be ready to receive you." The elder is blissfully oblivious to Swazi's anger but I'm feeling the heat. We have a lengthy conversation with him tell me about everything that has been happening in his *Inkhundla.* I always enjoy our talks.

"*Nkhosi,* unfortunately I can't stay. I have pressing business matters that I have to see to."

If I keep that old man waiting too long, he will want to know where I passed first. He's cunning like that and I don't want him to know that Swazi is here just yet. I can't bring myself to throw her to the wolves as yet, especially after her repulsion to just the surface of my demonic possession, she would probably bolt for good this time.

"Manana will see you out *ndvodzana.*" The chief says and I see Swazi biting her lower lip, stopping herself from saying anything.

Dutifully she escorts me outside and her anger is crackling in the air between us. I'm tempted to kiss her on the lips and pull that pouting lower lip but she'd probably bite me. So, I stand awkwardly instead and bear her stare.

"What the hell was that Hlongwane? Who said I want to remain married to you, let alone get re-married?" she hisses and I know she's tempted to poke my chest with her tiny fingers.

"Can we talk once I come back?" I'm being a coward plus I can see that someone is watching us behind the curtains.

"Talk? Talk Hlongwane? You had all the chance to talk to me in Durban and you left me only to come back smelling like a tavern. You had another chance to talk to me last night and you came back reeking of cheap female perfume! So excuse me but there's nothing I want to hear from you. I was doing just fine before you came. Now I feel like I'm in an unending train wreck. So the only thing I want from you is this, don't come back." Her eyes are glistening with unshed tears.

"*NaDlamini wami, NaNkosi,* like the fool that I am I was scared you would see my demons and run. Hearing your words right now is my worst nightmare. I don't deserve you, I never will but I don't see myself living without you. I knew you were the one for me all those years ago and that made me run. Now that I've spent some time with you, all I want is to build a home with you and create a legacy for our children. I'm done running, *ngiyacolisa* but nothing can keep me from coming back to you. *Ngikudzinga eceleni kwami sonkhe sikhatsi.* I know I messed up but please give me a chance to right my wrongs and be the best husband to you. Please let me send my uncles with the lobola."

She's shaking her head throughout my impassioned speech, refusing to let even a single tear fall and I'm getting desperate.

"I told you words are cheap. Yet you keep hurting me again and again. I'm better off on my own. I..." I kiss her like my life depends on it, at first she doesn't respond. I keep on going and I'm relieved when she kisses me back until I can feel myself getting so close to creaming my pants. When I break off the kiss we're both panting.

"Please, can we talk when I come back?" I ask against her lips after catching my breath.

"Ok." Her voice is breathless

She looks into my eyes for a full minute before breaking from my embrace. Then she proceeds to shake that delectable behind, knowing full well I'm watching her. Damn, I'm in trouble.

....

I rub my knuckles against my temple in frustration. As always Ntsikelelo has made a monumental fuck up of things during my absence. He has stepped on toes, lost accounts and generally has the Board in a frenzy. I had to douse fires and assure the board that I have it all under control. It seems like Siphiwe and I must throw an all-nighter just trying to determine which accounts are salvageable and which accounts have totally written us off. I hate how I always must clean up after my brother. If he didn't look so much like me, I would swear we don't share the same DNA. The imbecile doesn't have the sense he was born with.

He's out now probably terrorizing some unlucky prostitutes. His idea of kinky borders on sadistic. I still cringe when I remember the first time he called me, a crying mess because he had whipped a prostitute too hard and she had bled almost to death. I had to see to it that, she was taken to a very discreet private hospital and paid for her silence. I told him never to call me again and he hasn't. Though I have a niggling suspicion, that his father still cleans up after him.

Time swiftly burns by and drinking coffee keeps me awake as I muddle through Ntsikelelo's mess. Fuck! I totally forgot to call Swazi. I look at my watch and it's just after midnight. I call her anyway and the phone rings forever and just as its about to ring off, she picks up.

"Mmmmh?" her voice is groggy with sleep and I really

wish I was having sleepy sex with her right now.

"Hey baby, sorry I woke you up. Things got so hectic, I forgot to text you. I'm still at the office."

"Ok," she sounds like she didn't even hear a single word I said. Her husky sleepy voice is turning me on.

"Go back to sleep princess, Zikode wakho yakutsandza yeva?"

She responds with some incomprehensive gibberish and I smile to myself before ending the call, putting my queen out of her misery. Hearing her voice warms my heart.

There's a lot of discrepancies in the financial reports. It's evident that Ntsikelelo wasn't very good in covering the money trail. Yes, my father is a bloody cliché. He started his company on blood money. He would smuggle guns to war torn countries and he still smuggles guns to Nigeria and DRC, getting good bucks for it from rebels. He doesn't care that his guns are used by children to shoot and maim innocent civilians. As long as he gets his money. That's why he was so eager to have me marry Swazi. He has had his eye on Dlamini's mines for a long time. Not for the minerals but he wants to use the covered mine holes for safe keeping place of his guns.

When I first discovered my father's illegal dealings I was eleven years old and he wanted to rope me into the 'family side business'. I point blank refused, telling him that I wanted no part in his dealings. That earned me two broken ribs and a burst lip, but I didn't relent. He called me all sort of names, spineless and weak being more prominent. He could have killed me that night, but as always, my mother stepped in and made him stop. She and Mlandeli nursed me back to health.

Make told me she was proud of me for standing my ground, for knowing right from wrong at such a tender age. She had always prayed that we weren't sucked into the smuggling world. She said it changes a man, corrupts and kills his soul. She said my father wasn't always so callous or ruthless. I personally think he was born a cold son of a bitch, but I didn't dare voice that ever. The next year he shipped me and Ntsikelelo to a rebel camp in DRC where we were supposed to be taught to be men.

We were never the same after our year there, the things we saw and did. When my mother found out it broke her heart, yeah she might have died from leukemia but her heart never healed from what our father put us through. When I asked to go and study overseas, she forced my father to agree. She said she would miss me, but it was for the best. She wanted us both as far away as possible from the underworld.

Ntsikelelo wouldn't budge he wanted in on the fast cash. He stayed behind and became my father's wing man. Something he doesn't fail to rub in my face every time. I want no part in it, that life can miss me. Yet I'm forced from time to time, as much as I loathe it, to clean up their accounts. Hlongwane Logistics to a larger part is a legit business but from time to time they inject their dirty money into it to 'clean' up.

I hate my involvement, but the old man has me by the balls or so he thinks. He doesn't know I have been secretly investing money to start my own company. I just need to solidify my connections with a couple of investors back in the UK and some in Switzerland then I am finally free from this life. I refuse to have Swazi sucked into this life. I know the reason my father is so keen on her is because like the scavenger he is; he can't wait for her father to die so he can use her.

He initially wanted Ntsikelelo to marry her, because my brother is easier to manipulate than me. But my mother intervened and pointed out that I was the older and by right should get married first. That left a bitter taste in my brother's mouth and he tried to make it seem like he didn't want Swazi but deep down I know he wants her. More so because she is mine and my brother always craves what is mine.

CHAPTER ELEVEN

"Maswazi those chores won't do themselves now. Jo'burg has made you lazy, you forget you are a married woman now. Tsk." I grumble under my breath as Makhulu rumbles on about being a good wife.

I've been home for two weeks now and it's been amazing, but I have grown so accustomed to having my own space. I hate to admit this but I miss Hlongwane like hell. I haven't seen him since he dropped me off at home. The day after that, he called me, and he said he urgently needed to go overseas on business. To secure a tender and investment in Bangkok that will make him set for his new company. He hasn't come back, neither has he called after asking me to allow him to send his uncles. I just don't know how to feel about him going AWOL.

"Swazi are you even listening to me?" Makhulu sounds irritated now and I turn to look at her more fully.

"I am Makhulu I will do the chores just now," I try to soothe her.

She's been on edge lately. Aphelele, her granddaughter, is expecting. It doesn't help that the offspring is the illegitimate spawn of a well-known married business man. Aphelele is only 17, orphaned at two that's when she came to live with Makhulu and us. When I left she was still running around barefoot, in primary school. It came as a shock seeing her rounded belly. Aphi is also taking strain, being pregnant out of wedlock especially in rural Swaziland. The judgment was brutal that's why some girls die trying to abort their *'shame'*.

"Makhulu would you love a person who's confessed to you that they did something horrible? Something like killing a person." I rush to add when she looks at me quizzically. I can't come out and say rape, besides rape is high up there with murder in my books. It kills the victim's soul.

"Did you ask why they did that horrible thing?" she asks and Hlongwane's coldness flashes in my mind. He didn't even deny that it was woman's perfume that he was reeking of that day.

"I did and they wouldn't say. The person got very defensive and shut me out."

"Maswazi my child, love is not easy. A person may be and do horrible things but love you like you are the only woman in the world. The question is can you live with the horrible things they did? Will they do the same horrible things to you? The only guide we should have on love is God my child. His love is unconditional.

He loved David even when David killed another man because he had fallen in love with his wife. He loved Saul even when he had been actively persecuting believers. He blessed the children born from Lot's daughters even though they were conceived when the daughters got Lot drunk and had relations with their own father. Communicate my child with those you love and there won't be anything you won't be able to overcome." I let her words sink in and she squeezes my hand reassuringly.

"Get up now, your father needs to eat and drink his medication." Makhulu shoos me from the couch and I know better than to protest. I'm not too old to get my ears boxed or worse an arse whooping from her.

I'm grateful that Hlongwane brought me back home even though first few days back home were intense, I had to explain why I ran away. My parents took it badly when I told them that the morning I ran away, I bought rat poison and I almost drank it. The tormenting and whispered snubs got too much for my young self and moving to Jo'burg is the only thing that saved me.

"Why didn't you come to me and tell me you were suffering Manana?" my father asked with suspicious moisture in his eyes.

I didn't want to burden him back then and I still don't want to burden him now. I told him of my stay in another country and I down played how much I struggled before I met Akhona. I haven't spoken to Akhona since I left Jo'burg, I tried reaching out to her via WhatsApp again when we were in Jo'burg overnight but she just blue-ticked me. She doesn't even know I'm home. I'm not pushing her, when she wants to talk to me she will.

I cut vegetables under the watchful eyes of Makhulu while she knits some stuff for the baby and Aphi chats with me. Aphi wanted to help but she's ready to pop anytime, so I told her to rest and let me handle everything.

"Pregnancy isn't an illness; Swazi don't treat her like she's an egg. She's the one who decided to grow up before her time." Trust Makhulu to say something like that.

I haven't seen my siblings as yet. It's not weird at all, they prefer staying at our other houses in Mbabane. They don't like the country side, never have, even when we were growing up. I was the one who went to Maphalaleni High school, while they studied in some college in town. I also preferred it that way, because when they were around they always tormented me. Mostly my sister, my brother barely paid me any attention. Except when he was being egged on by my sister. Masomalenhle was easy going and he neither liked nor disliked me, I think, but Zamaswazi has always been like a vengeful shrew. I don't understand why my sister hates me so much. The more I tried to please her as a child, the more hurtful things she had to say to me.

"Smells wonderful in here, reminds me of your mother's cooking." *Babe* says wheeling himself into the kitchen.

I beam at my favorite man. He's stronger now than when I first saw him, even his doctor is impressed with his progress ever since I came back. He calls me his magic pill. *Babe* told the doctor that all he had needed was me back home. I'm happy that he's getting better, honestly, I don't think I'm ready to completely be an orphan. *Babe* is the only father and mother that I know, well and Makhulu of course.

"I'm preparing iSishwala with beef stew and your favorite pumpkin leaves *Babe.*"

His face lights up and I kiss his worn cheek. How I wish I'd come back earlier and had more moments like this.

"The way you cook, I must charge that boy 10 more cows," we all laugh at that comment. Besides missing Hlongwane, I'm at my happiest here in this kitchen with my family.

Aphi helps me set up and we have dinner over flowing

chatter and some laughter. I'm pleased that my father finishes his plate and I make sure he takes his medicine. His nurse is on a much-needed break and I'm taking care of him. At least now he's strong enough to bathe himself, but I do help him dress up.

"*Babe,* how did you and my mother meet?" I ask when we are alone, Makhulu and Aphi have gone to bed. My father doesn't like talking about my mother. That's something I learned growing up. He always looked pained whenever I brought her up. So, I stopped talking about her, even though I was curious about the woman who lost her life while bringing mine into the world.

"It was at the Umhlanga dance," oh we are talking today and he's even smiling at the memory. "The moment I looked at her flawless beauty and the way she held herself, I felt my blood boil. I was afraid to approach her though. Not only was she beautiful but she was also the niece and ward of *iNdlovukati.*" My eyes are popping out of their sockets by now. This explains why the King graced my wedding, he is cousins with my late mother. This leaves me wondering why the Queen Mother, my great aunt has never been in my life.

"So *iNdlovukati* is my great aunt? How come I've never seen her except at the dance and she never acknowledged me. Did they not approve of mother marrying you?" my curiosity gets the better of me.

Babe tries to say something but then has a coughing fit. It gets so bad; he's coughing up blood. I'm freaking out and panicking on the inside. Outwardly I manage to rub his back and hand him one of his handkerchiefs. The fit leaves him weak and drained. Fortunately, he was already bathed and dressed for bed. I wheel him to his bedroom and help him into his bed, tuck him in and kiss his forehead just as he did when I was young.

I go to bed with a lot of questions swimming in my head. I take out my phone and try to call Hlongwane before I fall asleep. My talk with Makhulu made me realize that yes, he is a monster but I love him. I can't help it and maybe if we talk I'll understand him more. It rings unanswered until it goes to voicemail. I sigh heavily feeling glum. I really need him, something about looking into his chiseled face and those pools of charcoal calms me. It makes me feel strong. I fall asleep with a heavy heart.

......

I've been up before the crack of dawn, I had to drive all the way to Lobamba to buy baby clothes with Aphi. I settled on Gables Shopping Centre because it has both Pick 'n Pay and Woolworths, I also need to do grocery shopping. There is no mall in Maphalaleni and you can't really buy baby clothes from Imbuyande Supermarket. The look on Aphi's face is priceless, she's so excited at all the little clothes.

□

When he left, Hlongwane sent his driver to give me his bank card. It's the one I'm using to buy the baby stuff. I'm hoping that the bank notifications will finally catch his attention. Desperate, I know. Holding a little romper just made me feel broody, I wonder how it will feel having a little Hlongwane inside me.

"Pretty soon we will be shopping for clothes for your baby, sis Swazi," as if she can read my thoughts Aphi says this with a wide smile on her face.

I smile back and lightly rub my tummy, some of her excitement rubbing off on me. Motherhood is so appealing to me; I can't wait to have my own babies. I was mostly on my own growing up and that was lonely, I want a whole brood of children at least seven. I don't know how Hlongwane feels about children. We haven't really gotten down to talking about kids. I'm reminded again of how little we know of each other.

Aphelele is tired I can tell so I suggest she waits for me in the car and I do the groceries on my own. I get the ingredients for my famous carrot cake. My dad being diabetic, I can't just buy one from the bakery, so I used to make them for him. He's been giving me hints all week.

"Nomaswazi I thought that was you!" it's too late to hide now so I turn towards the owner of the voice and smile.

"Mam' Deacon, what a pleasant surprise," nothing

pleasant about it. And I wonder why she always feel the need to wear her crisp white and blue Anglican uniform with that little navy hat and thoroughly pressed black skirt even when she's not going to church.

"I heard you came back two weeks ago but we haven't seen you at church." Her voice is accusing and she's raising her eyebrow like she's part of the celestial judgment panel.

"I have to take care of my father, he's very sick." I try to keep my voice respectful.

"Oh yes. He is in our prayers, we are all interceding for his health," by any luck she will walk away now. But nope, "So you come to your home with a man and kiss him in front of the whole of Maphalaleni to see."

I sigh inwardly, not sure how to respond. The old me wouldn't even say a word.

"Just because you were jilted at the altar my child does not mean you should start indulging in worldly things and give up on finding a man. You must come to church and the ladies will hold a prayer interception for you. There's also this diviner I know..."

At this point smoke is coming out of my flared nose and I have to keep my fist against my side to stop me from punching her. I have had it with these people treating me like I'm some special case just because I'm not wearing a ring.

"With all due respect ma'am, please reserve those

prayers for your own daughter. At the rate she is having abortions, she might be out of children to bear by the time you find someone you can fool into thinking she's pure." Even I am amazed at how cool my voice sounds.

She looks like she swallowed a whole sack of lemons. I leave her spluttering and calling me all kinds of names. The timid Swazi they knew, who took all their insults lying down is dead. There's a new Sherriff in town and she is learning to be her own woman.

......

When we get home, my father ropes me into going to a council meeting with his headmen. Growing up he took me to almost every meeting, I know how the system operates all its ins and outs. I love how even in a wheelchair *Babe* still commands respect and how open his council is.

"How did you find today's meeting Manana?" he always asks the same question.

"I think it's good that you are implementing crop rotation as you were taught by the Ministry of Agriculture. But I am not fully satisfied with the reports on how the funds are being spent in some of the villages. I suggest you select a team with an independent auditor and we do a surprise inspection of all the villages on the same day. Their records will be seized and given to the auditor to check for any misappropriation of funds, while the team assesses the state of the villages."

Babe has been listening attentively to everything I said and nodding at intervals. It still warms me even today how seriously he takes my suggestions. Even as a child he would listen to me as if I was the *iNdlovukati.*

"I also thought some of the reports given were a bit sketchy and exaggerated. When do you think I should arrange for this surprise inspection?"

"The sooner the better but even the team you select mustn't know its function until on the day of the inspection itself. I can look up independent auditors or ask Hlongwane to find us one."

My father is beaming, he really loves my idea and the pride he has in me is shining from his eyes.

"I'm glad you came back home, I missed sharing ideas with you all these years. Your brother and sister don't care much about the workings of *Inkhundla.*"

A lump suddenly lodges itself in my throat, so I don't respond, I squeeze his hand and we drive the rest of the way home in comfortable silence. We find another car parked in our yard and I wonder who it is. I park next to the unknown car and help my father into his chair. He wheels himself in and I follow behind smiling slightly, stubborn old man. I tried talking to him about amputating his leg. He said he would rather die with all his limbs intact, what if his forefathers don't recognize him without a limb. I gave up, he's my daddy I still love him.

"*Skoni*," my heart beats faster when I hear my father say that. Hlongwane is back! I'm happy he's back but I'm also dreading the conversation we're supposed to have.

I'm standing here conflicted while I watch Hlongwane converse with my father. He looks deadly in a black suit and tie. I wonder why he didn't come with his Bentley. He hasn't once looked in my direction, ok that's cold but maybe he's respecting my father.

"Go and pack Maswazi am sure your in-laws can't wait to see you," my father commands and I'm about to protest but he gives me the eye and I retreat to my room with a sulk. I come back with my bag and my so-called husband doesn't help me carry it to the car. Ok, whatever happened overseas couldn't have been good he's so cold. Not the man who left with a promise that nothing would stop him from having me by his side.

You're overanalyzing Swazi, he's probably tired and cranky. I try to rationalize as I roll my huge suitcase to his car. For some weird reason I don't feel safe with Hlongwane today. The usually fiery charcoals today are an icy pool. I hold on longer to my father than I should and Hlongwane clears his throat impatiently. Geez, what is this guy's problem? Had I not been so accustomed to him, I would think this is another guy altogether. Talk about multiple personalities, maybe he's bipolar.

......

"So how was the trip? Did you manage to get Bangkok on board?" I tentatively ask after about twenty minutes of riding in complete silence. He looks at me briefly but he's wearing sunglasses I can't read his expression.

"It went well. Yeah." Work with me here! I feel like slapping him. He's so irritable and moody today, I khant!

"Why didn't you bring *Inathi* today? Where's Bab' Mlandeli, I think he has a soft spot for me."

"Dammit woman do you ever stop talking?" he literally barks at me and I am left shook. Well shoot me for trying to lighten the tension.

I keep my mouth shut for the rest of the journey, fighting the tears that are threatening to fall. I know Hlongwane the devil himself, but does he have to be so cruel? When we arrive at his home, it's dark and I barely look at the building. I'm upset at my husband's callous disregard of my feelings.

He also ignores the servants who greet him, but unlike me they seem used to his cold demeanor. He leads me to his cottage which is just outside the main house and there's another a little distance from his. Mind you I'm still dragging my suitcase and sulking behind his long and sure strides. His place is cozy with its own well-equipped kitchen and the largest flat screen I have ever laid eyes on in the lounge. I stand nervously in the lounge not sure what to do or if I am even allowed to say anything.

Without warning he grabs me and kisses me, like some prostitute he bought for the night. His lips demanding and brutal on mine. I swear my mouth is already bruising from his onslaught. I will not be one of his rape victims! It just feels wrong and instinctively I clamp my teeth hard on his lower lip. I taste his blood as he hurls me away from him. He lets out a string of curses. It all happens so fast, it feels surreal.

"Bitch!" he snarls, and I feel a hot, stinging fist connecting with my cheek.

It's such a sudden and unexpected blow it knocks me off and I crush against the glass coffee table. The table gives in under my weight, the shards of broken glass cuts me. There's a ringing sound in my ear and I fight the tears which threaten to fall. He doesn't even bother checking up on me, he just bangs the door as he storms out. I'm too stunned to cry, as if on cue my nose starts bleeding. I was married off to a monster, I think as I drag my abused body to the bathroom. Once I see my disheveled state in the mirror, burst lips and bloody nose. I finally break down.

CHAPTER TWELVE

I am woken up by the coldness of the hard ceramic tiles, my head feels like someone is dragging a ton of bricks inside it. I try to get up and my whole body protests after a rough night sleeping on the bathroom floor. Recollections of last night come flooding back; Hlongwane almost mauling me, his blow before he left me there on the floor without even a backward glance. I have exhausted all my tears and all I want to do is curl up and die. I'm not being dramatic. Hlongwane knows, he was there when Ashton violated me, and he goes and does the same. He promised to protect me and then turns around and hits me.

My puffy eyes stare back at me from the warped reflection in the bathroom mirror. One eye is swollen almost shut, my cheek is also swollen, cut in some places and my burst lips look nasty. I have become a statistic; he has reduced me to a cowering battered woman. I can't stand my own reflection. I wince as I shower, my left side is bruised from where I banged the table.

I wonder how they do it. Show your face, hide the scars from the world while inside the wound is festering. My father must never know about this. The way he trusts this monster, it would kill him to know that he gave his youngest daughter to the devil himself. I cover up with a long-sleeved silk blouse, tucking it in a long flowing skirt and cover the cornrows Makhulu plaited with a head wrap.

I put on more concealer than usual and carefully apply nude lipstick on my burst lips. I will have to wear sunglasses for the swollen eye. Outside I hurt like hell but inside I'm dead. I take a deep breath and prepare to go and meet my in-laws. Getting him arrested only flirts through my mind but I reject that thought. I don't want more shame and ridicule.

Seeing the scattered glasses of the coffee table brings it all back. Yesterday wasn't a nightmare, it happened, and Hlongwane is nowhere to be seen. A white envelope catches my eye, it's underneath a disk next to the flat screen. My hands shake as I reach for the letter. I'm hoping for an explanation of sorts, an apology for the monster I saw last night.

You think your cunt is all that?

Sweetheart, I've had better.

N

I have to re-read those two lines repeatedly, I even look behind the note for a side note. Or something, anything less hurtful. It all comes crashing down. He used me. Now he is discarding me like some used condom. He even signed the damn note.

My hands are shaking violently now as I pick up the disk, it's written 'Watch Me'. I don't even know how to operate the bloody machine and my hands shaking makes it even harder. After some struggle, everything is good to go, and I grab the remote. I sit at the edge of the couch, my back rigid as I press play.

Once the video starts playing, I'm grateful that I'm sitting. I feel so weak, I can't even summon the strength to press the pause button to make the horrible and disgusting sounds stop. I can't watch this! But my eyes remain glued to the big screen even as each moan deepens the knife in my chest.

......

"*NaDlamini wami, NaNkosi,* like the fool that I am I was scared you would see my demons and run. Hearing your words right now is my worst nightmare. I don't deserve you, I never will but I don't see myself living without you. I knew you were the one for me all those years ago and that made me run. Now that I've spent some time with you, all I want is to build a home with you and create a legacy for our children. I'm done running, *ngiyacolisa* but nothing can keep me from coming back to you. *Ngikudzinga eceleni kwami sonkhe sikhatsi.* I know I messed up but please give me a chance to right my wrongs and be the best husband to you. Please let me send my uncles with the lobola."

His voice as he was looking deep in my eyes rings in my mind as I watch him sink balls deep inside my only sister. The recording shows my sister clearly; I would know her anywhere. I also have a feeling it's a recent video. While I thought he was overseas building an empire for our children, he was screwing my sister. He is grunting and making guttural sounds while she screams her pleasure. I wish I knew that pleasure, him inside me and giving me the same pleasure. I wish it was me screaming at his touch and not my sister.

I thought we had our very own soul connection, how wrong was I? The joke is on me; we haven't even been together a month. Then he picks her up like she doesn't weigh anything, well she doesn't really. She's tall and lithe with a beautiful light complexion, everything I am not. She places both legs on his shoulders until she is hanging just above his beautiful huge cock. Mine! Everything in me screams and I wish I could close my eyes.

I watch his strong muscled legs spread slightly apart, he lowers her to my *Zikode* and proceeds to pound the living daylights out of her. I can hear clearly the slapping sounds, that quicken as they progress. I can't see his face or hers, I'm looking at her yellow arse and his huge black balls. The deeper he drives into her, the louder she screams.

My traitorous body is responding to his wild thrusts and then she comes like a waterfall all over his magnificent cock. Her legs jerk uncontrollably but he doesn't relent. When her jerky movements stop, he tosses her on the bed, Zikode is still achingly erect and huge. He turns her over and her clean-shaven business is shown as clear as day in the screen. He hovers in between her legs stroking himself, his back towards me.

She giggles and then moans as he inserts himself into her. I feel anger twisting my soul. It's so intense it gives me the strength to pause the blasted sex tape. The names my sister used to call me all come back and I'm like a bull seeing red. Then there's my so-called husband, the man my father entrusted me to. The man asking my father to send his uncles so that he can pay lobola for me for the second time. I was fine before he came back into my life and made me fall in love with him. Then he abuses me and makes me watch this, this, this... arghhh I feel like pulling out my hair.

I am done letting people walk all over me and doing as they please. I am tired of being told I'm ugly, too dark, too fat. My inner child is screaming for vengeance; I want to hurt him as much as he hurt me. I want him to feel some of the pain I have carried with me all my life. I am rummaging through the house looking for something, anything that can hurt him as he hurt me. Before I know it, I'm thrashing the place but it's not enough.

......

I stand uncertain with a brick in my hand, Hlongwane will definitely kill me if I do this. Zama's giggles and moans fill my ears and I see him inside her. The anger comes back in full force and I throw the first brick. I couldn't find a bat like Beyoncé in **Hold Up**, the bricks will have to do. The splintering of the windshield and the car alarm going off brings the servants running and they stop when they see that it's me.

I don't stop, I throw another brick this time at the bonnet. No one makes a move to stop me. I must look crazy with my bare feet and mascara running down my face. I want him to feel my pain as I slash each tire. My crazy rage gives me so much power, the wipes in the windshield come off, the windscreen by now is cracked open. The doors look like they were involved in an accident, there are no more functioning lights.

Bab' Mlandeli stops me when I start pouring petrol all over the car. I break down and sob into his fatherly arms and he just lets me. The anger is being replaced by a searing pain. It's like I'm back in primary school, hiding in the toilets and bowling my eyes out. Why me? Am I never meant to be happy like everyone else? The pain of his blows and the sex tape flood me and I sob until I'm out of breath and have full blown hiccups.

Bab' Mlandeli offers to take me back to the cottage and I panic. I left the cottage turned upside down, when Hlongwane comes back he is going to kill me. I must leave this place. I can't go home like this, my father would have a heart attack. I don't have friends and I can't go to my siblings and have Zama gloat seeing me in this state. I wish I was back in my flat in Berea with Akhona.

"Please take me to *Ludzidzini,*" my voice is scratchy.

The old man is surprised by my request but doesn't question it. We take another car, a white Benz this time. I sag into the back seat, my whole-body aches. My feet are bleeding and my hands have blisters. But it's my heart which has suffered the most abuse. The tears fall as we leave the huge Hlongwane estate. I hope to never see this place again, I'm glad Bab' Mlandeli doesn't say anything even though he keeps checking me in the rearview mirror.

......

I must have cried myself to sleep because I'm woken up by Bab' Mlandeli. We are outside the intimidating gates of Ludzidzini Royal Residence. It feels weird to be here when it's not *Umhlanga* and there's not a lot of people milling around. As always there are royal guards at the gate and Bab' Mlandeli says they refused to let him in without an appointment or royal summons.

"I'm here to see *INdlovukati* please. I'm her granddaughter," I try to plead with the burly guard.

He looks me up and down probably taking in my torn skirt, the blood caked on my bare feet, my battered face and my blistered hands. I can see how little he thinks of me.

"Little girl go and play somewhere else. We know all the princesses, if you are a *nkosatana* where is your royal guard? If you want help go to the UN offices, they are in town."

"You don't understand the Queen Mother is my great aunt. I am the daughter of Chief Sobhuza Dlamini..." by now other guards have also come to see the free show and they burst out laughing when I mention my father. Bab' Mlandeli is incensed next to me but I place my hand on his arm to calm him.

Some ladies come out of the gate and the guards immediately stop their sneering and stand at attention. The youngest and most expensively dressed looks at me with compassion and addresses me directly.

"Hi, I'm Khanyisa, can I help you?" her voice is friendly, and her eyes are warm while all the others seem to defer to her, even the rude Royal guards.

"I am Nomaswazi, I would like an audience with her majesty," one guard sneers when I say this and Khanyisa gives him an eye and he immediately stops.

"May I ask why?" Khanyisa is so polite and soft spoken.

"I recently learnt that she's my great aunt. My mother was her niece and ward, but she passed away." I hope she won't send the guards to throw us out and she believes me. I sag in relief when she tells the guard to let me in. She takes my bruised hand and tucks it in the crook of her arm. Bab' Mlandeli gives me a questioning look and I mouth to him *"thank you, you can go"* I have a feeling I will be fine now.

"So that means we are cousins then. Oh, grandma will be so happy!" I don't share Khanyisa's enthusiasm. Her grandmother has known about me all of 24 years and has never tried to look for me. I try to keep up with Khanyisa's bouncy strides but I'm barefoot and the gravel has no mercy on my already injured feet. I flinch in pain but don't make a sound. Khanyisa is such a beautiful and humble princess.

□

She's chatting like she's known me her whole life, had it been any other day I would have enjoyed her company. Today however, I'm in physical pain and my spirit is crushed. Maybe coming here wasn't such a good idea, in my state. It's too late to turn back now. The palace is gorgeous, the building simple with a cheerful almost peach colour. It's a single story building, it's not as huge or extravagant as the King's actual Residence but it's still beautiful and stately. We pass the water fountain, the other ladies following us at a distance.

The interior is just as spectacular with a fresh modern style. I don't get to admire it much because Khanyisa is dragging me along. One of the ladies tries cautioning her but is ignored. She's screaming *"Makhulu!"* into every room.

"I'm here *Nobamba* no need to scream the house down," a voice primly responds in the room to our left.

A little pretty girl bursts out of the room before we even enter.

"Khanyi! Khanyi! Are you here to take me on your walk?" I've never seen a more beautiful child, with her round cheeks. She flashes her white teeth and dimples as she talks animatedly.

"No Nombuso, I only brought back Makhulu's guest." The little angel looks at me and then takes my hand and kisses it.

"Kissing the bubu always makes it better," she says her big clear eyes eyeing me solemnly. I smile back at her or try to; my lips feel like they barely stretched.

I don't know what I was expecting, maybe I expected her to be regal and aloof, something screaming her royal highness. Not this comely elderly lady in her light cashmere jersey, a throw blanket around her knees and glasses perched on the bridge of her nose. She's holding a copy of **Sing Thando, Sing!** She smiles warmly at Nombuso who goes sprinting to her and kisses both her cheeks. As if sensing my stare, she looks up and looks like she's seeing a ghost.

"*Tsandzile*!" the name comes out as a croak.

"No, I'm her daughter Nomaswazi." My voice is also shaking with emotion. I have been deprived a mother's life my whole life and she's been here. Reading stories to her other grandchildren.

"For a moment there I thought you were her ghost. Oh my child. My poor child." She opens her arms and I find myself in them, bawling my eyes out. She hushes me and rubs my back soothingly. And it feels like home.

......

"Why? Why did you abandon us?" I finally ask the question that has been burning in my mind ever since my father told me she was my great aunt.

It's evening now, I have been given a warm bath. Because I couldn't fit Khanyisa's clothes, I was given the Queen Mother's *lihiya* to wrap around me. At least now I look a little presentable not like some hobo. I've been forced to eat even though I had no appetite whatsoever, but my great-aunt has been fussing over me.

"My sister died when she was pretty young, but she left me the most beautiful gift; Tsandzile, your mother. You look exactly like her when she was your age, with the same dimples, fire in her eyes and lovable spirit." Oh, so she's going to completely disregard my question? I let her speak.

"She was like a daughter to me, I raised her as my own child right here until she fell in love and I married her off to your father." My mind is brimming with so many questions right now, but I let her talk.

"After she got married, it was never the same again. Of course, she visited here and there but I also had my duties and commitments to the State and to my family. I was regent and there were rumors of a takeover. She had troubles in her marriage, troubles she tried to tell me about. But I sent her back each time and told her to be strong, she needed to be patient. Until she died. I failed her as a mother."

"I thought she died giving birth to me?" it comes out like a question. I'm even more confused than before I came here. What problems? Was my father a woman basher as well?

No! my mind rejects that thought, not *Babe* my knight in shining armour.

"Is that what Sobhuza told you?" she asks with a frown and I shake my head quickly.

"No, *Babe* never talks about my mother. He only told me recently that she was your niece. I heard about her death from my sister." I don't add how nasty she was when she told me this or the other nasty things she has been saying to me my whole freaking life.

"Mmmmh then it's not my place to tell you child, your father has to tell you himself." And then? Why all this secrecy?

"But why did you abandon me? I needed a mother figure so badly growing up!" the anger is simmering underneath but I'm still talking to the Queen Mother after all I can't exactly shout.

"After your mother's funeral, I wanted nothing more to do with your father's family. I wanted to take you with me, but your father begged and begged until I relented. I'm so sorry for neglecting you along the years."

Sigh. The healing will take a while but the first step towards reconciliation has been taken. I hug her, and she holds me for the longest time.

"What happened to you? Who hurt you?" great-aunt asks touching my eye. Tears which haven't been far, well up and cloud my vision. Before I can respond there is commotion outside, shouting comes from the corridor. It sounds like a struggle and the voices are heated.

"I'm not leaving here without my wife!" I start shivering uncontrollably as I recognize that voice. I would know it even in my grave. The tears which had been on the verge of falling, burst out uncontrollably. I'm scared for my life. The devil is here to claim my soul.

CHAPTER THIRTEEN

The last two weeks have been an abso-fucken hell. I haven't been able to enjoy fully the opulence of The Okura Prestige Bangkok where I'm currently staying. Or a chance to fully explore the architectural contrast of Bangkok, from the modern buildings to the heritage sites and museums, the gorgeous landscaping as well as the religious houses which are mostly influenced by Buddhism. Bangkok is said to have some of the most elaborate temples.

I've only seen the Tetris Building, since I've been working in it. It's such a technologically-advanced place, the way it's built it seems to have a spiraling pixel-like effect on its glass façade. I'd love to show it to Swazi one day, show her the building that seems like its dissolving downwards, like parts of the building are being eaten away and it can collapse at any moment. I can just see her excitement now, her craning her neck to take it all in.

Leading two lives is draining and all I want is to get home and send my uncles with lobola so that I can finally bury myself inside my wife. I had a tip that my investors were looking to give a building tender for a resort that could potentially be the Eighth wonder of the world. Packing up and leaving was the hardest thing I have ever done. It was different from all the other times, I have Swazi now, a reason to want to go home every night.

Winning this tender will set my portfolio on the right path, a chance of a lifetime. So, I've been working around the clock creating designs. Something about Chief Sobhuza's homestead gave me inspiration. Something to look traditional and timeless on the outside, an interior with a modern and uptown funk edge. A blend of Swati rustiness and Asian futurism. When I'm designing, hours tend to blend into each other and I can go for over twenty-four hours straight with little breaks in between.

I can't have my father know what I am up to, so I also have to carry on my CEO duties which are draining as hell. I'm still cleaning up Ntsikelelo's mess, smoothing over ruffled feathers. My candle is burning on both ends and I am this close to losing it. I haven't been eating right, barely sleep and don't even have time for a run. What hurts me most is that I'm neglecting my bride-to-be.

She surprised me by being understanding, not throwing a tantrum as I expected. When I called her to tell her of my departure she was more curious about my work than angry or disappointed. I had to tell her that I wanted to branch out on my own and about the Bangkok tender. Mostly she listened, asked questions here and there then the praises came stroking my ego no end. I felt like a peacock with my chest swelling at all her compliments.

That call lasted two hours. Our longest call yet. I curse at times when I finished work at odd hours and I couldn't call her. I always tell myself I will call her, but I have been burning myself to the ground literally. I never get around to calling her. Shitty, I know but I'm new to this committed relationship thing and I'm doing a pretty messed up job.

It's my last night here and I agreed to a night out with my potential investors. They promised me that the bright pink neon lights of Soi Cowboy are were the dark side of Bangkok's nightlife are. We're at a Thai go-go bar, a combo of a bar and strip club. It's raunchier than your average strip club, it's a live show and the waitresses are serving us naked. Our table has a pole and two girls are giving us a show. I turned down a personal lap dance but I've had to constantly adjust Hlongwane in my pants.

I spot Ramona, she's sitting by the bar with her girlfriends and she spotted me just a fraction before I spotted her. I'm not surprised, Ramona has always been one to travel and she loves eroticism. A place like this is perfect for her. Damn she still looks hot with those endless legs. She opens her legs flashing me with her pink, waxed cookie and I chock on my whisky. I spill some of it on my jeans.

"Are you oright?" Asao asks in his heavy Japanese accent and I have to come up with some lame excuse. I don't even know what I'm saying to him, my mind is on Ramona with her glistening cookie. I haven't had any in a while and Zikode is painfully reminding me.

I excuse myself and head to the Gents room to fix myself. After doing my business, I come out of the toilet only to be ambushed by Ramona. She drags me back into the stall and locks us in. Then she's all over me like some nasty rash. Her every touch is skilled and designed to feed my lust, she knows which buttons to click. I'm almost undone at just her touch.

It's not as fulfilling as Swazi's eager fumbling, her un-crafted passion as she tentatively touched me. Just the thought of my baby douses out any lust I'm feeling. Calmly I unwrap Ramona from me just as she's about to take Zikode into her mouth and do my zip. She looks at me the way African courts react to stock theft. The old me would have jumped her and not regretted it. Maybe I am whipped.

"It was nice meeting you Ramona, but we can't take off from where we left, I am married now." I want to laugh at her expression when she looks at my empty ring finger. I didn't need some gold band reminding me of my commitment and promises to my woman. Swazi is all I crave and I unlock the door and leave Ramona cursing me in the toilet stall. I apologize to my investors and spend the rest of the night discussing buildings over good whisky.

......

Our house which I plan to gift Swazi as a wedding gift is under construction. I swear I developed an ulcer in the past two weeks. At least the head of the team seems to have everything under control. He's been sending me daily reports over emails and every building material is accounted for. I'm thinking of hiring him and his team full time under my new company. I've had to call in a lot of favours to get the house built in record time.

The day of submissions is finally here. I am nervous as hell and wish I had brought Swazi along. I'm too tense; it doesn't help that I haven't had sex since that random woman in Jo'burg. I refuse to resort to self-service, I want Swazi.

I'm not worried much about my submissions. I know my design is unique, it offers that African edge I'm sure isn't offered by any of the other bidders. I researched my competition. I did my research on the tender and I have provided similar services on some of my projects under my portfolio when I was still an independent contractor. I have reference details of clients that the evaluator can contact. I set up profiles of my team, their skills and qualifications including mine. We might be a start-up company, but I have been very picky in my selection.

My connections through my father's Logistics company have finally paid off. I managed to secure bio-friendly material quotes at a much-discounted price. My solution offers cost savings to the investors. My contract management processes are in minute detail from project initiation, day-to-day operations, review points, my company quality points and the works.

I make the presentation and can't wait to leave and go back home. We're told that we'll getting the response in the next ten working days. I call the office as soon as I land at Manzini airport after a long arse forty-seven-hour flight, we had two stops and changed airways. Unfortunately, I have to pass through the office first.

My body is almost shutting down but I have to dose out some fires. Siphiwe has been doing a great job but there are still things I need to sign off. The company needs more trucks and I have to ensure that we get the funding. Everything is haywire, I'm exhausted and all I want is to go home, bathe and go see my Swazi.

"You look like hell Mr. N," Siphiwe notes while giving me another cup of coffee. I barely smile back that's how exhausted I am. Still I push myself and only leave the office at 6pm, bone weary.

I decide to take a shower first before going to take Swazi. I can feel something is amiss from the curious stares I'm getting from the servants. I ignore them only to be shocked when I find my whole cottage smashed. Scratch that it's like a tornado had gone through every room. The only thing left intact is the television. It looks like someone was watching something. I pick the remote from one of the slashed sofas and press play.

I feel my blood boil when I see the content of the video. I want to kill someone so badly. I pause the filth and decide to just go and shower, knock off some steam. It's obvious Nomaswazi was here. Her suitcase is in my bedroom, her scent in my bathroom. My first crippling thought is that if Nomaswazi was here that means she saw the video too. My blood grows cold. *Fuck! On top of all my demons now this, I've lost her forever this time.* The thought alone drives me to punch the bedroom wall.

I don't even take a shower, I rush to the garage and get another shock. My car. My beautiful Inathi ruined! I come close to sobbing. I can imagine her fury as she slashed the tires and wrecked my windscreen. My mind races to many scenarios of her driving off in a rage, tears blinding her and causing her to skid off the road. She's probably lying in a ditch somewhere dead.

The thought of my Swazi lying dead in a ditch somewhere because of me does make me sob. My wounded cry brings Mlandeli running to check what's happening in the garage. Mistakenly he thinks I'm crying for my car.

"She almost burnt the whole thing, I stopped her in the nick of time." He says trying to hide his grin.

I don't give two flying fucks about the blasted car right now. All I want to know is, where is she? Is she safe? Is she hurt? Mlandeli seems to find the whole thing amusing. Mostly my tears. Eventually he tells me that he took her to Ludzidzini, I don't even wait for him to finish telling me about how the guards treated them. I rush to get the next available car.

......

Here I am, throwing a tantrum at the Royal Palace. No one keeps me from what's mine not even the royal guards, not in the enraged state I'm in.

"Sir we are asking you to leave before we shoot, you are trespassing on Royal grounds," one of the guards bellow while the others are trying to push me out.

"I'm not leaving here without my wife!" they will have to kill me first. I hear my suit tear, but I keep on struggling to get out of their grasp.

Abruptly I'm let go and the guards stand at attention. The Queen Mother is standing by the door a look of haughty anger plastered on her face. I give my salutations and drop my eyes even though everything in me is screaming in protest.

"What is the meaning of all this commotion?" her voice carries quiet authority.

"I mean no disrespect your majesty, I just want my wife then I will leave." I try to muster as much deference as I can in my voice.

"You are certain your lost wife is here because?" my teeth grind at the bite in her voice.

"My driver dropped her here in the morning. I just want to see that she's ok," even if it means I get arrested.

"I will ask you to leave child, your wife will come to you when she feels like coming to you." I'm about to protest when my Swazi comes from behind the Queen Mother.

My heart clenches at the fear I see in her eyes. What the hell did he do to her? Her one eye is swollen shut and her beautiful lips are burst and also swollen. The left side of her face is peppered with cuts and shiny bruises.

He's gone too far this time. I'm going to kill him. I try to shield the anger I feel; I don't want to scare her. I move towards her and she recoils, hiding behind the Queen Mother and one of the guards hold me.

"Baby, I would never hurt you like that please let's go home and I can explain everything. Please." I wish I didn't have to beg in front of all these people, but I am desperate. I can't stand how scared she looks. She's even visibly shivering. When I get hold of his neck I'm going to wring it until it snaps in two.

"Do you want to go with him my baby?" the Queen Mother's voice softens marginally when she's talking to Swazi. Like she is talking to a three-year-old.

Swazi shakes her head vehemently, fat tears spilling on her cheeks. Every fiber of my body wants to wrap my hands around her and hold on to her. I'm not the monster she now thinks I am. I love her too much to even raise my hand at her.

"Please leave or I will have you thrown in jail where you belong." The Queen isn't joking, my shoulders sag in defeat.

"Swazi, I love you. I swear I would never hurt you like this. I just need a chance to prove myself. I will give you space but I won't be far from the royal gates. I'm not leaving you here, I can't function knowing you are hurting like this." My eyes are cloudy too. I should have taken her with me.

My steps are heavy as I head over to my car. One thing is sure I am killing him. I feel my rage brimming again and I find myself driving back home. He's crossed a line this time.

......

"Ntsikelelo!" I bellow as I get to his cottage.

He comes out half naked with an evil smirk on his face. I don't say another word, I just lunge at him and deck him with my right hook and follow him down. All I'm seeing is red as my fists and legs connect with his flesh. The crunching sound as my hand connects with is nose is satisfying, so is the spurt of blood that immediately comes from his nose.

I strangle him and he's scratching my hands trying to get me to loosen them but I only tighten them. He twists my arm and somehow manages to flip us over. He starts fighting back. He throws a mean punch but I'm quicker and I am going to kill him with my own bare hands. Images of Swazi's face keep flashing in my mind fueling my anger and I knee him in the groin and he doubles over in pain and topples to the floor. I kick him again and again until I zone out. I only come to when I'm being held by Mlandeli and another driver while my father is checking Ntsikelelo's pulse.

"When will the two of you stop fighting like a bunch of savages? He'll live." My father says clinically.

Supporting his words Ntsikelelo weakly sits up and doubles over as he vomits blood. He retches for a while before flashing a bloodied grin at me. His face is barely recognizable but he's enjoying the pain. I want to punch him all over again but Mlandeli and the other guy are holding me firmly in place.

"*Stay the fuck away from my wife, or I swear I'll kill you with my bare hands.*" I hiss at him and we all know I mean it.

CHAPTER FOURTEEN

I have been sleeping in my car for three straight nights. My muscles cringe in protest as I wake up. I'm still in my torn, bloody suit and I haven't bathed since day 1. At least they bring me food. But it's never my wife. I haven't seen her since I burst into the palace. I wonder why she chose to come here instead of her home. I've had blue balls for so long I think my balls have either shrunk to oblivion or fallen off, Zikode has never been more traumatized.

I've been flooding her phone with messages and calls. She never responds nor answers my calls, but I haven't given up. I've also been working from my car, fortunately my laptop was in the car. To stretch my legs at times I walk around the Royal Kraal and grounds just around sunset. It is beautiful and peaceful, but I'm just riddled with too much pain and anger to properly enjoy it.

It had always been like this even as kids, he would fuck up and I would get blamed. Only my mother ever believed me, but my father just said she babied me and couldn't see that she was nursing a viper. I'm startled from my thoughts by a tap on my window. When I see Swazi my heart leaps in my chest. I sit up straight and open the passenger door for my Queen.

She's wearing *lihiya* again today and she looks as terrible as I feel. Somehow that mollifies me. The swelling has gone down but her lips are not fully healed yet. I crave her touch so much, I tentatively touch her hand and she doesn't snatch it away. Feeling a little bolder I take both her hands and stare at them. Her lovely soft hands are bruised, cut and have blisters. I feel like such a failure I couldn't protect her.

She clears her throat and when I look into her eyes, they are glassy.

"I need you to go home and not sleep here outside the palace gates. You're making things awkward for the Queen Mother." Her voice is quiet, resolute like she's rehashed this speech in her mind a lot of times.

"I'm not going anywhere without you. I know I messed up..." she breaks in as I'm talking.

"No you didn't mess up, you showed me who you really are. My heart stupidly loved you through it all but this, this I can't forgive or accept. You slept with my sister. Not only that you also filmed it and threw it in my face after you violated me and left me battered in your home." Her voice is breaking but she stubbornly blinks back the tears.

"Swazi it wasn't me, I can..." she laughs but it's not her usual magical laughter, this one is jaded and bitter.

"Please Hlongwane don't insult my intelligence on top of everything else. I was with you. I saw you with my own two eyes. I wish it was something I heard from someone else but I saw you." There's a finality in her voice which tells me she doesn't want to hear whatever I have to say.

Somehow I'd hoped she would, like my mother, believe me just because I said so. All conviction and fight I had just depleted and all I can do is just look at her. Inexplicable emotions fill me and the only tangible one is defeat.

"I'm sorry that I've been such a nuisance, I promise not to bother you again." A look of hurt flashes through her eyes but she tries covering it by clearing her throat and offering a weak smile.

"Then that's it I guess. I'll ask my father to send back your cows since the marriage was never consummated. I just need the bruises to go down and then I'll go home. Plus, I've been bonding with Khanyi..." her voice trails off finally and she looks down while biting her lower lip.

I've noticed that she tends to blabber when she's nervous or emotional. I'm slowly closing the shatters of my heart so all I want is her out of my car. I feel suffocated by her presence.

"That won't be necessary. Goodbye Nomaswazi, I hope you find a man deserving and worthy of your love."

She looks at me like I just slapped her in the face and then she's huffing as she gets out of my car and bangs my door. I don't stay to watch her walk back into the royal gates because I'm afraid I might do something stupid like run after her. I drive away and I don't look back.

......

It's peaceful here, I can feel her all around me. Her warmth and serene aura lingers around her headstone. I crouch and place the fresh bouquet of lilies among the others which have dried. I drove around restlessly until I found myself at my mother's final resting place.

"I wish *Babe* left us instead of you. Maybe you would have told me what to do or you would have been able to help me control my demons. She's hurting. I finally found her *Make*, the woman whose arms feel like home and she's hurting in the worst possible way because of me. I don't know what to do, how to get through to her. How to make her understand that I could never hurt her like that intentionally. I don't have your gentleness or your patience. I'm impatient you always said so, I want to be better for you and for her. But I think I've lost her, for good this time and it hurts so bad."

Words fail me but I know she understands. Here at her deserted graveyard I can cry freely. I sob for the childhood I never had, the evil things they made us do and the loss of the love of my life. I'm kneeling beside her tombstone, the gravel is cutting my suit and hurting my knees but that barely registers in my mind. I sob until all my tears are spent and I rest my head on her granite headstone. I don't feel better even after my tears are spent, my heart is heavy.

"What do you want?" I ask without even turning my head.

"She was my mother too you know," he snaps back sounding like he did when we were ten.

I grunt and ignore him looking at the simple headstone. It suits our mother; she was the epitome of simple elegance. Nomaswazi reminds me of her sometimes, her effortless style and her warmth. I still remember her ever present gentle smile; death be not proud. I start uprooting some of the grass that has sneaked into her tombstone ignoring this moron.

He grunts as he lowers his body to the spot just next to

the tombstone and he joins me in uprooting the weeds. We work in silence and her calm seems to have descended on us. Ntsikelelo shifts his eyes and looks straight at mine. I stare back at him. He looks a mess, his face is swollen, the left eye swollen almost shut and his nose is broken. I really did a number on him.

"You followed me here because you know it's the one place where I won't snap your neck," I've always been able to read him like I'm reading myself. And the unfortunate thing is, he can read me just as well. He can feel my pain and my darkness the same way I can feel his. Growing up our connection was so strong it felt like we could share thoughts but as we grew apart, the connection also weakened. I can only feel his extreme emotions now, same applies to him.

"You broke my ribs which almost punctured my lungs. My whole body hurts like a bitch" He always speaks the most when it's just the two of us. When others are around he doesn't say much.

"I didn't do a good enough job, you're still standing here looking ugly," he smirks and for a minute, I see the boy who used to make us skinny dip in the river where the girls bathed.

"At least I don't look old and grey like you. I've never seen you this whipped before, she's making you weak. You really love her don't you." It's a statement and we haven't broken eye contact.

"I love her and you just ruined any chance I have with her the way you always ruin everything for me. How did you even know I brought her back?" I can't keep the bitterness from my voice.

"Now that's unfair I haven't been ruining everything for you, some of the things you ruined on your own. It's my business to know everything about you so I told my men to keep an eye on you. For your safety." I really want to punch him now but I can't disrespect my mother's grave like that.

"I always got blamed for your mess. I always had to clean up your mess. I always had to make sure that you're ok. Yet you hurt the one woman who means something to me."

"I didn't ask you to! I needed you to be my brother not my father. You are my half and you left me without so much as a backward glance. Getting into trouble seems to be the only thing that always gets your attention. You even replaced me with those idiots from your college days." This is the most passionate I've ever seen him but it doesn't make what he did right.

"I had to go away you know how I feel about the gun smuggling. I had to look out for you, I'm older..."

"By three minutes! Only three, you and your father never let me forget that. I work hard to be his right wing man but all he wants is to give everything to you. Even that wife you hit me for was supposed to be mine!" his voice has gone up an octave but I'm even angrier than him.

"I want no part of your blood empire, I never did and you know that! You can have it all. I want nothing that involves turning innocent children into monsters. As for Swazi, she's mine! I will kill for her," and I mean it.

I might not have joined the family's underworld business but our father trained us well, from when we were just kids. I'm faster and a better shot than Ntsikelelo, we both know it. He nods once. He won't try another stunt to hurt her to get to me. That's a relief because I wouldn't hesitate killing him the next time.

"You know the Beast still has plans for her right?" he says quietly, searching for my reaction. The Beast is our father's name in the underworld. He is known for his ruthlessness and it was rumoured that he once ripped a man's heart out of his chest for double-crossing him.

"He can only get to her over my dead body." Now it's his turn to grunt, he knows I mean this. "There's no marriage or union between us anymore so his plan has failed."

"What do you mean? You just admitted you love her enough to kill for her." His question is genuine.

"She believes that I was you in that video and I raised

my hand at her. There's no way we can come back from that." Just admitting defeat out loud makes it all real.

"Did you explain to her that it was me and not you?" now it's my turn to grunt.

"She wouldn't listen to me. Besides no one ever believed me whenever you created trouble except *Make.*" I shrug as I smooth over her headstone, nostalgia gripping my heart.

"So what? Your ego got bruised and you're just going to give up? That's stupid man, especially for you. Does she even know we're identical twins? Or did you spin me off as your brother like you always do." I hate the sneer in his voice but it does get me thinking.

I'm brought out of my thoughts by Ntsikelelo offering me his hand. I look at the hand then up at him blankly.

"Come on let's go get your woman back."

......

If the *iNdlovukati* doesn't call the police on me this time, it will be a small miracle. I haven't been out in public with Ntsikelelo in a long time, I forgot the stares we get when we're together. It's worse today because we both look a mess and yet we are in the Royal grounds. We wait for a while before Swazi comes out with one of the princesses I think, I've seen her on the news and during State events.

She stops in her tracks when she lays her eyes on us. Swazi opens her mouth as if to say something and closes it again. She looks at Ntsikelelo then at me then back at Ntsikelelo. She's clutching at the princess's hand and she looks so lost its not even cute. I remember how we used to confuse people for fun when we were younger, our parents were called to our school the first week of our first grade.

She finds my eyes and stares at them as if searching for something and I can't believe I'd even thought of giving up on her. That I'd given up on this connection that makes me want to live again, to face my demons and conquer. Even with a burst lip she is still effortlessly graceful. We stare at each other like there's no one else in the room until Ntsikelelo clears his throat.

"Hlongwane?" she's uncertain who she's talking to as she looks at me then at Ntsikelelo.

"NaDlamini can we talk? Privately." I hear Ntsikelelo tittering under his breath and I jab his injured ribs.

She leads me to the Royal Kraal. Without the dust from the many participants of *Incwala, Umhlanga* and the *Sibhanca* Dances the Kraal is huge and intimidating. The livestock has returned from the open veld and is locked inside its kraals. The animals move around restlessly as they prepare for nightfall. The rays from the setting sun dance across the trees turning the leaves golden.

It also thrusts a hue on Swazi's skin warming her already rich, chocolate looks. She's sitting on a rock, hugging her legs to her chest while her face rests on her knees and looking at me expectantly. Only the occasional moo and bleat break the silence hanging between us. I'm not sure where to start so I go back to the beginning of my nightmare.

"We were twelve years-old when we were forced to hold down a sixteen-year-old girl and take turns raping her. A week later I was standing over the corpse of the first man I ever killed. His lifeless eyes staring blankly at me haunt me to this day."

CHAPTER FIFTEEN

My heart is pounding almost out of my chest and I hope he can't hear it. I don't think he's even here with me right now, he's closed off. As his voice continues narrating, I see the scared little boy he must have been then, almost a man but still very much a boy.

"I wish that was the worst thing we did or saw but it wasn't. My father provided and still provides weaponry for the different rebel groups in Congo, Uganda, anywhere in Africa as long as they are willing to pay good money for it. He spoke to the leaders of the Mai Mai Cheka to initiate us into manhood. He wanted us to be tough and ruthless enough to take over his empire someday. He told our mother he was sending us to a military boarding school."

The bitterness in his voice is highly acidic and for a moment he struggles with his emotions. He forcibly closes his eyes, like he doesn't want to see whatever he's seeing. When he opens his eyes they are bloodshot and harrowed. I want to hold him and tell him its ok but I know he wants his space now, so I hug my knees even tighter.

"We went from Pofi to Kashibere along the Walike road all the way to Goma, recruiting boys. Some of them were as young as six years-old. I remember this one boy in Pofi they took him to his homestead that was rundown and ordered him to kill his father who had been partially crippled by a stroke. I remember his cries, begging them not to make him do it. They hit him with a *panga*, he had to man up or else they would slit his mother's throat. He did it, right there in front of us and in front of his mother, he took the *panga* and cut his father up. And you want to know the really fucked up part?"

Why isn't he crying? My eyes are now blurry with tears and I have snort running down my face and I wasn't even there. I shake my head blindly and he continues as though he was waiting for my input.

"They still slit his mother's throat, only after raping her in front of him. He was younger than us maybe ten or eleven years-old. Three weeks later in one of the Mai Mai camps, a little girl tried to escape, and they made us kill her. They kicked her like she was a stray dog, then they gave us big pieces of firewood and made each of us beat her with them. She didn't even scream or cry out, she was whimpering the whole time. She was bleeding from the mouth and she was coughing up blood from her little lungs until she died. Then they made us lie down and beat us with fifteen strokes each from long bamboo canes. They said we knew that she wanted to escape."

I want him to stop now, I can't hear anymore. I want to hold his inner child and hug him, shield him from all the horrible things he had to see. I want him to break down and cry. I want to tell him he doesn't have to be strong and hold it together for me. But I can't. So I rock myself instead and let my tears flow silently for the end of all those children's lives, even Hlongwane's. What those rebels made them do killed their childhood, it robbed them of their innocence.

"They gave us drugs to numb us and turn us into unthinking killing machines. The drugs helped with the nightmares, but Ntsikelelo's nightmares were worse than mine. He'd wake up screaming and wet the blankets. The men would pour a bucket of ice-cold water on him and make him sleep on the bare ground. I couldn't watch him suffer like that, so I would give him my share of the drugs as well. While that stopped his nightmares, I didn't know I was turning my brother into an addict and I had to do all those killings with a clear mind. I remember everything, some nights I relive it in my dreams..."

A sob escapes my mouth, startling both of us. Once it's out I can't seem to stop the other sobs from coming out of my mouth. I try stuffing my fist to muffle the sobs until I feel Hlongwane lifting me from the boulder I'm sitting on and cradling me in his arms.

"Shhh its ok. We were only there for a year, yes it left us twisted and ugly on the inside. Ntsikelelo enjoys pain and he's a misogynist that's why he hurt you and I'm so sorry *nkosatana.* What he did to you is unforgivable I just want you to understand why he's so twisted. I'm also broken Swazi, they broke us." My sobs intensify as he says this and he continues rocking me while brushing my back.

I've never imagined that such horrors exist, that they are children who go through all that. I mean we see it on television but it all seems far-fetched until you meet someone who's personally gone through it all. My childhood woes pale in comparison to what Hlongwane and Ntsikelelo went through. I don't know if it makes me forgive him but it makes me understand him a little. I'm glad Hlongwane told me all this even though it tore my heart into a million pieces.

"Hey." He says when my sobs and hiccups have gone

down, he's cleaning my face with his hands and I feel self-conscious now.

"Hi." I croak back, my voice sounds so scratchy and horrible.

"Promise me you'll never cry again, you're so ugly when you cry." My devil is slowly coming back to me. I laugh as I hide my face against his neck.

......

'Rent due today. You coming back, or should I look for another flat mate?'

I stare at the text from Akhona and wonder whether our friendship really meant so little to her. I don't know whether I should pay or just give the flat up. A part of me wants to go back and chase my dream of getting a qualification. Another part of me wants to stay and take care of my father, I've already wasted six years away from him.

Then there's Hlongwane. He and I have made things up, I think. I'm not sure really, we kissed and talked until it was late and the insistent buzzing of the mosquitos eventually chased us away from the Kraal. Today I'm going back home and its easier because the Queen Mother is away on State business and she took Khanyi with. I hate goodbyes and I've started this amazing bond with Khanyi.

Hlongwane is taking me home since he's the one who 'asked for me to visit his home' in the first place. I don't know how to feel about him being an identical twin. I mean I've already mistaken him for his twin in the cruelest way. Plus, how sure can I be that its Ntsikelelo in that video. I mean Hlongwane clearly loves sex, which I haven't given him yet. The man left me alone in his bed to go and have sex with a random woman, I also have to count that lawyer who reminded me of Zama. Clearly, my sister is more his taste than me.

"What are you thinking of? You've been quiet since I picked you up." His voice breaks into my thoughts. I turn my head and collide with his intense grey gaze.

"You have the most beautiful eyes," I blurt out and he grunts. I can't tell him that I'm doubting him.

"They remind me of *Make*, at times when I miss her I just look at my eyes in the mirror."

He loosens up whenever he talks of his mother and this warmth engulfs his whole countenance. I envy his obvious devotion to his mother, I never got to know my mother and my father barely ever talks about her. I spent my whole life missing something I've never had but it felt like a huge chunk of me was missing. I listen to him speak fondly of his mother until we park inside our yard.

"About what Ntsikelelo did," he sounds nervous and his eyes are pleading, "please don't tell your father." I hadn't been planning to but hearing him ask it makes me mad.

"Had he killed me, would you have been able to keep it from *Babe* then?" I click my tongue when I don't get a response and I get out of his car.

……

"My children, a man knows he is wealthy when his children visit him twice in one month." *Babe* exclaims as he wheels himself into the sitting area, he looks stronger than the last time I saw him. He's beaming at Hlongwane as he shakes his hand. Never mind my earlier outburst, I'm glad I didn't run home; it would have ruined their relationship. As it is my great aunt is very skeptical of Hlongwane even though I didn't divulge what happened.

It feels good to be back home, my father squeezes me in his embrace and I kiss him. At least Zama never visits home, I know Hlongwane said it was Ntsikelelo in that video but still. It's just wrong on so many levels. Did she know it was Ntsikelelo and not Hlongwane? Did she know he was filming the whole thing? I cringe at the thought that my own sister set out to deliberately hurt me like that.

After Hlongwane leaves my father asks me to take him to our favorite spot, the tallest of the Malandela hills. We haven't been there in years and navigating his wheelchair up the hill is hard. I remember when I was young he'd climb the hill at first with me on his neck and as I grew fatter on his back. We don't say much until we're on top of it and I plop myself on the grass trying to catch my breath. I had forgotten how calm it is up here and how refreshingly crisp the air is.

"Why do you love it so much up here *Babe*?" I ask and he smiles at me wrinkling the corners of his eyes.

"I get to see the whole of Maphalaleni up here and I feel closer to my ancestors." He's right about being able to see the whole of Maphalaleni. From up here I can see all the homesteads. The women look like ants in the rivers as they wash their clothes. The cattle grazing while the herd boys play soccer close to them. I don't know about the ancestors though; I've never been that spiritual.

"What do you think makes a good leader Manana?" his kind gaze is piercing my soul as he asks this. I ponder his question as I lie on my back, starring at the clear sky.

"Someone who is smart, emphatic and commands respect with his actions." *Babe* keeps quiet for so long I even start to think he's dozed off when he starts speaking.

"You know I've led my people, the people of our forefathers for over thirty years and I've learnt that what makes one truly a great leader is empathy and accountability. You have to be able to feel what your people are feeling in order to make decisions that will truly benefit them. Your choices won't always be what everyone wants but as long as you are willing to be held accountable for the consequences of your actions then always go with your gut."

I love this, our talks up here are always random and deep. "Would you have loved *Make* let's say she had a really scary past and so many demons raging within her. Demons that could have hurt you and her."

"We all have demons Swazi, some of them rage on the surface for everyone to see but the deadly ones are the demons that silently eat away at one's soul without anyone else seeing them."

I look up at him and he has this faraway pained look in his face and I bite back my next question and we sit in silence until he breaks it.

"When I met your mother, Tsandzile, I already had someone who was promised in marriage to me. She was of the Matsebula clan; her name was Lomawa. So, when I fell in love with your mother I couldn't bring myself to marry Lomawa anymore, so I told my father and the elders, they weren't happy. They said Tsandzile would have to be my second wife after Lomawa.

But I was young and adamant in my love, so I refused. That strained relations among our families. We got married and that was the happiest time of my life. Tsandzile was everything that I needed in a woman and more. She was kind hearted and had this fire in her soul.

A year passed and Tsandzile hadn't fallen pregnant. A family meeting was called and since she didn't have any sisters that could perform her duties for her, I was told I had to marry Lomawa. The news hit Tsandzile hard, it dulled some of the fire in her eyes. I needed an heir, so I agreed to marry Lomawa. We were married and within a year we had Zamaswazi. Although Lomawa had given me a child my heart belonged to Tsandzile and my folly was not hiding that fact.

We kept trying for a baby with Tsandzile without any luck. Any egg that attached dissolved before it even reached three months. This killed your mother and in turn killed me. Three years later, Lomawa again blessed me with another child this time a son, Masomalenhle. Lomawa couldn't understand why after giving me children I still favoured Tsandzile over her. I tried loving her as my wife, but my heart belonged to Tsandzile." The implications of what he just said hit me hard and I sit up but he continues talking.

"Years passed and Tsandzile never gave up hope of bearing me a child. It was hard on her, but we stood by each other. Then one day she went to visit her aunt and she told me when we returned that they had consulted the royal seer. A year later, Zamaswazi was eight then and Masomalenhle was five, you were born but unfortunately, we lost your mother. She held on long enough to hold you in her arms and she named you then she took her last breath." I feel it the blow of my mother's death on him, he stutters for a while and blinks back tears, I hold his withered hand.

"I was devastated. I never got to say goodbye and a part of me died that day with her. The Queen Mother was incensed. She said I failed to protect her niece and I let them kill her. I had no idea what she meant, I loved Tsandzile with my whole being. But she was adamant about her claim. She came with the royal healer and they sprinkled some water on your mother's grave.

She wanted to take you and raise you, but I begged her. You were the only link I had left with Tsandzile, if I lost you too I would have lost everything. She relented and left. A week later Lomawa started complaining of a headache. The headache grew so severe she became blind. That wasn't all, she started having a nose bleed and when she was coughing up blood, she finally confessed." Babe's voice has become bitter as he gets to this part of the story, there's so much anger on his face.

"She hated that I had married Tsandzile instead of her, so she went to a witchdoctor who tied up your mother's womb. That's why your mother couldn't conceive for the longest time, until she visited the Royal healer. When Lomawa saw that her muti had failed she went to another witchdoctor and this time wanted Tsandzile dead. You protected your mother while you were in her womb but the moment you were born that sorcerer won and I lost my Tsandzile. After her confession Lomawa also took her last breath."

By the time he is done narrating, we are both a crying mess. I crawl onto his lap and break down. I cry for my unborn siblings, for the pain my mother must have endured, and I cry for her stolen life.

It all suddenly makes a lot of sense. The reason my sister hates me so much and can't stand the sight of me. Her mother had left the seed of poison in her heart. In her own twisted way, she blames me for her mother's death. I had been a baby! I always assumed we shared the same mother.

I wish I had known earlier then I would have understood her animosity. Maybe I wouldn't have tried so hard to make her love me. Maybe her insults wouldn't have had that much bite, her taunts less destructive. It doesn't help thinking of what ifs. It is what it is and I'm glad I finally know.

CHAPTER SIXTEEN

"I don't understand why you are paying lobola for the second time!"

Meeting my father always leaves me on an emotional high. My mother begged me to forgive him on her death bed. This is the one thing I can't do, even for her. How do you accept an apology that was never given? He hasn't once shown remorse for what he put us through. Instead he tries to control and manipulate us every chance he gets.

"You don't have to understand anything, she's my wife and I'm paying lobola with my livestock." Ntsikelelo throws me a cautioning eye but I am not afraid of the man we call a father.

"Then you should have just returned the cows I used

paying lobola for her in the first place."

It's the day before the lobola negotiations and my father is all over my case like a bad rash. I already instructed my uncles to pay whatever amount is asked for, the only thing I want them to negotiate is Swazi coming to stay with me tomorrow. I haven't seen her since I dropped her off from the palace and it feels like it's been a year. She sounded down on the phone but assured me it had nothing to do with me.

"You can claim your herd of cattle from whomever you gave them to. I don't owe you anything." I respond while checking my watch and the next thing I know my back is against the wall and my father's elbow is pressed against my wind pipe.

"Paying lobola again won't change the fact that she's the wife *I chose for you.* Neither will me stopping supplying the renegades with armory stop them using children and killing people, they'd just get another supplier. So get off your judgmental horse and show me some respect and appreciation. *I made you!*" his face is so close to me I can see his Adam's apple bobbing up and down as he spits the words.

He clicks his tongue then lets me go and I try to fill my air-deprived lungs with oxygen. He storms out of the house. I feel a blackout approaching but I focus all my energy in blocking it out and I succeed. Ntsikelelo looks at me with the biggest smirk in his face. I'm grateful that I received a call earlier letting me know that the house is almost ready. I can't wait to get out of this toxic house.

"Are you sure you are ready for marriage? Won't you end up hurting her when your urges come back?" he asks while looking me dead in the eye.

"I don't know but one thing I know for sure is this; Nomaswazi is the one good thing in my life right now. There's nowhere in hell I'm letting her go."

……

I was feeling restless after my encounter with the old man so I decided I need a breather. I drove around until I found myself here, close to her house. I know I'm not supposed to see her until after the lobola negotiations but I still take out my phone and dial her number.

"Hello." Her voice is soft and breathless and it does things to my loins.

"I'm parked next to *linchitsamuti kwenu.*" I almost curse myself for how detached I sound right now. She pauses for so long without responding, I almost think she's hung up on me. At least I can hear her breath cackling over the line.

"Fine, I'm coming." She hangs up and I lower my seat as I wait for her.

It's a good thirty minutes later when I hear a slight knock on my windows, it's her. I was dozing off. I sit up straight then I open the door for her. Her watermelon and peaches scent fill my car the moment she gets in and closes the door. It's the weirdest combo but I picked it up when we were in Durban together and I love the scent on her. She's a welcome breath of freshness. She greets then looks at me expectantly.

"Don't I even get an I missed you kiss?" she flushes at my words and tries to pull off an affronted look.

"No Hlongwane what will people say?"

"First off, my windows are darkened no one can see anything inside even if they were standing right next to the car. Secondly, I couldn't care less what people think or say about us. Now can I have my kiss." I don't wait for her to protest; I was already leaning in as I was talking. I claim her lips and they are soft and pliable under my lips.

"*Sawubona nhlitiyo yami,*" I murmur against her lips and I feel her whole face heating up.

I try to stifle my chuckle as she buries her burning face against my neck. She really has captured my heart with her bold innocence. Outwardly she's this shy, uncertain woman but I've had the chance to dig deeper into her soul and experience the fire she buries at the depths of her soul. I can't help but laugh when I remember the night I saw her at my club in Jo'burg. Nomaswazi just pushes all my buttons and she does it so effortlessly. I feel lighter already just by being in her presence.

"You don't have to do it you know." I look at her in confusion and she elaborates. "You don't have to pay lobola for the second time. It's crazy, I mean who does that?"

"A man who has a lot to atone for. I hurt not only you but also your father Swazi. He's a chief and he could have gotten any man to marry you off to, but he chose me and I broke that trust in front of everyone. Also a man who finds himself deeply in love. The first lobola was paid by my father for his own agenda. This time, it's me showing you the depth of my feelings for you and that I choose you to be my wife. I can't afford to give you the wedding of your dreams right now, but I'm working on it. I promise I'll give you the best wedding in the whole of eSwatini."

"Oh." She says while biting her lower lip. Not quite the reaction a man expects after pouring out what little heart he has to his woman.

"Did I say something that's bothering you?"

"No, no its nothing. Really." I may be fresh in this committed relationship thing but I'm as sure as hell that its nothing means something is bothering her.

"*Nkosatana* talk before I make you talk." Stubborn Swazi needs my boardroom glare. She sighs and slumps her shoulders sinking slightly into her seat.

"It's just that this whole lobola thing has brought back my anxieties in full force. We've been here before

Hlongwane and it ended with me alone at the altar, humiliated and suicidal. What if you walk out on me again? I don't think I'll be able to bear such rejection again. Then there's Zamaswazi, my father told me he called her to come and support me tomorrow. I couldn't find it in my heart to tell him about the video, you know. Is it so bad of me to wish my own sister stays as far from me as possible?" her eyes are swimming in unshed tears.

I can't tell her that Zamaswazi thinks she slept with me. Ntsikelelo told me that she came onto him thinking it was me and he never corrected her besides he "could never turn away free pussy." He took the video because well he's a twisted pervert, she didn't know he was recording. It all happened a year ago and according to him Zamaswazi is obsessed with me. She was blowing up his phone until he blocked her and stopped answering unsaved numbers.

As for her fear of me running again, I realize that nothing I say will ease her fear. My actions hurt her deeply and I can only show her my intentions.

"Buckle up, I want to show you something." I tell her even as I lean over and buckle her seat belt.

"Hlongwane I shouldn't even be with you right now. If makhulu notices I'm gone she..." she protests as she wipes her tears away with the back of her hand.

"I'm not taking you far we'll be back within the hour."

She wants to protest more so I just start my engine droning out her protests.

……

Ten minutes later we're driving up the hillside. The terrain is a bit steep but it was the best site I found, nestled and tucked away at the top of a hill. We meet the constructor and his team leaving at the gate, he honks at us and the men at the back of his bakkie take off their hats. I honk back and Swazi looks at me skeptically. I can tell she has a lot of questions but she chooses not to ask.

I open her door and take her hand as she alights. Her face is filled with the same animated curiosity that she had when we were in Durban. I inspect the progress of the house with a critical eye. I must say I'm impressed by their workmanship, they are now at second window level and they are doing a neat job. I love how they are bringing my design to life.

"What is this place Hlongwane?" I grin when she finally can't hold in the curiosity.

"Do you like it?" I ask bringing her closer to me. With heels on, the top of her head reaches just under my chin. Today she's much shorter yet she still fits me like a glove.

"Like it? I love it! The air is much fresher up here. Look at all that greenery. Look at that mountain behind us and those hills around us. *Babe* and I have a similar spot at

Malandela, we usually sit there and look at all of Maphalaleni. Imagine living up here and getting to see this view every day." Her excitement calms my nerves; I was a bit anxious thinking that she might not like it.

"This is my wedding present to you, it was meant to be a surprise. As you can see its still under construction. It's close enough to your home so that you can check up on your father whenever. There'll be a lawn there and your garden, you can plant those flowers you love so much. There's also going to be a basketball court around there and it'll be joined to a tennis court. I'll teach our sons how to play or even our daughter. We can have as many boys as possible but only one princess. The swimming pool will be on the roof of your house, I know you love water and you can curl up on the deck with one of those books you love so much. Maybe we can shag under the stars while the children are sleeping." I'm trying hard to sell her my dream.

"Hlongwane, this is... wow this is just..." she shocks me when she starts crying and I panic.

"It's ok if you don't like it *nkosatana* I can design another house, one that you want. This plot is yours, the title deeds are in your name. I can get them to demolish this and we start afresh. Just please stop crying." She's shaking her head vehemently against my chest.

"It's not that I hate the house, I love it. I'm just scared

that like my mother I might struggle to give you kids or even worse be barren."

I'm lost and in between hiccups she tells me about her father's unfortunate polygamy. I had no idea that the old man had two wives, all he ever talks about is Swazi's mother. I can tell that the news broke her and she's torn up.

"I grew up being told I killed my mother you know. Then I heard all this, it still feels like she died because of me. Had she remained barren maybe Zama's mother wouldn't have done what she did. Hearing you talking about children scares me Hlongwane. I feel like even from birth, I wasn't meant to be happy. My birth brought about tragedy and my life has been one misfortune after the other." The pain in her voice is so raw and it makes me want to kill whoever caused her this much pain.

"I'm sorry that I became part of your misfortunes in the past Swazi. I brought you here to show you that I'm committed to you. I can't wait for us to turn this house into a home. I've never thought of myself as a parent because I'm too screwed up but with you Swazi, I want to be better. A better man and a better father to our children. If we don't have any children, I still want to walk into this house and find you barefoot in our kitchen and preparing my favourite meal in just an apron." She giggles sweetly at the last part.

She stands on her toes and brushes her lips against mine. "I love you," she breathes against my lips and I deepen the kiss. Devouring all the love from her lips and pouring my love into hers.

"Speaking about the future my two months' leave is up next week, I need to go back to work." I'm now parked at the tree close to her home again.

"You can do your Accounting course this side, I'll get you into the same program via correspondence." I'm paying lobola for her tomorrow, I'm not letting her jet off to another country.

"Sangweni, you can't keep me by your side forever." I want to snap and say, *Watch me.* Her calm voice and her using my clan name put me off kilter. So I let her talk.

"Growing up my father made sure I lacked for nothing and shielded me a lot. That made me spoilt and soft. He couldn't shield me from the bullying and name calling or from getting my heart broken. The morning I ran away from home I had bought rat poison. I was so weak I wanted to take my own life. Going to Jo'burg and having to fend for myself made me grow up and become stronger. I know you want to protect me but please let me do it on my own."

I feel like shit now. I'm torn between the need to have her with me and protect her and the need to let her grow on her own. If I do get the Bangkok deal I will be up and down a lot. It would be selfish of me to ask her to give up her dreams and follow me around as I fulfill mine. I've gotten so used to having her around me in the past two months.

I sigh. A deep despondent sigh.

"Fine. You can go..." she doesn't even let me finish she swoops in and places wet kisses all over my face. That simple gesture makes the love I have for her solidify.

"Only on condition that you won't be staying in that unsafe flat. I choose and pay for your new apartment in a secure area with beefed up security."

"Secure area and beefed up security, Hlongwane? Isn't that over the top even for you," the exasperation in her voice is clear but I don't care she will just have to accept that.

"No negotiation *nkosatana*, take it or leave it." My father has probably made enemies along the way and I don't want Swazi becoming a pawn in their dirty games. She huffs and pouts.

"Fine you win, you pigheaded moron!" she pokes my head and I hide my laughter. *I always win baby.* Always.

CHAPTER SEVENTEEN

"I'm the talk of the village again," I grumble as I hand my favourite man his chamomile tea.

Already the women from around have come to "assist" in the cooking and preparation for the lobola negotiations. If you ask me they are just here to get another scoop to gossip about around the water holes. *Babe* chuckles, at least he seems happy with everything. I don't know I'm just dreading this whole thing.

"Their princess is getting married, of course they should talk. It's a joyous occasion Manana." He says while Makhulu makes approving noises.

If it were up to me they'd be the only people present for the negotiations. That's just wishful thinking on my part. We're African after all, everyone has to be present.

"They were the first people to laugh and talk about me last time when my wedding fell through." Yes, I have every reason to be resentful of them right now.

"Even Jesus was crucified by the same people he performed miracles for. They rejected him time and again but he still gave his life up to cleanse their sins." Makhulu pipes in as she continues taking stuff for the ladies to prepare in the older kitchen.

"For once I agree with her white god. You were born to serve this community whether they love you or not Swazi. You are not their friend *ungumake webantfu besiSwati.* You will love them with all that is in you, even when they don't see or appreciate it. That is the power of your name." there's a beauty in the tone of his voice that I can't quite describe. It makes me all sappy.

"I'm your daughter of course both of you will only have great things to say about me!" I tease them and break the deep moment we are having.

Makhulu drags me to her house where I will be sitting with Khanyi, Aphelele and some of my distant cousins until they call us. The rest of the girls keep ogling Khanyi but she ignores them and is telling me about the event they went to.

□

I wish Akhona was here, she was the one friend I made in a foreign country. I'm grateful that Khanyi and I are growing closer.

A loud shrill cry breaks the light banter the girls are having and makhulu instantly looks worried. She leaves us to go and check what's happening outside since there's sudden activity.

Aphelele gave birth the day before yesterday to the most beautiful angel in the whole world. Her pale skin is almost white but it quickly wrinkles when she cries and turns a bright red. She has a full head of flaxen almost gold wispy curls. Her milky eyes look like someone inserted a chalcedony inside the irises causing her to blink rapidly.

"This can't be a good omen," Aphi says when the baby keeps piercing our hearts with her shrill cries.

I'm now cradling Labotsibeni close to my chest and she won't stop crying, her whole face is red and Aphi is also crying. My anxiety is beginning to cripple me and I make a bargain with God. If my lobola negotiations go well, I'll start going to church more often. There's commotion and shouting outside and my heart beat is now erratic. The baby's cries have weakened and she's hiccupping. I go and peak by the window.

"I won't give you my great-grandchild, you hear me. I won't let you mutilate her for your evil ways." Makhulu's voice is charged with emotion and I can't see the person she's screaming at.

"You can't keep my husband from his child! We want my husband's daughter."

My hold tightens on Labotsibeni while the bickering continues, they'll have to pry her from my cold fingers. I hear my father's authoritative voice instructing the guards to take them out. After some swearing they finally leave and the baby is now quiet, only then do I relax my hold.

I look at Aphi holding Labo while she suckles as if her little life depends on it. To think someone would want to hurt such a beautiful soul is sickening. My anxiety has lessened a bit, the baby was probably feeling the bad aura from her father and his wife. Some of the tension around my chest eases and I continue praying for my lobola negotiations to go smoothly.

......

It feels like I'm doing this for the first time. I guess I am because now I know the man paying lobola for me. He is no longer my knight in shining armour, I'm not even sure he's capable of loving me the way my father loves me. If anything he is the perpetrator of unimaginable evils. He tends to be controlling and he has a short temper. He's aggressive and thinks he can intimidate me to do anything. He has an identical twin who slept with my sister. The worst is he left me in his bed while he went to screw a random woman.

In the same breath he's fiercely protective of those he loves. He makes me feel good about my body and has told me so many times that I'm beautiful I've ended up believing it. He calls me princess and treats me like one. His laugh gives me tingles all the way to my toes. He has flashes of childlike joy that make me want to stay young with him forever. He has nightmares that make me cringe and want to hug him and never let him go.

If I have any sense at all I'll be the one walking away this time around. Yet one look from those smoldering charcoal eyes and I know I'm incarcerated for life. His gravelly voice when he's speaking siSwati, *Nkhosi*! SiSwati is the love language of Africa just as Italian is the love language of Europe. Every Casanova should speak some siSwati even if it's just a few love phrases.

His dream of teaching our children how to play ball reeled me in; hook, line and sinker. I want to have little a little Hlongwane or a dozen, with his bone structure and those compelling eyes. Some melanin dripping babies that will bring us both endless joy. We're both not perfect but both of us deserve love and a shot at happiness.

A sharp nudge from Makhulu's elbow brings me back from my land of fairytales. There are whistles and the sound of joyous ululation, it looks like the whole of Maphalaleni is here! Simple lobola negotiations have turned into a celebration of some sort. It's no use complaining to *Babe*, he will simply tell me that the whole of Maphalaleni is his family. Growing up, it didn't matter what time it was, he would drop everything to resolve a dispute among his people.

I look at him now next to his kraal and he is in his element, ever the benevolent host. His face is writhed in the biggest of grins as he tells a story to Hlongwane senior and the men around them. He even looks taller on his wheelchair much like the proud, Sobhuza the Great who raised me. I try hard not to look at my father-in-law for too long. He's the older version of the twins but with normal dark brown eyes like the rest of us.

I have to serve them food and I do so with my eyes averted and I get complimented a lot. Trouble starts when I have to serve my husband to be, these morons are sitting side by side and wearing identical smirks. It's eerie how alike they are. They sit with their backs straight and shoulders squared, they are even wearing similar suits. People notice my dilemma and there is good natured laughter at my expense.

I look into their eyes, identical pools of charcoal but Ntsikelelo's eyes are cooler when regarding me while Hlongwane's eyes are molten lava. They are scorching my soul as I hand him the plate of food I'm carrying.

"NaDlamini," he grunts softly as our hands brush sparking some current between us and I know I made the right selection.

A big gleaming Jeep Cherokee drives in as I make a return trip from the kitchen, I have more food to serve my in-laws. I don't pay much attention to the car it could be one of my father or father-in-law's friends from Parliament. I am serving one of the uncles when there's a sudden lull in the animated conversations and a pregnant silence befalls our homestead. I turn to see what has sparked the silence and I almost drop the plate of food in shock.

There stands my sister Zamaswazi, in the flesh and dressed to the nines. She has on a dazzling white dress, hugging what little curves she has tastefully, she has on a traditional red Swati skin apron on top of the dress but like someone with a child it is raised over one shoulder. Her hair is tied into a neat bun on top of her head and she has on professional looking make-up. She's standing there in all her splendor like a regal bride.

I spy Masomalenhle's back, he is leaning inside the back seat of their car. He is struggling to get something out of the car. I feel light headed and hot flushes rip through my body as she walks past me without even the slightest acknowledgement. She makes a beeline to where *Babe* and

Hlongwane senior are sitting and bows in greeting. I can't catch what she's saying but my father looks like he's about to have a heart attack.

Breathe Swazi, the voice in my head rings and I try to count to ten. I read somewhere that it works when anxiety is crippling your body. Why isn't it working for me? Flashes of the taunts and all the nasty words she's ever said to me keep ringing in my head and I feel faint. I can't breathe.

"Look at me *nkosatana*. You have to breathe." I can hear his voice but I can't breathe let alone reply and its causing me more agitation.

"Nomaswazi here take this water, it has sugar in it." It could have salt or ash for all the taste I feel in my mouth right now. By some miracle I manage to drink the water and I'm wheezing. I don't know what's happening to my body right now, I have no control over it.

"Swazi, baby please focus on me. I swear I'm not the father of her babies."

What?! It feels like someone doused me with a bucket of icy water and my labored breathing is replaced by searing chest pains. What does he mean babies? The fog in my mind is fast disappearing and I look up to see Zamaswazi holding one little replica of Hlongwane, complete with charcoal eyes. While Masomalenhle is now next to her holding another baby.

......

□

I wish this was a dream. A horrible dream I can wake up from but the stares I'm getting from the whole community are real. As are the identical twins my sister brought to disrupt my lobola. She claims they are Hlongwane's babies and demands that the Hlongwane family do right by her. I'd think it was about the babies if it weren't for the victorious smirk she keeps throwing my way. The babies are about four, five months and she could have brought them to their family a long time ago.

She stole my dream of having those cute chubby babies! I feel anger burning inside me, a red amber fueled more by the looks I keep receiving. I am tired of all the crap Zamaswazi keeps dishing my way that I'm supposed to just take. I feel anger that has been building up for over twenty years. Anger I had no idea I had. Anger that propels me and I find myself in front of her breathing heavily. She stares at me coldly, unfazed.

"Why?" in my mind I sounded louder, I try clearing my throat and she laughs at my face.

"Why? Is that what you came flying to ask me? Your fat body is even taxed, you're sweating and you want to know *nywayi*?" I bite my tongue to stop the tears which are about to spring into my eyes. Her mocking tone is still as acidic as it was when I was six years-old.

"Why do you hate me so much? Why have you always treated me like I'm a cockroach to be squashed under your shoe? Why do you gain so much satisfaction from my pain? Why Zamaswazi? Why??!" this time my voice doesn't let me down, it doesn't crack or break. She looks bored.

"Not everything is about you princess. You run away from your home all these years and now that you're back you expect us to roll down the red carpet and throw you a feast? Who was taking care of your father? Who was taking care of the man who just paid lobola for you? I did, I even bore him heirs that you probably never will. So please enough with the sob story already!" anger bubbles in my soul again and it makes me laugh.

"You're so stupid Zama. You are beautiful and you can get any man that you want. Yet you're so resentful and bitter you thought you could hurt me but you ended up sleeping with the wrong twin." The look on her face tells me that she didn't know that she played herself.

"I saw the video Zamaswazi, you played yourself. You're so sick and twisted with this hatred that you are clinging onto. I didn't kill your mother and I lost a mother too! You don't see me doing all sorts of messed up stuff to you."

Her bloodshot eyes are sending laser beams my way and she's clutching on that poor baby too tight.

"You only lost a mother that you don't even know, while I lost both my parents the day you were born. At least before you, your precious father paid us some attention even when he was neglecting my mother. When you came it was like we didn't exist. I was eight years old and I had to mourn the death of my mother alone and raise my brother. While all your father cared about was his precious baby from his precious wife. He kept us because he couldn't kick us out and when I was old enough he shipped us off to Mbabane. So don't you ever compare your loss to mine *princess*. I wish you died at birth with your mother!"

The venom in her voice depletes my anger and I just stare at her as she wipes the tears with the back of her hand. Her nose is red and for once I see a vulnerable side to her. I see her pain and I don't know what to do about it. Mixed with the pain is such raw resentment just staring at her eyes makes shivers run up and down my spine.

I am reminded that we have an audience when there's a loud gasp from the people around us. All I ever wanted was the love and acceptance from my sister. I saw this confrontation ending with forgiveness and all I get is rejection in front of everyone. It's all overwhelming, fatigue is now holding my body hostage and I just want to curl up into a ball until this whole nightmare ends.

My first instinct is to run, this time not to another country but to my bedroom. I lock myself in the bathroom. I feel suffocated like the walls are closing in. Today didn't turn into my worst nightmare as I feared, it turned into a burial of whatever hopes I had of me and Zama ever reconciling. Maybe I should have died at birth like she said. Then I wouldn't have suffered from this constant pain of rejection.

Babe should have named me Lahliwe instead. Clearly, nobody wants me, not the people of my forefathers and definitely not my siblings. I'm searching frantically for a razor blade and I can't find it. I catch sight of my crazy eyes in the mirror and I slam my fist into it. The pain in my hand as I get the splinters of glass out of it and put my hand under running water is nothing compared to the dull throbbing pain in my heart.

CHAPTER EIGHTEEN

"...I wish you died at birth with your mother!" Zamaswazi's words hang over all of us and for a split second hold us all hostage.

Then I watch as emotions flood Swazi's eyes and the tears she had been valiantly holding onto tumble down. The second passes and there's chaos. I want to run after my bride who rushes through the people who had formed a circle around her and her sister. Just as I'm about to take off I hear a grunt which turns into a growl and I watch helplessly as the chief keels over while clutching his chest.

Zamaswazi looks at him and clicks her tongue before

handing me the baby she is carrying. She forcibly takes the baby her brother is carrying and hands it over to Ntsikelelo. We all look, stupefied at her retreating back while the brother looks at us almost apologetically. He looks longingly at his father.

"Lenhle!" Zamaswazi's shrill voice is like a whiplash and her brother scurries to her before coming back with a big suitcase. He then scurries back and they drive off at high speed, without any care for their father who could be having a heart attack and the babies who have begun wailing.

Swazi's grandmother takes the baby from me and I rush to where the chief is laying and my father is feeling for his pulse. It takes a while and I am now frantic with worry. This is all my fault. I shouldn't have insisted on paying lobola for the second time, none of this would have happened.

"I can feel a pulse, its low but I can feel one." My father says and I heave a sigh of relief.

He looks me straight in the eye and I know that look. He's instructing me to pull myself together. Just like that, my guard is back up and I am rational and clear headed. Ntsikelelo helps me carry the chief into my car while the villagers are swarming around us like angry bees. People can be insensitive in their curiosity. At least in rural Maphalaleni, there is no one without sense to film all this on their smart phone. I have no doubt though that what just transpired will be a conversation starter for most of them.

□

"Which hospital should I drive to? Mbabane or Piggs Peak?" Ntsikelelo asks and I try to think which is closer or better.

"Piggs Peak is smaller but it's the closest, let's get him there for now."

"Are you sure? I mean Piggs Peak is a glorified clinic, we may as well just take him to the clinic here or the one in Hhukwini. Besides, I can get him to Mbabane in the same time," he argues while eyeing me in the rearview mirror.

"Then why did you even ask me? Just get to the stupid hospital!" I grit through my teeth. He eyes me coolly through the mirror and I want to choke him.

"Can you believe we are fathers now? The little fuckers look just like us." He says stealing glances at me. I grunt ignoring him as I try to call Swazi. Her phone rings unanswered.

"Man, I messed up big time. I have no interest whatsoever in that whore, now she's the mother of our children. She's bitter and psycho. I don't know what to do with those kids." His voice is downright pleading now.

I know what he's asking of me, but I can't. Not at the cost of my Swazi. I can only imagine how she's feeling right now. Those babies will be a reminder of her sister's ultimate betrayal. I can't hurt her by forcing her to care for those babies, even though they are mine as much as they are his.

"You are a father now; you'll figure something out. No. I'm not helping you out with this one. You did complain that I parent you, this time I won't be parenting you on how to parent your children." I ignore his thunderous look and try calling Swazi again.

We reach the hospital in record time and the chief is taken into intensive care. Swazi is still not answering her phone. I try one last time and finally it's picked up.

"Swazi's phone hello," answers a chirpy voice at this point I'm just relieved someone is answering.

"May I speak to Swazi?"

"I'm sorry but Swazi can't come to the phone right now."

"Please, it's her husband. I really need to talk to her."

"Hlongwane? You're speaking to her cousin, Khanyi. Swazi is still locked in her bedroom; she won't open or talk to anyone. How is the chief?"

"He's stable for now." I lie before hanging up and swearing. I hope Swazi hasn't done anything drastic. I refuse to even entertain the thoughts of her committing suicide.

I ask Ntsikelelo to keep me updated about the chief's health while I take his car back to Maphalaleni. He isn't impressed with me but he'll live.

"Thank you." I say to him placing my hand on his shoulder. He places his head on top of mine and nods lightly. It feels good to be able to talk with my brother again.

□

Swazi was right, it's never too late to mend fences with family. I don't know if the same principle can be applied to my relationship with my father but right now, I'm just glad I have my brother back.

……

The past two days haven't been easy on me and Swazi, our relationship is back to being strained. It's like every time we move two steps forward we are dragged ten steps back. I found her locked in her bathroom and she only opened up when I promised to break down the door. She hurt her hand but wouldn't say what happened, the mirror was also broken. I'm worried about her, she's shutting everyone out including me.

I wish she'd let me in but she has been by her father's bedside since he came out of ICU last night. I'm watching her now as she cradles his limp hand. I've been asking her what she wants to eat for the past five minutes but she simply stares at her father and strokes his cheek with her other hand. I'm two seconds from snapping when my phone goes off. Inwardly I wince when I check the caller ID.

"Meet me in thirty minutes, my office." Then the line goes dead.

I guess he's been handed my resignation letter then. I sent it in this morning, my resignation is effective immediately. I might be jumping the gun since the Bangkok deal hasn't come through yet but even if it does fall through I know my company will be ok.

I put my phone back into my pocket as I look defeated at Swazi. She's still shutting me out but I would rather just be here with her than go to that man. It's not like I have much of a choice in the matter.

"Baby I need to pop in the office for a while, I will be back soon with your lunch." I say as I brush my lips on her forehead.

She barely acknowledges my touch. I wish I knew what is going on in her mind right now. I wonder why his other children haven't come to check on him. Zamaswazi hasn't even called to ask about her babies. Some mother she is; it's bad enough that Ntsikelelo slept with her and impregnated her. Now we are stuck with her for life.

I park my car in my usual spot and sit for a minute giving myself the pep talk. At the reception there's utter chaos and everything is in a frenzy, I ignore the mayhem and proceed to my meeting. The PA seems relieved to see me and waves me in. I don't bother knocking but just get in and take a sit without being offered one.

He's in a bad mood. I can tell by the lines around his mouth and the vein popping on his forehead. He's on the phone, probably with one of the board members because he's not barking orders and he's trying to be as pleasant as possible. I realize for the first time that he has really aged. To be honest, he aged a lot with my mother's death that's when his grey hairs started showing. And he became even colder. My mother managed to make him, a bit more human.

"You can't resign, who is going to run this company?" As always, he's not asking.

But some of my wife's stubborn streak has rubbed off on me. I try to mask how much he intimidates me and I stare him in the eye without flinching.

"I don't have to do anything, father. I have to focus on my own company now" My voice is as flat as his.

"After all that I've done for you, this is how you repay me? I took you to the best schools..."

"That was your duty as my father. You were supposed to take care of me, besides you ruined all that when you let them turn us into animals. You broke us and yet I have been paying my dues in the last six years. I have demons that have not given me peace my whole life, that is what you did for me. I don't owe you anything." My voice gets progressively gruffer as I talk, and my anger awakens.

For the first time my father seems shocked. This is the second time I cut in while he's talking and talked back to him.

"You think I don't know how much I messed up? I lost my wife! She hated what I did to you. I was doing it for you,

I was just the son of a village drunk and I had to fight to where I am today. In my world you kill or be killed and I wanted you to be ready to take over the empire I built for you from scratch. I lost the one thing I loved and it was all for you!" his Adam's apple is bobbing up and down in agitation.

"That's the thing I don't want your empire. Ntsikelelo deserves everything, he has been working under you all this time. I don't even want to be part of this company. I'm done being your skivvy." A staring contest ensues between us and I don't blink nor look away until he talks again.

"You don't get it do you? If we go down, you go down with us." I chuckle at his threat; he narrows his eyes at me, but I'm done being his pawn.

"No I don't. I made copies of the company files while I was working here, and they are as clean as spring water. You and Ntsikelelo are on your own on this one. Let me save you some breath, disown me I don't want your money. If you ever try to harm my wife or use her, I will be the one ripping off your heart. Good day, father."

I don't give him a chance to reply. I walk out of the office like I didn't just sign my death certificate.

……

I end up going to my hotel room. I booked into the Royal Swazi Sun, to be closer to the hospital so that Swazi will be close to her father. She refused to come. This hotel reminds me a lot of the one we were to get married at, in Ezulwini. Nomaswazi has been making it abundantly clear that she doesn't want, nor need my help and my patience has finally worn off so I left her at the hospital.

I have to wait up for the conference call from Bangkok. I'm worried and nervous about it, I mean I just resigned from my job and getting that deal will really set the tone of my new company. I've also been working on other deals, none as big as the Bangkok deal.

I ask to use the hotel conference room, I have to look as professional as possible and that includes taking a bath at 1am and wearing a suit which says competent architect. I feel an adrenaline rush I have never felt back at my father's logistics company. I took a gamble and I really hope it pays off.

"Mr. Hlongwane."

He didn't really say Hlongwane, it came out sounding like Sho-nga-re but because it's a conference call I keep my face passive. I offer a brief smile to the other board member sitting around the conference table. I'm glad I decided to bath and dress professionally.

"It is with great pleasure that I would like to inform you that your bid has been accepted and you have won the tender to build Bang Kho Laem Luxury Resort. We loved your idea of

mixing futuristic plan with the traditional Swati architecture. We are looking forward to seeing your vision come to life. You are advised to start working as soon as possible before our rainy season commences."

What! We're in April already and their rainy season starts mid-May or late May latest that gives me a month and a half at most! Inside I'm panicking but outwardly I'm smiling, well my version of a business smile.

"Thank you so much Mr. Paribatra for the opportunity, you won't be disappointed."

I spend another thirty minutes going through the brief on the conference call and by the time I'm done it's almost nearing 3am local time, while in Bangkok it's almost 8am.

I punch the air in celebration and I wish I was celebrating with Swazi. I send her a text telling her I got the deal. I also text Melusi, Ntsikelelo and Mpho. My brat of a brother calls back immediately and I'm surprised.

"Way to go man. This will kill the Beast!" I laugh at the excitement in his voice.

"Hey that's your father show some respect. What are you doing up this late?"

"These little demons shit a lot, I'm up changing their diapers and they want their bottles too."

It's great seeing him stepping up like this for his babies. We spend a few more minutes on the phone making fun of each other. There's no response from Swazi, maybe she hasn't seen the message yet. I wonder whether we are going to be able to survive this setback as I make my way to my room.

CHAPTER NIGHTEEN

The rate at which *Babe* is slipping away from me is the scariest thing I have ever gone through in my life. He woke up after being admitted two days and he was visibly hurt that Zamaswazi and Masomalenhle weren't at the hospital. He blames himself for the rift between us and Zama having babies with my intended's twin. When he talks about them his eyes are filled with pain, at times his eyes are vacant, and he stares out at nothing.

He hates hospitals and he would have complained by now demanding to be discharged. He isn't even aware of his surroundings and it breaks my heart. Feeding and bathing him is a struggle because unlike before, he doesn't put any effort to help.

He drifts between unconsciousness and lucidity. For the past two days he thinks I'm my mother. He's been chirper and tells his Tsandzile all that has been happening ever since she left him. I asked the doctor and he said it might be the medication they gave him, or he just misses my mother. They say his heart as well as his sugar levels are critical but stable. What does that even mean? Are they critical or are they stable?

The seizures are the worst like the one he's having now. They usually start with him twitching restlessly and mumbling incoherent things as sweat drips down his back. Then progress to full blown thrashing. I help the nurse hold him down as tears pour down my eyes. I can't stand seeing him in so much pain. His whole body is convulsing, his eyes rolling to the back of his head. The nurse injects some insulin into him and the convulsions lessen until he lies still.

I take a warm wet cloth and wipe his clammy skin. He opens his eyes and they are clouded with confusion and my poor father looks like a lost child. I can see that he's struggling to place my face.

"Maswazi? When did you come back?" his raspy voice breaks my heart and I swallow the lump in my throat.

"Yes, it's me Babe, I came yesterday." I don't want to confuse him any further.

"Please tell Zama I don't hate her. I sent them away when they continued tormenting you and throwing you down that closed mine scared me. She has her mother's hate Tsandzile, she would have hurt our Swazi. Lomawa I'm sorry for neglecting you and our children, you deserved a better man. One who would love you the way you desired. I... I..." I put my hand over his trembling hand and swallow the lump in my throat.

"Shhh it's ok Lobamba, you don't have to say anything." My voice is shaky from my unshed tears.

"Where is that Hlongwane boy? He made a mistake but he cares for you Swazi, he will take care of you, don't shut him out." As if saying all these words was taxing to him or the meds are kicking in, he falls asleep.

I can finally let the tears out and sob as silently as I can. I smell him before I feel his hand on my shoulder. He makes me stand up and I bury my face on his chest which muffles my sobs. I don't deserve his comfort; I've been dreadfully cold towards him. I'm scared he'll leave and I'll be alone.

"Seeing him look so frail and engulfed by all these machines is too much Hlongwane. I can't lose him. If I lose *Babe*, who am I left with in this world?"

□

He lets me cry my eyes out then forces me to eat breakfast. He has to rush somewhere, he's busy setting up his new company. I'm proud of him, I want to tell him that but my heart is just too heavy. When lunch arrives Makhulu comes to see *Babe* and he has another seizure, they ask us to step out and I feel like I'm drowning.

The doctors said the seizures are provoked by low sugar levels when the brain neurons lack glucose they short circuit. The heart attack he suffered from isn't helping matters either. The seizures usually leave his brain muddled, him weak and a back headache follows. He is back to slurring his words when they let us back in.

"You look just like Tsandzile; your mother was so beautiful. I saw her just now she was holding me close to her and singing. She sang like an angel. So beautiful." I can't stop the tears from flowing down my cheek at the serene look on his face.

"Don't cry Swazi. Ndlovu ezidl'ekhaya ngokuswela abelusi ... You are stronger than you think. There's a fire inside you, don't be afraid to let it blaze..." his voice trails off and I realize that he's fallen back to sleep.

Makhulu beckons me outside and I unwillingly leave his side. The beeping machines keep reminding me that this is not a nightmare. Makhulu is holding a vanity bag when I find her in the corridor.

"Go and bath my child, you stink and that poor boy has to see you like this." I have no energy to argue with her so I take the bag. As I'm about to turn she holds my hand gently.

"I know you don't want to hear this. You have to let him go child, he's tired now." Before I protest she puts a hand over my mouth.

"He has always put you first from the moment you were born. I saw him fight for you, I was there when he raised you single-handedly. He has always put your happiness first and he found you the most noble husband. He has done his part now; he is tired let him rest with the love of his life. That man has pinned after your mother all these years but only held on because he wanted to see you grown and well taken care of. Let him go."

I want to wail and scream that I'm not ready, but I just shrug her hand away instead and head to the hospital bathrooms. I know she's right but how do I even begin to let go of the man who has been the love of my life for so long? My first love.

......

I'm sitting in the hospital park bench. I needed the air plus the nurses needed to clean *Babe*'s room while he was out for some tests. It's peaceful here, there are a few children in hospital gowns playing quietly. I feel someone sitting next to me and I turn and look at him. This time he smiles and it's creepy how alike they are.

"What do you want Ntsikelelo?" I'm proud of how calm my voice is right now.

He smirks, and I remind myself that he's not my husband. It's so damn hard though.

"Ah so she can finally tell us part. What gave me away? My charming good looks?" I snort at his corky response.

I'm still not over how they also seem to dress similarly even though they don't even stay together. Their voices are the same and their gaits are also similar, it's almost impossible telling them apart. I don't tell him that his scent gave him away. Hlongwane always smells of woodsy musk masculinity while he smells of leather accord and spicy cinnamon.

"What do you want?" I haven't forgiven him for the stunt he pulled, he hurt me physically and emotionally.

Call me stupid and all other names or blame the Hlongwane charm but ten minutes later I find myself following him to his car. I'm curious to see what he needs my help with. I tell him that this time if he hurts me, Hlongwane will kill him and I will help him bury his body. He laughs and tells me to buckle my seatbelt.

He passes by the mall and asks what I will like to have. I tell him I'm fine but he claims his brother will kill him if he doesn't feed me. I end up telling him my favourite pizza flavour. I'm eating meaty pizza at the back of his car and he keeps checking me on the rearview mirror and telling me what he and his twin got up to when they were in grade school. I laugh at their escapades but I'm not offering him any of my pizza, we are not friends.

We park inside the old Hlongwane residence and this time he leads me to the main house. We are in the nursery and I'm looking at tiny replicas of my husband, they are so beautiful with their charcoal eyes and chubby cheeks. They are dressed up in matching grey rompers with teddy bears in their chests. They look like catalogue babies.

I wish I can say I instantly fell in love with them, children are innocent right? But all I can see when I look at them is that video and my sister's taunting face during my lobola negotiations. I see the burning hatred in her eyes and I hear her wishing me death.

"I try looking after them as best as I can and they have a nanny and maids taking care of them. It's far from enough though. They need a mother NaDlamini," he says cradling both babies in his arms. They are gurgling at him, making the same noise and it's the most beautiful sight.

"They have a mother," I say past the lump in my throat, "unfortunately I'm not their mother."

I walk out of that nursery as if the devil is on my heels before I crumble in front of them. I wait next to the car to be taken back to Mbabane Hospital, back to my fading father.

□

......

Today *Babe* is more lucid than he's been ever since they admitted him. He asked me to make his favourite meal and I had to beg one of the nurses to let me cook in her room at the staff quarters. Luckily she agreed and it was worth it because *Babe* ate everything. He even had carrot cake for his dessert.

I am hopeful now that they will be discharging him soon since he seems to be better tonight. He's complaining about being in hospital. He says he wants me to take him to our spot in the hills. I see the man who raised me in *Babe* tonight.

"Remember that time you climbed up that mango tree but then you wouldn't come down because you were afraid to even look down?" He asks with laughter in his voice. I also laugh at the memory.

"You had to coax me down when it became dusk, and I still wouldn't come down." We both share a laugh and it feels like old times.

"You have a gentle heart Manana and that's your biggest strength. But it's also your weakness," he's suddenly became serious and I let him talk.

"I've shielded you all your life, but you still turned out strong. A silent fighter like your mother. Don't try to always keep it in and always be strong, not with your husband. Allow him to see you break down and let him help you figure out how to patch the broken pieces. You must be strong now my princess, a storm is coming, and I will be there guiding you through it. You have your mother's fire and my love for our people, never doubt yourself. They chose you for a reason."

I'm confused but know better than to ask him to be less cryptic. He's silent for so long while I stroke his hand. I think he's fallen asleep, but he speaks again.

"Don't blame yourself for your sister's hatred. She inherited it from her mother. There are some things you can never change my darling and you must not beat yourself up about that. I know her actions hurt you but those babies she carried were never meant to be hers.

They are your children Manana and I know you felt the love burning in your chest when you saw them. All you wanted to do was hold them. Don't let the hurt keep you from your children." I hate where his speech is going but I listen silently.

"Fight Maswazi. Fight for what is rightfully yours. Fight for what you want and fight for what you believe in. Do you hear me?" he is clutching my hand and looking into my eyes. I suddenly feel emotional as I nod repeatedly, tears blinding me. "I am tired my child, allow me to rest now."

"You're getting better *Babe*, today you haven't once

flinched in pain. We'll even take you to those Asian doctors that are keeping Mugabe alive. Maybe we'll fly you to England, just please don't ask me to let you rest." I try to bargain with him my voice has a plea in it even as it is breaking.

"Nothing can keep here now little one. Abo Dlamini o *Lokothwayo, bo Mlangeni, Sobhuza, Mntungwa, Kunene bayengibita.* It's time." The compassion in his voice tears my heart apart.

I shake my head vehemently; no I can't let him slip away from me. He can't leave me an orphan. He's getting better!

"You can't go now *Babe,* remember you promised that you will be the one walking me down the aisle on my wedding. You promised you will play with my kids. You promised you'll never leave me!" my voice rises as hysteria grips me. He has to keep his promises.

"Shhh little one. I'll always be there; I'll never leave you even when you can't see me I'll be right here." He weakly taps my chest and coughs for a while before talking again. "A new sun can't rise while the old one is still up and shining. I have to bow down now my angel. I love you, carry my love with you always."

This is it my ultimate heartbreak. I thought Hlongwane walking away and leaving me alone at the altar was my worst heartbreak. This right here, is not breaking my heart but shredding it into nothingness. My heart and my head are at war with each other. I see how tired he is and Makhulu's words ring in my head as tears blind my eyes.

"I love you Babe, thank you for always being there for me. I love you so much." I choke out, feeling a burning need to pour my heart to him. He smiles and wipes away my tears before kissing me all over my face. "Rest now *Babe*, I will be right here." I kiss him for the last time.

Just like when I was a kid, I take of my shoes and scramble onto the narrow hospital bed. I snuggle next to him, only this time I am the one cradling him in my arms. I hold him as tears course down my face as his breath evens out. His body tenses and I feel the exact moment that he stops breathing. I don't let go of him even as he grows cold in my arms. I hold on until Hlongwane gently breaks me away and I break down sobbing uncontrollably in his warm arms.

CHAPTER TWENTY

The yard is teeming with people from all around the country, a few from outside have also come to pay their last respects. The chief was a well know, loved and respected man. I am hearing tale after tale of his wit, bravery and kindness across the fire in the kraal. The smell of meat hangs around the yard, some of the meat is being braai-ed on the open fire while some is being cooked in drums. The conversation is livelier in the kraal while around the yard muted conversations are being carried on.

It's the night of the vigil and I am exhausted from

running around trying to get everything together for the funeral. Strangely Ntsikelelo has been with me throughout, helping me buy food, slaughter the beasts needed for the funeral. An easy truce has been called between us and its great having my brother with me. Of course, my father is also here, looking important and telling anyone willing to listen how close he and the chief were.

The people I'm most grateful for are my squad. Melusi and Nokwanda flew in the morning after he passed on and even though they hadn't met before, Nokwanda hasn't left Swazi's side since. At least I know that someone is taking care of her, forcing her to eat and hopefully being a shoulder to cry on. What worries me is I haven't seen Swazi cry since I found her sobbing in that narrow hospital bed while cradling the chief's corpse.

Mostly she stares dry-eyed into space, she's gone back to that dark corner in her head. She has completely shut me out and that scares me, I feel like I am slowly losing her. I have come to rely heavily on her. Her love and warmth have become my substitute crutches instead of how I used sex and women's attention before. Nomaswazi isn't aware of it yet but she's slowly driving me back to the brink of my darkness.

I signal Ntsikelelo to take my place, no one will notice he's not me. It's dark now so I make my way away from the kraal unnoticed. I find Nokwanda with Swazi in her hut. She leaves after squeezing my shoulder and kissing me on the cheek. I take Swazi's hands in mine and they are icy cold, and I force her to look at me. Recognition lights up her eyes a bit, I'm scared about how lost she looks.

"I can't believe he's gone. He's really gone. He left me, after he promised he'd never leave me." Her voice is broken, and I scoop her up and cradle her on my lap.

"Shhh baby it's ok. He's resting now, he's finally at peace with his heart." I think if the chief loved his wife as I love mine, he's finally complete in death.

Nomaswazi's chest heaves before she breaks down and cries. I hold her and let her cry. Inside these walls, in my arms she allows herself to be vulnerable and to drown her despair in tears. I'm glad that I can be that, she's finally allowing me to be that safe place for her. Maybe there's still hope for us after all.

She cries until the tears are spent and the hiccups fade. She has let it all out and didn't hold back. When she's done I go into the shower with her and help her bath.

She's so fragile right now it breaks my heart. I wish I could take her pain and feel it for her, but I can't all I can do is be here for her. All I want is to draw her into my arms and let her cry the whole night. To hold her close to me, lend her some of my strength. But of course, I can't. The singing has already begun, and we must leave before her Makhulu sends out a search party for her.

"Thank you Hlongwane," she says quietly looking at me with her puffy eyes.

"That's what husbands are for." I see a ghost of a smile on her face and I can't help myself. I kiss her shortly and she doesn't kiss me back. It stings but I have to understand that she's grieving the man she loved so dearly.

I wait for her to leave before I also step out and head back to the kraal to join the vigil.

......

As the prayers and remembrances of the Chief's life are being recalled our last conversation flashes through my mind. More like what he said to me because mostly I listened.

"Son, thank you for caring for my child like you have. I don't regret choosing you to be her father, husband and protector. I can rest easy knowing that you are here watching out for her. Maswazi is strong and very stubborn. She won't ask for help even when she needs it. I know I'm leaving her amongst vultures. She's kind, so she will want to help them. Make her stand her ground, it's her birthright. You are not your past, forgive yourself. Forgive your father, in his own way he loves you. Always know that I am proud of you. You are the son I always prayed for. Thank you for proving me right."

I have a lump in my throat just remembering his words.

□

I choose not to share my memories of him because they are so precious. He was a father to me even after I left his daughter by the altar. He didn't blame me or lash out, instead he made me take care of her trust fund. He always looked for the good in people, I think my wife inherited that from him. For all he knew I could have blown away all her money, but I didn't.

"*Nkhosi, Dlamini, wena wekunene. Hamba kahle Ndlovu ezidl'ekhaya ngokuswela abelusi, uyidlalile indzima yakho walucedza lubanga lwakho. Sengiso sekutsi siyolahla leLilangeni.*" An elderly wrinkled man is leading the somber procession.

It's still early hours of dawn, roosters are crowing but that doesn't chase away the cold. It's true what they say, upon the burial of a great chief everyone can feel it in their marrow. His elder daughter screams upon the words of the elder, rolling in the ground while thrashing her arms around. I would have bought her act had she cared to call and check on him while he was in hospital, lying on his death bed.

The spirit of loss lingers as I help a few council members to carry him on the wooden royal chair. He's seated upright as if at any moment he will flash his kind smile. An *Imbongi* is chanting Dlamini clan names. Elders lead the way; the men know where to go. All the Dlaminis are leading the way even my brother-in-law who looks lost and out of place and the rest of the community follows. The singing and wailing continues until we reach the point where women can go no further.

My eyes land on Nomaswazi, she seems so lost and empty. She looks like she is carrying the weight of the world on her shoulders. She heads back too, but keeps looking back at her father's corpse longingly. The singing has gone down as the elders take turns speaking to the chief, informing him that they are taking him to his place of rest and that he will finally join his ancestors.

We are left standing at the bottom of the mountain while only the Dlamini elders proceed to his resting place. Like every royal before him, he will be buried while sitting as culture demands. I watch as their lamps disappear up the mountain and I feel a loss as acute as the day my mother died.

Once the people start heading back I immediately go in search of my wife. I find her busy serving people tea and scones. I mean I hired a catering company so that she wouldn't suffer. Yet no, Swazi must be Wonder Woman. My first instinct is to go and pull her away, she needs to rest, and I know she's hurting. Melusi beats me to it and steers me away to sit under my late father-in-law's favourite tree.

"Leave her alone, she's dealing with her pain the best way she knows how." I hate it when he's right.

□

"It's just that... I don't want to see her suffer." He pats me on the shoulder. He gets me.

Mpho joins us with a stupid grin on his face. He is still the free spirit in the group.

"Man, why didn't you tell me about all the pussy on hot legs you have this side? What in hell are you feeding your women? Look at those curves. Oh, wait I forget you are now pussy whipped like this fool Melusi." He speaks fast, his eyes running around the yard and we just let him run his mouth.

I see Ntsikelelo looking lost and I wave him over and introduce him to my other brothers. They chat up a storm, but my eye constantly wanders to Nomaswazi. She looks so pale and the queue for food is so bloody long. Ignoring Melusi's restraining hand on my arm, I get up to go get my wife.

Just as I am about to reach her, a well-dressed elderly man in a three-piece suit reaches her first. I recognize him, it's her father's attorney. They move away from the food table and I follow them. My first instinct will always be to protect Swazi.

"...so, I need to see you and your siblings on Monday. It would be best if you could all come to my office." I catch the tail of what he's saying, and I figure it's to do with the Chief's will.

Swazi nods and accepts his card, she looks so drained. I

forestall her as she's about to go back to serving. She doesn't put up a fight and that's how I know I'm doing the right thing as I lead her to her hut. She's out like a light when I come back with our plates of food. There are tear stains on her face. I cover her with a light blanket and head back to see to the mourners.

......

Its Monday today and I'm waiting for Swazi to finish dressing up. She has barely said two sentences to me since the funeral and it's been days. I need her to say something even if it is to lash out. She spends most of her time locked in her bathroom and that worries me. I'm afraid she'll try to commit suicide and I am not sure I will survive it if she dies. I hate how vulnerable her love has made me.

I have to go to Bangkok. I was supposed to leave this morning but I couldn't because I have a feeling she will need my support at the will reading. Luckily, her siblings left soon after the burial but she's going to meet them today. I wish I can put off the Bangkok trip but I can't I'm already operating on a very tight schedule and it can't be avoided.

"I need to leave for Bangkok tomorrow morning and fix some specs. I will try to squeeze everything in a week, if I can't then two weeks at most." I say when we're driving out. She looks at me then looks out of the window.

"Go Hlongwane. Leave me like everyone else." The

bitterness in her voice makes something in me snap and I stop the car so suddenly she almost hits the dashboard.

"I am here Nomaswazi, because I love you. I have been here since he became sick but you have continually shut me out! So don't you dare paint me to be the monster here." I am hissing, hoping to get some reaction from her but she only looks at me for a while before staring out of the window again. I sigh in resignation and start the car.

Forty minutes later we reach the attorney's office and no word has been exchanged between us. We are ushered into the conference room where everyone else is already sitting.

"Great, now that everyone is here we can begin." Mr. Ndlovu, the attorney says after we take our seats.

My eyes move quickly around the conference table. There's the slutty, obsessed sister, the clueless brother, Makhulu and a few of the council members. I wonder what the council members are doing at the reading of the will, but the lawyer is talking again.

"The last will and testament of Chief Sobhuza Dlamini, is in the form of a video he made a year ago on the date displayed on the screen." He signals to one of his assistants and the screen in front of us comes alive.

The chief looks strong on the screen; clearly of sound mind. He stares blankly at the screen before a voice prompts him to start.

"Oh is it recording?" voice in the background responds yes and only then does he start talking. His gaze is so direct it feels like he's looking at us. Swazi stiffens next to me and grips my hand, I squeeze her hand back to assure her that I'm here.

"MaKheswa, you have been with us from when I married my first wife and you have taken care of my family since then. You became a mother to my children when they lost their mothers. I can never fully repay you for your kindness, but I leave you the cottage where you have lived most of your life. You and your descendants can stay there for as long as you want or build on the strip of land I have left you. I also leave you one hundred thousand as your retirement package. You have served me loyally all these years, it's time that you rest as well.

To my children, I have nothing left to give you. Five years ago, I liquefied all my assets except for the houses we stay in. Meaning I sold the mines, the company I had and other lands, even my herd of cattle except for Nomaswazi's lobola and cashed in all my life policies. I took the money in all its entirety and divided it equally among the three of you and set up trust funds in your names.

Zamaswazi and Masomalenhle, I gave you full control of your trust funds when you turned twenty-four while Nomaswazi's trust fund is in the hands of her husband, Hlongwane. That my children is your inheritance, I didn't want you to wait for me to die before you started pursuing your dreams. As for the houses, I think it's only fair that you each get the house you have been living in. They are all under your names already.

Zamaswazi, my child. My first born, I am sorry if you ever felt like I neglected you while you were growing up. I tried to make it up to you by arranging for you to marry Chief Lokothwayo's son, but you plainly refused. I couldn't force you. I hope one day you find the love that you seek. I am sorry about your mother; it is all my fault. I wish you could let go of the bitterness now and live your life free from the past. I love you Zama and I'm sorry that I never told you this enough.

Masomalenhle, my only son. I rejoiced when you were born because I thought that in you I had found someone to take over from me. From an early age you have never shown any interest in our Inkhundla. You would rather chase after the council's daughters. The amount of damages I've had to pay for you were another trust fund on their own. You are my son I still love you. I hope someday you can grow a spine and stand up to your sister, Zamaswazi. You haven't worked a day in your life even with the degrees I made sure you got. You are a man Masomalenhle, it's time you start working, settle down and take a wife. Find all your children and raise them before it's too late.

Nomaswazi, my baby girl. I've had to raise you from when

you were a child and I often worried that I sheltered you too much, that you would become too gullible. I realized that you naturally always see the good in people even after they hurt you repeatedly. I've seen you struggle to gain favour with your siblings and no matter how mean they are to you, you still run after them and are kind to them. Such a forgiving heart is a strength and a weakness. From when you were young, you looked forward to accompanying me to the council meetings, you have loved our home and most of the projects undertaken were your initiatives. I'm proud of your love for our people. Your leaving nearly killed me but I'm so proud of how you've grown and how you were able to take care of yourself.

Can I have some water?" he asks coughing and someone behind the camera rushes over with a glass.

I take the opportunity to look around the room. My wife next to me is as pale as a ghost and holding my hand. The brother is emotionless, and the sister looks like a volcano that's about to erupt. The lawyer looks unfazed as he sorts through the papers in front of him. The council members look like varying degrees of how I feel, confused yet intrigued about what is yet to unfold.

In the video, the chief is done drinking his glass of water, he wipes his face with a crisp handkerchief before he resumes talking.

"Mpiyakhe, Sicelo and Maloyi I couldn't have asked for better spiritual advisors, I didn't only view you as iBandla lami

but you were my brothers and you molded me into the chief that I am. I know what I am about to ask you goes against our traditions, but my spirit tells me that the wellbeing of our people depends on this. My son and only heir apparent is a wimp and he has no inclination to rule our people. I tried training him, but he was more interested in spending my money on girls. I have no faith in him as his father and I can't ask you to have faith in him as a leader either.

Then there's my daughter. My Swazi, she has the heart of a lion and over the years she has kept surprising me with the depth of her love for our people and our ways. The introduction of crop rotation, solar panels were some of her ideas as young as she was. I would rest easier knowing that our people are in such capable hands. What I am saying is I have chosen my youngest, Nomaswazi to succeed me as your Inkhosatana. When you look past the fact that she is a young woman, you will see what I also see, she is more than capable of leading you. My last plea to you my spiritual advisors is to stand by her and help her lead our people..."

The rest of what he's saying is cut off by Zamaswazi charging towards Swazi. There's commotion and she's being held back by her brother and Swazi is just as frozen as I am. Zamaswazi lets out a string of curses but all I can think is how all this is going to affect Nomaswazi.

CHAPTER TWENTY-ONE

I've never felt so alone in my life. When I ran away to South Africa at the back of my mind I knew *Babe* was here, missing me and I could always find my way back home. Now he's gone with no hope of returning. My siblings hate me more than they did when I was growing up. To top it all I have managed to push away the one man who was in my corner. He really stepped up with the funeral, I didn't even thank him. I was selfish in my grief. If only death had a manual; easy steps on dealing with grief for beginners.

I just got a call from the council that my succession matter has been set up for a week from now. I'm nervous and I don't know which way the vote will sway. I really wish Hlongwane was here right now or at least give me a call. I take a leap of faith and call him. His number rings unanswered until it reaches voicemail. I awkwardly keep quiet after the beep until I hang up without saying anything.

I'm visiting my mother's grave today, something I have never done on my own. When I was younger my father would take me and we would bring her favourite flowers. He would talk to her so lovingly and I would obediently stand next to him without saying a word. I always felt so guilty. Zamaswazi had led me to believe that my birth had led to my mother's death. So, I always assumed that she died while giving birth to me.

What do you say to someone you never knew your whole life? With *Babe* it is easier it's as if I'm talking to him again and everything makes sense. I struggle a couple of times with words until I just give up and brush her tombstone. I hope she can feel the yearning in my heart. I hope she can feel the love and the regret that I never got to know her. To drive her crazy as a teenager and to be her best friend. I hope she's happy now that her love has finally joined her.

I'm not sure how they will meet with one buried on the mountain top and she is buried all the way down here. Death is so confusing for an African. On one hand we are taught that the dead become ancestors and they look out for us. Is it automatic that you turn into an ancestor or is there some criterion used? On the other hand, Christianity has taught us of heaven and hell. So, are the ancestors in heaven or in hell? I hope wherever my parents' souls are they have found peace.

I drive back home or what's left of home, it's just so empty without my king. The last of the relatives finally left yesterday. We were all relieved. The requests were outrageous. They wanted livestock to be slaughtered so that they have meat to carry back to their homes. My livestock I might add, yet they had no qualms saying how the ancestors must be turning in outrage at my father's request.

I shudder when I find the huge Cherokee car in my yard. I don't have the strength right now for Zamaswazi and her acidity. I have a mind to drive off but my father's last words ring in my ears and I get out of my car. I square my shoulders as I get into the living room. I am taken aback to find my brother sitting alone with Makhulu's scones in front of him. Maybe his sister is somewhere in the main house.

I greet him awkwardly and perch my butt on the couch. I had forgotten how just like my father Masomalenhle is. He is just as tall and his nose is flared, but instead of my father's authoritative gait, he is slightly a hunchback his shoulders bowed in perpetual apology. He used to walk straight when we were younger. I wonder what happened to that carefree boy who loved peeking at girls bathing in the stream.

□

"Nomaswazi," he says by way of greeting and he can't look me in the eye.

"Masomalenhle," I respond in kind and wait for him to say something.

"I'm sorry for your loss." Ok this is awkward for us both. I wish I can reach out and hug him.

"He was your father too," I say softly not sure how to navigate through a conversation with my own blood brother.

"I was a constant disappointment to him, never was the son that he craved for," he says bitterly, and I feel the need to reach out and hold his hand.

"He loved you and he blamed himself for pushing you and Zama away. He really wanted a relationship with you Lenhle." The look he is giving me is hopeful and my heart twists.

"What are you doing here?" I ask him when we've spent close to five minutes just staring at each other in comfortable silence. He sighs and rubs his eyes, something he always did when he was nervous back when we were young.

"I came to apologize for not being a good brother to you all those years ago and mostly recently when we came to dump my nephews on your lobola day. I have no excuse, I'm sorry. I also want you to know that you are not stealing anything from me by accepting *Babe*'s instructions. I never wanted to be chief, it feels like a huge burden has been lifted off my shoulders."

He speaks fast, words tumbling onto each other as if he's scared he might leave some words out. I'm an emotional mess so his words trigger the tears which aren't that far from my eyelids. I swear my tear ducts are faulty these days. I get up and launch myself at him the way I always did with *Babe*. For a moment he remains frozen but the he hugs me to him.

Thank you Babe.

I whisper in my heart and I know for sure he's keeping his promise; he is still with me. I felt guilty because I thought Lenhle wanted to be chief and this just lifted one burden off my shoulders.

......

Yesterday was a revelation with Lenhle, seeing him in his own light not behind our sister's spotlight. She kept blowing up his phone, he tried to hide it but I saw her name flashing on his phone a couple of times before he switched it off. Call me gullible but I enjoyed having my brother over even just for a day. We talked of old stories about our father, careful to leave out the painful memories.

He shared with me his love for minerals, he studied metallurgy and now he wants to supplement it with either quantity surveying or mining engineering via correspondence. His whole face lights up when he talks of mining, I had no idea that Lenhle is such a nerd. I told him about my failed attempt to study Accounting. He encouraged me not to give up on that dream even when I'm now chief.

I'm still glowing from the memory of our conversation when there's a knock on my door. Its Aphelele and she lets me know that my father-in-law is requesting my audience in the living room. To say I am shocked is an understatement but I still scramble to dress and look a tiny bit representable.

"*Makoti wakami.*" He responds to my greeting and I sit awkwardly on the floor next to him. I just hope I'm bowing my head right.

"I need you to tell that husband of yours to come back and work on the legacy I built from scratch for him and his children." He gets right into it after declining my offer of tea.

"With all due respect, my husband is his own man and he makes his own decisions which I respect as his wife." He grunts at my words and because I can't see his face right now it gives me the courage to say my next words. "Furthermore, he hasn't fully healed from what you made them go through as twelve-year olds and you insisting on him taking over from you is only derailing him."

"He told you about that?" he sounds more shocked than offended which is a relief.

"He still has nightmares and blackouts from their memories down there. When I confronted him he told me everything." Not the gospel truth but I still say it.

"I see. Get up and sit on that sofa." My head shoots up in confusion and he offers me a warm smile. "A chief doesn't bow for any of her subjects makoti, even for her old father-in-law."

Odd but I do as I'm told. It is really weird looking into his eyes because I find myself wishing they were charcoal instead of dark brown. One thing for sure my man is going to mature like fine wine, it is written in the genes. Without saying a word, he opens his briefcase and takes out a manila folder and stretches it towards me. Now it's my turn to stare at his proffered hand in shock.

"Take it," he barks out an order and I take the manila folder and flip through it. My eyes shoot up in shock when I see the contents and my father-in-law is looking at me with that knowing glint in his eye.

"Why are you giving me this?" I ask eyeing him suspiciously.

"You need leverage and I just gave it to you." He says stapling his fingers together.

"Yes but why? What's in it for you? I must tell you now I refuse to be anyone's puppet, I am my father's daughter

□

and Sobhuza was no one's pawn." he chuckles at my accusing tone and reclines on his chair.

"You remind me of my wife, seemingly sweet and shy but feisty and quick to sting when pushed into a corner. I can see my son is in great hands." The Universe has decided to throw me shock after shock, who knew Hlongwane Snr has such a beautiful smile! I totally see where my Hlongwane gets his smile from.

"He has been plotting to have your father's dynasty overthrown, so my advice to you is cut off the snake's salivary glands and it becomes your pet. I cannot erase what my children went through, I thought I was preparing them for my world so I can secure their children's future. All I ask for in return is to be involved in my grandchildren's lives. Old age tends to get lonely sometimes." I am used to my father's cryptic way of talking so his words make perfect sense to me.

I thank him and insist on him staying for supper. I'm surprised when he holds Labo and plays with her. I should try harder to help Hlongwane mend relations with his father while he is still alive. So he won't have the same regrets that I have. Every day I regret running away to Jo'burg, that action cost me six years away from my father, years that I will never gain back. I got to see him but only for a short two months. Then he died.

……

I hate confrontations, they make me nervous and half the time I end up chocking. I almost turn my car and heard back home but one of his wives has already spotted me and it wouldn't do my reputation any good to turn around now. *Babe*'s words of fighting square my shoulders and I walk out of my car and head into the homestead I haven't been in, since I was a teenager.

I find the headman as his youngest wife serves him breakfast, she's young enough to be his daughter. A man with a potbelly his size and probably high cholesterol shouldn't be eating that much grease. I am angry at his disloyalty but because I was raised right, I greet him and sit on one of his sofas. Unlike in the past I do not cast my eyes down or bow my head, my father-in-law's words ringing in my head.

"You can't just come into my house unannounced child," he huffs at me and I ignore his insolence. He doesn't bother acting like he supports me because he has garnered quite the backing to overthrow me and my father's lineage. I give him my ugliest and most intimidating look or try to imitate Hlongwane's look until he squirms. I caution my anger until its only simmering before I speak.

"Maloyi, you served my late father well throughout his reign and it would be in your best interests to also serve me with the same loyalty, otherwise we wouldn't want a respected man like you being investigated for tax fraud." While he's spluttering I throw the incriminating manila folder on the table in front of him.

"Don't worry, you can keep those copies, I have the originals." I leave him hissing like an angry mamba and hurry out before I lose whatever bravado I had.

I drive out of his yard and park just before the fork that joins the road home. My whole body is shaking from delayed nerves. I clutch the steering wheels as the adrenaline rush courses through my body. I just blackmailed one of the many "uncles" I had growing up. What if this backfires? What was I thinking following my father-in-law's advice? The man is a hardened weaponry smuggler for crying out loud!

What's done is done and now all I can do is hope that he doesn't call my bluff and he backs down. Instead of driving back home I find myself driving towards the Hlongwane mansion. The truth is I'm running away from the memories of *Babe* that home carry. I see him laughing in the kitchen as I cook and pretend not to see him as he helps himself to a second serving of my carrot cake. His easy banter with makhulu on religion and what he termed her white gods.

I'm ashamed to say that I cut myself or hurt myself every day now. Sometimes twice a day. It is my only outlet of my emotional pain, physical pain I can stand not the emptiness in my heart. I'm always careful not to cut a vein. Yes, the burden of ruling over Maphalaleni is a daunting one for me but not enough to make me want to take my own life.

I find myself in the main house, Bab' Mlandeli let me in. at least he wasn't awkward and he didn't ask me what I am doing here. I head to the nursery and I find the nanny washing one of the twins while the other one is quietly sucking on his toe. She smiles her welcome and I watch closely as she carefully washes every joint of his chubby little body before taking him out when he starts kicking the water angrily. She wraps him in one of the identical bathing towels with an elephant on the top corner which she makes him wear like a hat. She quickly dresses him before reaching for the second one.

"May I?" I ask and she hands me the baby with a big smile.

"Sure, Langa is easy-going unlike Mthiyane over there. That's why I bathed him first." As if to validate her words Langa gives me a beautiful wide gummy smile. Langa and Mthiyane, how typical of Nguni men to name their children after the clan names. The names are beautiful and they fit the next generation of Hlongwanes perfectly.

Langa holds my finger as I wash his face and looks into my eyes with his milky white eyes and dancing charcoal irises. His gurgling sounds make my heart constrict. I guess the cure of a heart numbed by death is the unconditional love of a new life. As I wash his tiny energetic body, I feel lighter and more at peace than I've been in years.

CHAPTER TWENTY-TWO

"You're nothing but a spineless pussy!" the snide snarl still booms in my head. "Imbecile get up and stop shivering like a toothless dog! Is that the best you can do? Look at me you little fucker! You're so weak they are going to rip your heart out before roasting it on an open fire before they eat it. Vomit one more time and I will make you eat your own vomit! Get up and fight! Fight! Fight you little worthless piece of shit!"

The punch even feels real. Another punch and Ntsikelelo screaming in my face bring me back from the torture dungeon that was my childhood. I had totally zoned out.

"What the fuck is wrong with you?" I wince at Ntsikelelo's harsh voice, slowly coming back to full consciousness.

Only when I'm fully aware of my surroundings do I notice Swazi slumped on the floor of our bathroom. It all comes flooding back. Christ! No, no, no! Thick blood is seeping out of her nose. Her body is limp and lifeless. What if I have lost her? I stay crouched down with her in my arms and her blood on my t-shirt. I don't know how long I stay there or when Ntsikelelo called the ambulance, but I only hear them asking me to step aside. Only when Ntsikelelo tears me away, are they able to take Swazi and put her gently on the stretcher.

I want to fight them, but he holds me back and they wheel her to the ambulance. My brother takes over driving and we follow the ambulance.

"What happened?" he asks as we get out of the gate.

"I came back from Bangkok and came straight to her home. Her Makhulu said she is locked in her room. I came into her room and called out her name but she didn't respond which was weird. I found her slumped over the bathroom floor. I saw the blood and the razor blades, and I... I thought she was dead...that she committed suicide. The next thing I know I was having an intense flashback and I just zoned out."

I drop my face in my hands, appalled by what I came home to. It felt like she had already died on me too. I've been riddled by intense nightmares from our time in Congo since I went to Bangkok and I even resorted to not sleeping some nights and working nonstop. Thinking Nomaswazi was dead just pushed me over the edge.

"I felt it, that dark place and I just knew something was horribly wrong and I rushed over to check on you. Why didn't you call an ambulance or something?" Ntsikelelo says quietly and I feel like such an arse. For once I'm grateful that Ntsikelelo always has his goons following me and giving him my exact location all the time.

After what seems like an eternity we make it to the hospital and aren't allowed to follow Swazi into the emergency room. So, we alternate between pacing down the hallway of Mbabane Hospital and sitting in the couches with our faces buried in our faces.

"Nomaswazi Dlamini?" the doctor calls out and we both jump to our feet and she looks perplexed from Ntsikelelo to me.

□

"I'm her husband," Ntsikelelo offers when I haven't said a word. I don't trust myself to say anything right now and I can't talk past through the lump in my throat.

"Your wife's nose bleed is quite serious and that isn't good in her condition."

"What condition?" Ntsikelelo blurts out, I swear I'm feeling hot flushes right now and I seem to have been rendered mute.

"She is borderline anemic; her red blood cell count is low and so we infused some blood into her. Fortunately, her blood type is an easy match but still we would like to keep her for observation. Her blood pressure is also too low." The relief which floods my body is staggering, I lean against the wall to stop myself from collapsing on the floor. For a moment there I was scared she would say my Swazi has cancer.

My relief is short-lived as the doctor continues speaking, "However, I did see some fresh cuts, scratches and burns which suggested that your wife has been inflicting self-injury on herself. Has she ever been suicidal or is she going through traumatic events?" I feel the breath seeping out of my lungs again.

"Yes..." my voice barely comes out in a whisper and the doctor looks at me quizzically and I clear my throat. "...she once tried to commit suicide about six years ago, but she didn't go through with it and her father recently died... she is not suicidal, she is not harming herself. I would know, I would have seen it." My voice trails off and I'm trying to convince myself that my Swazi wouldn't want to take her own life and leave me.

"Self-injury is typically not meant as a suicide attempt, rather it's an unhealthy way to cope with emotional pain and it comes with the possibility of more serious and even fatal self-aggressive actions. I believe her intense nose bleed was also brought on by her mental imbalances or stress," the doctor tries to re-assure us but I'm back to being mute.

"Can we see her?" Ntsikelelo asks again and I could kiss him right now.

"Sure but she still hasn't regained consciousness. Good thing is she's breathing on her own. Please convince her to see an in-house therapist when she does wake up, otherwise she won't be discharged as she's on suicidal watch." the doctor has a warm and easy smile.

I wonder how she does it, it's fast approaching midnight. She shows us Swazi's room and the nurses are unashamedly checking us out and whispering as we pass. I couldn't care less; all I want right now is my wife. We find her resting peacefully in her private room, they even changed her into a hospital gown.

She has drips attached to her arm, one for blood and the other a colourless liquid which I'm guessing is water. She looks pale and guilt niggles at me like a bitch. I should have noticed that she was suffering and taking strain but instead I flew half-across the world to work on getting my company off the ground. I kiss her all over her face until Ntsikelelo clears his throat.

"Stop acting so whipped," he has his classic corky half-smile on and for the first time this evening, I feel lighter.

"Thank you for being here. It's fine you can go now," I offer even though I know he's going to refuse.

The idiot has the nerve to say I can't throw him out of his wife's room. He's stupid but I'm still grateful to have him here. Jet leg and the emotional exhaustion of the past evening are finally sinking in and I can barely keep my eyes open. I climb onto the hospital bed, careful not to hurt Swazi and exhaustion finally claims me too as I cuddle her.

......

I'm roused from the deepest sleep I've had in a while by voices.

"He will never survive without you. You are his lifeline now," it's that idiot's voice but it sounds gruffer than usual.

"He's my lifeline too." Swazi's voice is weak yet it manages to spread warmth throughout my body. Without opening my eyes, I hug her to me, a little too tightly because I hear her soft "ouch".

I open my eyes and I find her face so close to mine and I steal a kiss before she can complain of morning breath. The kiss is short and I inspect her in the glare of morning light. Her face is haggard and when my eyes land on the blood and liquid transfusion needles on her arm my breath hitches as I remember the state I found her in.

"I'm fine Hlongwane, this doesn't hurt." She tries to reassure me and raise her hand to solidify her lie.

It hurts, even though she tries hard not to wince or show any sign of pain, I can tell it hurts. I pull her roughly into my arms and this time the wince comes out louder. I don't let go. I hug her tightly not saying a word and neither does she. We only break apart when Ntsikelelo clears his throat noisily.

"That's my cue to leave," he is already standing, and he awkwardly squeezes Swazi's shoulder before leaving.

"He doesn't have a girlfriend, does he?" she asks and we both burst out laughing.

Our laughter is short-lived. I make her snuggle against my broad chest. Her heartbeat is a bit erratic in sync with mine. I kiss the top of her head not and struggle to find anything to say for a whole minute.

"Why?" I ask the question I've been struggling with ever since I found her lying there, all bloody.

"The cutting makes me feel physical pain and it helps me forget...everything. The first cut was an honest mistake when I was fourteen, but it made me forget the taunting and name calling and I focused on the physical pain. Then I started cutting my inner thighs whenever I was hurting or numb. I once burnt my arm with an iron on purpose." She pauses as if it's all too much and she's breathing heavily. I rub her back until her breathing evens.

"I had stopped while I was in Jo'burg. Then we met again, I cut myself the night you left me alone and went...all night. I thought it was a random act. I did it again when Ntsikelelo hurt me and Zama disrupted our lobola. Ever since Babe passed on, I've been hurting myself every day. Sometimes twice a day." I stare at her eyes which are swimming with tears and I am shocked.

"It's all too much Hlongwane, I feel trapped. The pain of losing Babe is crippling my heart. Maybe we should run away, go and settle in Durban. You can open your offices there and I will finish my degree and work with you like you wanted. I don't think I'm cut out to rule over anyone, they hate me. They're already plotting against me and I had to blackmail Maloyi. I don't think I can fight!" she breaks down into sobs and I hold her so close to me as I try to assimilate all the she has said to me. I only talk when her sobs have subdued into whimpers.

"I know you are scared baby and I'm so sorry NaDlamini. I shut you out when you needed me the most, I failed you. I almost lost you and that's the scariest thing I have ever gone through in my life. I know how it's like to be in a dark place. The past week has been hell for me too, the nightmares and when I found you passed out I had a full blown zone-out. If Ntsikelelo hadn't snapped me out of it when he did, you could have died Nomaswazi and left me with the guilt that I was too broken to help you." The thought alone makes my voice catch and I have to clear my throat before I talk.

"What I'm trying to say is, it's time we stopped running from our demons. They won't leave us Swazi until we face them head on. I want us to have children one day and they don't deserve our broken pieces. They deserve our healing; we are going to heal so that our broken pieces don't make our children bleed too." I lift her chin in between my thumb and fore-finger.

"You don't need to be stronger and more aggressive. You already carry so much strength in your stubborn yet calm and gentle way. In the way you authentically love and laugh. The way you can be sassy when you want to be. And in the way you respect those around you. You are a good woman Nomaswazi. My woman." I stroke her face and she leans into my caress.

"So here's how this is going to pen out, you are going to walk confidently into that council room. You won't be afraid to fall because if you do fall, I will be right by your side, ready to catch you. Whenever you need me nkosatana I will be here, ready to serve you. So, no more cutting, you need to speak to a professional." She shakes her head at my last statement.

"I'd rather talk to you," her voice is barely above a whisper.

"You can't my heart, you are on suicidal watch. They won't be discharge you unless you speak to an in-house therapist."

"Please be there when I talk to the therapist." I sigh as I look into her begging eyes. I never saw myself seeing a shrink, but I will do anything for this woman in my arms. I agree and she nestles back into my arms and we remain in silence until we both drift to sleep again.

……

I find him reclining on his chair in his office and he doesn't acknowledge my knock or offer me a sit. I don't waste my time with pleasantries because I have a therapy session with Nomaswazi in a bit. I just came to clear a few things with the old man first.

"My wife will not be a pawn in your twisted games and you will not turn her into a blackmailer." He looks up from his papers and takes off his reading glasses.

"She already told me that she won't be anybody's pawn.

I was only looking out for the woman you love. When you promised to rip my heart out, I knew then that you love her just the way I loved your mother or even more." He smiles, a full blown smile that even reaches his eyes and I am shocked.

"Your mother was my world; I would have killed for her without blinking. I wanted to give her the world, but she didn't want the world. She just wanted me at home with her and our children. I always justified my actions by saying I was doing it for her, building an empire for her and our sons. She wanted no part in it, she even refused to travel abroad with me or go to the spa and splurge on my money. She said that it was blood money and that it killed my soul." His voice is wistful almost poignant.

"I should have listened to her but instead I hurt her in the worst way possible. When I sent you to DRC, that was the last straw for your mother. She never forgave me. I am sorry son, for all I put you through. I don't want to die while we're estranged or you're angry at me like your mother. I will understand if you can never forgive me." I never saw this day coming and I know it's time to let go.

"I will forgive you, if you apologize to Ntsikelelo as well and hand over all your shady dealings to him. Plus, this doesn't mean I will ever come back and work for you." He is grinning like he is pleased with himself.

"Consider it done if I get to taste your wife's home

cooked meals at least twice a month." I look at his proffered hand for a second before I accept it.

"Deal."

I came here expecting war but instead formed a truce with the Beast, Ntsikelelo won't believe this. I don't know if I'll ever be able to forget and live a normal life, but the first step to healing has been taken.

CHAPTER TWENTY-THREE

"What has caused your pain and how do you deal with the pain?" It's our fourth and final session with the therapist who insists we call her Donna.

The first session was awkward and barely lasted thirty minutes. Donna had to firmly let us know that if I don't participate, she would recommend psychiatric evaluation at the Mental Hospital all the way in Manzini.

I still remember Hlongwane's words after that horrible session. He wasn't angry or frustrated with me. He looked at me with so much understanding, understanding that I have never experienced in my life. Understanding that I didn't expect. I expected judgment and maybe even ridicule. Swazi the dramatic 'princess', that's what I have been called most of my life.

"We have to try right? I promise it gets better. I need you to get better for you, but mostly for me. With you in my life, I've experienced a better version of me and I want us to be better together."

Nothing has ever made more sense to me. Our problems won't fade away, neither will our anxieties but we'll get better and do better. The second session was a whole emotional rollercoaster that lasted over five hours. Donna called it unpacking our emotions. Boy did it feel like a movie of some sort, my feelings were all over the place and some of them in boxes. The resentment, fear of rejection, the hurt, insecurities, love, hate and some that I couldn't put a label on.

Then yesterday we were talking of relationships and we started with family. Donna made us understand that family usually sets the groundwork on our mental health and especially for me that it's ok to let go of family that threatens my mental stability. I felt yesterday's exercises. I'm surprised at how involved Hlongwane has been throughout this, he's not only present but also participating like right now.

"My pain stems from not being in control, the first time I fully let down my guard with Nomaswazi was the time we were at Ushaka Marine World. Being there and doing activities that I didn't get to do made me so happy and that made me feel guilty. That's when I had that horrible nightmare of the time they made us gang rape a sixteen year-old when we were barely twelve."

"Was that you subconsciously reminding yourself that you're a monster and you don't deserve happiness?" Donna asks quoting his words from our unpacking session.

"I guess so," Hlongwane says uncertainly after a moment of silent introspection.

"How do you deal with the pain?" he shifts uncomfortably at that question and looks at me, I nod my head slightly and he sighs, scrunching his nose with his index and fore-finger.

"I have sex. Lots of hard and fast sex, I only feel appeased when my sexual partner has many orgasms, her pleasure somehow makes me feel better for the pain we caused that girl and other women we raped." His explanation sends chills down my spine and not the good ones.

"You couldn't have that with Nomaswazi?" Donna presses on ignoring the intensity blanketing this room right now.

"I couldn't and I can't ever since I discovered her purity, I've felt like I don't deserve her." He chuckles mirthlessly before continuing to talk. "The fucked up part is that now I can't seem to be able to have meaningless sex with other women because then I see Nomaswazi's face. The hurt in her face when she discovered that I'd slept with another woman, that hurt made me feel a different kind of guilt from the one I've been living with. So yeah, this is the longest I have stayed without sex since I was twelve years-old."

Silence hangs over us and Donna purposely lets us stew in our thoughts allowing his revelation to sink in.

"Nomaswazi, how does what he just said make you feel?" she steers the spotlight back to me and now it's my turn to squirm.

"Insecure," I say the first emotion that comes to the fore, "crazy jealous and inadequate. I've seen one of his former sexual partner and she is everything I'm not and everything that my sister is. I feel inadequate because when I offered myself to him, he walked away. That time I thought he was rejecting me again. Then later I saw a video of him, turns out it was his twin, having sex with my sister. I had a major melt-down and now I'm just scared to have sex with him because I might never measure up to the women he's had."

I'm avoiding looking at Hlongwane, even though I feel the intensity of his eyes on me. We continue talking like this, Donna asking us questions until she's satisfied.

"I'm taking you off the suicide watch Nomaswazi. I have to commend you and your partner for opening up. While I feel that there's so much more we still have to get into, I can't continue keeping you here. I urge you to continue these sessions with me as an outpatient. Good luck on your council meeting tomorrow. Remember you're only as worthy as your mind sees you.

……

It's the day of the council meeting and having both set of twins around me is helping with my nerves. I must say, Ntsikelelo is doing a great job with the babies. They look healthy and content. Yesterday he just turned up unannounced and said he's sleeping over with the twins. I find all my boys in the kitchen island, bathed and the twins being fed by their fathers on the granite countertops. When Mthiyane spots me he starts screaming, banging one hand on the counter while the other is stretched towards me.

"I told you Mthiyane is a mommy's boy like you," Ntsikelelo pokes Hlongwane as I lift the little guy up and he starts showing off his two teeth. I also lift Langa up even though he's quietly watching me, it's a miracle I can even carry both of them at the same time. I kiss their chubby little cheeks.

"Now they are even getting my morning kisses,"

□

Hlongwane grumbles and I know he's not joking. Hlongwane doesn't like sharing me with anyone even his babies. I inwardly roll my eyes as I give my big baby a kiss. It was supposed to be a short kiss, but the devil had to drag it entrapping my head with his huge hand.

"Hey not in front of my children!" Ntsikelelo complains but the twins are giggling in my arms unaffected. Just having all of them around me lifts my spirits. For once I don't feel suffocated with memories in my own home.

My spirits plummet on the drive to Maphalaleni council hall along the backroad between Luve and Mbabane. Rain pelts down the windscreen fogging it only to be cleared by the wipes. Grey fog hangs over the mountain tops shrouding the vegetation and making everything look dreary.

It's hard to make out the passing scenery but I know it like the back of my hand. The steep slopes merging beautifully with the rolling hills. The occasional herd of cattle we would pass in the mornings as we made our way to school, the morning dew clinging onto our shoes. I walked these mountains for the best part of my life. In summer the shrubbery comes alive in a refreshing green and the hills aren't as grey.

I was always on the fringe looking in and I mistook that to mean I'm an outsider. That couldn't be further from the truth, these hills are in my blood. I remember once *Babe* took me to Mantenga Falls near Ezulwini and I was awed by the strength of the water as it whooshed into Usutu River. He said that the seemingly calm water in the middle of the river ran even deeper than the fierce water fall. His exact words were,

"Remember Manana, it is the calm and silent water that drowns a man not the loud waterfalls." I didn't understand what he meant then because in my mind, I reasoned that you could still fall and crush your head on the rocks underneath the waterfall.

"Baby, we are here." Hlongwane's voice breaks into my thoughts and I smile at him.

I know he's worried about me and I'm trying to assure him that I'm fine. I noticed that all the razor blades are gone from my bathroom. I talk to him whenever I feel suffocated, but I guess he's not taking any chances. He didn't have any nightmares last night, we're both taking baby steps. We find the council hall full and nerves flood me even more.

I've been sitting here listening to them shred my character to that of a young, impetuous and empty minded doll. They made me sit on the floor "with other women" and Hlongwane wasn't impressed. If they think I will hang my head in shame, then clearly, they don't know me. I am staring into their eyes as they speak of me like I didn't grow up in front of their eyes. They won't meet my eyes when they talk about me and I've had to coach myself to breathe to calm myself.

it is now Maloyi's turn to speak and he has been clearing his throat a million times until he looks into my eyes and I give him an unflinching look. He starts talking.

"I served under Sobhuza Dlamini his whole reign and we must all agree that he was the wisest and kindest chief we could have asked for." The grunts of approval comically change with his next words.

"He knew what we needed before we did and if his dying wishes are that we make his younger daughter our chief then I say we follow his leadership as we have always done and surely we won't go wrong."

The roars of disapproval at that are immediate. Shouts of blasphemy, abomination and the wrath of the ancestors fill the council room until the Queen Mother demands silence. That's the one highlight of this meeting, my great-aunt came through for me. Her presence lends me some strength and a mother's comfort.

The Chairman of the Council of Chiefs is also present. The Council of Chiefs is composed of twelve Chiefs drawn from the four regions of the Kingdom appointed by the *iNgwenyama* on a rotational basis. *Babe* was part of the Council and it is also the responsibility of the Council to advise the King on customary issues and any matter relating to or affecting chieftaincy including chieftaincy disputes.

Not that my chieftaincy is in dispute Masomalenhle has made it known that he is not contesting our late father's decision and if looks could kill, he would have died from the glare he received from Zama. My big brother even put in a good word for me and I was touched to learn that he thinks there is *"no one as capable and who loves Maphalaleni and all it stands for as Nomaswazi."* Of course, his kind words were drowned out by the outcry of the people.

I keep hearing how me succeeding my father will anger the ancestors, how displeased the ancestors are at even the notion. Some have predicted drought and severe famine should I ever ascend to his seat. Honestly, it's exhausting how they keep repeating the same thing in different words and voices. Only today I don't have the luxury of tuning out their voices, I'm forced to listen to each comment as snide as it may be.

After what seems like hours later of the back and forth, the Chairman of the Council finally gives me an opportunity to say something. Nerves clog my throat as I get up from the floor. Not an easy feat I must add, my behind feels like someone was throwing stones at it. I say a short prayer reminding *Babe* that he got me into this and begging him to give me the strength to see it through.

My voice as I utter my greetings and salutations comes out shaky and unconvincing. I feel defeated I may as well sit down and hang my head in shame. Then Hlongwane comes to my rescue by chanting my clan names in his sure, commanding voice.

"*NaNkosi, Sidlubula Dledle sika Nobamba, Lokothwayo, Ludonga luka Mavuso, Sidwaba Siluthuli, Mlangeni, Mntungwa, Kunene. Ndlovu ezidl'ekhaya ngokuswela abelusi, Sibhahuza sika Mawawa, Mlangeni, Sobhuza.*" By the time he is done Ntsikelelo, Masomalenhle, my great-aunt and others had joined in and I smile gratefully at him. Just a brief stretch of the lips to show him that he's my rock

"My earliest memories are of my father carrying me on his knees during every council meeting. Even as I grew older and wouldn't want to sit still, he still perched me on his knees and made me listen. I became curious as I grew older and I would ask him questions and he always answered no matter how odd my questions were. He listened to my ideas; from the solar panels, crop rotation and fodder crop." I keep quiet for a moment and look around all these people, most of which benefit from the projects I have mentioned. Yet today they stare at me with resentment.

“To him it didn't matter that I was young and a girl if it was for the good of his people he would at least try. I, at times had the worst ideas and he would patiently tell me why they wouldn't work for our people. Yes, I am young and yes, I am a woman but the love I have for Maphalaleni runs deep in my blood. I offer nothing but a mother's love, I promise to love and nurture our people and preserve their ways while adopting ways that will make us grow. I also don't know why my father chose me, but he saw something in me and I won't let him down."

It's hard to determine from their faces whether they are moved or not and I'm just standing here looking into their eyes. At least now they are meeting my gaze.

"Be that as it may the ancestors will never accept this, it's taboo. We know that the first male in the family is the one to inherit." *Make'* Sebenele, the oldest spinster speaks up while chewing on her snuff then she spits the disgusting stuff next to her.

"Why should we speak for the ancestors let them make their own decision," my head whips to look at Mashila, the traditional healer. He seems unbothered even as murmuring breaks out throughout the hall.

"Mashila stop talking in riddles and tell us what the ancestors have said." Maloyi says impatiently and Mashila ignores him while he keeps drawing circles on the floor. The whole hall is now tense, my eyes seek Hlongwane and he has a fierce scowl on his face and that has me even more on edge.

"It is said that when we are unsure about a leader, that leader must sit on the throne and if it is not theirs, the ancestors will strike them down with lightning." Mashila says slowly not looking up.

Gasps and whispers fill the hall. I am so shocked I find myself sliding back to the floor. Is this their plan? To strike me with lightning? I look at Zama and she has this smirk on her face. Ntsikelelo is restraining Hlongwane, everything is just in turmoil.

I need a sign *Babe,* I silently plead but there is nothing that calms my fear. A whole me struck down by lightning, is this to be my fate? Deep down I know I must go through with this. This is my storm and I can't run away from it and this is my birthright I must fight for it. I clear my throat and stand up again.

"I will do it; I will sit on the throne." My voice comes out calm and certain, but I am anything but calm. A storm is raging within me and I ignore it just as I avoid looking into Hlongwane's eyes. I look instead at my great-aunt and she nods at me. That reassures me somewhat.

Hlongwane is by my side in a minute and much like my disciplinary hearing at Van Gogh, this time he is dragging me out of the hall. I can see from the deep lines on his forehead that he is frustrated and he's not sure what to say, he keeps opening his mouth and closing it.

I let him be mostly because I also don't know what to say to him. *Hey this might be the last time I talk to you before the lightning strikes me down, but I love you ok?* He will strangle me if I even utter those words.

"Swazi I can't lose you, not like this. We can leave right now. You don't need this." Shame my man sounds so scared and I know I'm also shit scared.

I still take his hands in mine and look into his beautiful charcoal eyes. I love his eyes, I love him. He has become my heart and my soul in the short time since we reconnected.

"I love you Hlongwane, so much and nothing can drag me away from you not even lightning." He doesn't even crack a smile, ohkay maybe it's still too soon.

"No more running, remember? This is one fight I have to see to the end, I know I am worthy to be a good leader to my people. Surely the ancestors know this too otherwise *Babe* wouldn't have said they chose me. I need you to stand by me even as I go through this. I'm scared but something deep inside me says I must see this through."

He sighs, a long-suffering sigh then he pulls me into one of his bone crushing embraces. Too soon he releases me and taking my hand walks me back to the hall, to face my fate.

CHAPTER TWENTY-FOUR

Narrated...

The anger, hatred and disgust in her eyes chilled Masomalenhle to the bone and he was shivering even though it was a damp and dreary Swati day. He had always been intimidated by his sister, but it had graduated to fear as they grew older.

"I know that witch has Mashila under her payroll! I should have known that she'd use the greatest seer in all of Maphalaleni." Zamaswazi was speaking so fast even froth was coming out of the corners of her mouth.

"We were all there Zama. We saw her being led to the chair set in the middle of the yard in nothing but animal skin. We were all expecting lightning to come from the angry clouds, but instead a bright beam of sunlight streamed through the rain and shone on Nomaswazi. Just accept, she is the Chosen one." Masomalenhle spoke up and Zamaswazi was shocked that he even dared to speak back at her.

Zamaswazi's face turned into a hideous sneer. She raised her hand as if to strike him but this time he didn't flinch. He looked into her eyes daring her to lay her hand on him. She was surprised and lowered her hand, she could tell that she had to change her strategy.

"Come on Lenhle, we both know it is you who is supposed to take over that throne and with her out of the way we can contest Babe's will and get our inheritance. Aren't you tired of living in near poverty? Pretty soon the banks will repossess even your house and cars. Help me get what is rightfully yours." Her voice could be quite persuasive when she wanted it to be like the serpent in the Garden of Eden. She tried hard to cover the desperation in her eyes and smiled winningly at her wimp of a brother.

"Aren't you tired of living with all this bitterness Zama? Our mother killed her mother, but Swazi has put that behind her. Why don't you just let it go? Manana is our little sister, for how long should we hold on to our mother's grudge. I am done fighting battles that aren't mine. It's time I grew up and become my own man and father to my children. You should too." He said firmly, not swayed by her manipulative tongue.

Zamaswazi hissed fiercely and the glass of gin and tonic she had been drinking went flying across the room breaking into countless fragments as it hit the wall.

"Are you crazy?!" Lenhle's voice was shaking, the crazy gleam in his sister's eyes terrified him and the glass missed his ears only by a tiny distance. He heard it wheeze past him and he feared for his life.

"You know nothing of being a man! I have looked out for you since our mother died. I have prepared you to take over when that selfish man who sired us finally died and this is how you repay me? By rolling over and saying you are letting go because she is the Chosen one? Who chose her? When the hell will we ever be chosen huh? Who chooses us Masomalenhle!"

Zamaswazi was a woman deranged and she kept pacing frantically mumbling things to herself that Lenhle couldn't make head nor tail of. He stayed rooted to the spot watching rage and bitterness twist his sister's beautiful face into an ugly mask of hatred. He wanted to reach out to her, but he was afraid.

She was like a ticking time bomb. Ever since they returned from the council meeting she seemed unhinged, her eyes had a wild look. The froth appeared at the corner of her mouth kept bubbling and Masomalenhle just watched her vent. He wasn't a confrontational person and all his life he had listened to what his elder sister said but he was tired of the plotting and the hatred. He wanted to start over his life.

"I need to be somewhere..." his voice was hesitant and pleading like a child pleading with a parent to go outside and play. She stopped her pacing and stared at him with a look of pure hatred.

"You're going to her, aren't you?" She pointed an accusing finger at him and he couldn't deny her accusation, so he hung his head instead. Zama felt betrayed by the last person she thought would always be by her corner. She uttered a mirthless laugh that sounded like a choking hyena.

"*Make* was right, that girl and her mother are witches and now she has even bewitched you. I mean how else could she have stayed married that long to Babe without giving him a child and now even her daughter is also doing the same to that poor man. But it's fine, I see right through her and I will save you all from the clutches of that barren witch." That wild look again was in her eyes and Masomalenhle was scared for Swazi, maybe he should warn her and her husband he thought.

Without uttering another word, Zama picked up her new season Valentino blue rock stud spike bag and let herself out banging the door loudly. Her eyes landed on her Range Rover that the bank could be repossessing any moment now and the hatred she had for Nomaswazi solidified.

It was time she got rid of Nomaswazi, the way her mother got rid of her father's favourite wife. The only person who could help her now was Nkambule, her mother's witchdoctor. She checked her purse and she had just enough money to cover the consultation fee and diesel. She drove to his worn down hut which was at the edge of the Maphalaleni forest, hidden from the rest of the village.

Her eyes only smarted for a while from the smoke in the dingy room, then they had grown accustomed to the semi-darkness as they had over the years. She no longer shivered when she saw the numerous amulets around Nkambule's neck and arms. The first time she had seen the human hand on his neck she had thrown up and her mother had scolded her and made her clean up her own vomit. She had been six then.

Now even when Nkambule's eyes rolled into his head until only the whites appeared, and froth bubbled from his mouth as his body violently convulsed in a fit of sorts, she wasn't scared. She impatiently waited for him to be done and tell her that, the witch would be dead by morning. The trance lasted longer than usual intensifying the putrid smell in the room crowded with all sorts of portions and animal parts.

Zama fought hard not to gag as Nkambule spit out the froth laced with blood. His eyes were popped out and eerily white like he had just seen a ghost, which in all essence he probably had.

"Blood... blood covers her," his voice which was usually a booming thunder had shrunk into a thin wasp. From experience Zama refrained from questioning him and waited for him to say more.

"A life for a life. Her mother gave up her life for hers and whoever tries to take hers will pay with their life." Zama become impatient then and broke the cardinal rule.

"But you managed to take the mother's life away surely there has to be a way!" she cried out in frustration. Nkambule glared at her and gone was the confident sneer that seemed perpetually plastered on his face.

"I dare not touch her and if you knew what's good for you, you wouldn't either. Come, I can make you a powerful love portion and you can make any rich man lust after you." Zama clicked her tongue in annoyance but still took the portion, she had wasted her last money going there.

Her last option was if the King refused to appoint Nomaswazi. As per custom once a chief has been selected by *lusendvo* then the matter is deliberated by the King who is the one who appoints chiefs. So even though the council meeting ended well everything was now balancing on the

King's verdict. Chances of the King's verdict coming out in favour of that brat were high, the *INdlovukati* had been present at her deliberation for crying out loud.

Maybe she should use the love portion on that brat's husband. That would surely break Swazi's spirit. After all *she* should have been married to the powerful Hlongwane heir because *she* was older. But of course, her father had bended every rule to make sure that his favourite child had the best of everything, while she had been chosen for a mere chief!

She discarded the love portion idea because she might use it on the wrong brother just as she had been impregnated by the wrong twin. The sex had been the best she had ever had but she was done settling for second best while that witch's daughter lived lavishly.

Ironic how she had gotten a foreclosure notice on her house that very morning while her brat of her sister was living it up in that huge arse homestead that they were kicked out of. Night was finally encroaching, and Zama looked at the place she used to call home in disgust. When Swazi died she would use the love portion on her widower. All this will belong to me, she thought as she rubbed the chill from her hands.

……

She had had the rest of the afternoon to come up with a plan of action and she was satisfied with what she had come up with. No one would suspect she was responsible, and she would cry during her funeral; the way she cried for that worthless man who fathered them. She was parked next to the *nchitsamuti* tree. Checking for any movement outside, she stealthily opened the car door when she was satisfied that there was no one, she approached the yard.

Stealthily, she made her way to the gleaming Range Rover that Nomaswazi now drove. The moon shone and was reflected on the bonnet of the car. Zama tried opening it but of course it was locked, and she didn't have the key to open.

Think Zama, she chided herself silently and looked around for something to open the bonnet with.

She returned to her car and opened the boot, she impatiently discarded everything until her hand landed on a crowbar. It was perfect. She returned to the other car and tried as quietly as possible to open the bonnet. Her hands were clammy and her heart pounding in her chest, but the gods were with her because she managed to open the bonnet. She stifled her excitement and wasn't sure what the purpose of the wires was.

Taking out her tweezers from her bag, she pondered which wire to cut. She had to cut the ones which won't be easily detected and there was no way that stupid Swazi would check her engine before driving the car. She finally found one wire and quickly cut it then cut another just to be sure and hid them underneath the other wires. Admiring her handiwork, she slowly lowered the bonnet making sure to be as quiet as possible.

“Beautiful car isn’t it?” Zama almost jumped out of her skin when she heard the quiet baritone.

Swiveling around she came face to face with one of the Hlongwane twins. He was casually resting his tall length against the door of a hut not far from her. Zama wondered whether it was her worthless sister’s husband or her babies’ father. She wondered how long he had been there and had he seen her cutting the wires?

Darting her tongue across her suddenly patchy lips, she looked around wondering if she could make a run for it.

“Thinking of going somewhere?” he purred as he untangled his long limbs from the hut and prowled towards her.

Zama broke into a run but didn’t get that far, after five laps she was hauled from the ground and thrust over his shoulders. She began sweating in earnest and searched her mind for a story to cover up her crime. It was hard to think while she was held upside down. Without any warning she was set on her feet and she swayed unsteadily on her feet. He made no effort to steady her.

In the darkness his face looked emotionless and the

moon cast part of his face into the shadow. His eyes were glowing, and his stance was rigid. Zama tried steadying herself by holding on to him and he shrugged her hands from him.

"I was just checking... checking the new car." Her voice was scratchy and hesitant.

His white teeth flashed in the moonlight sending a chill down Zama's spine. She was trapped she realized and for once in her life she wasn't sure how she was going to wiggle herself out of this one.

"Is it? Then I'm sure you are dying to go on a test drive." His voice held no emotion whatsoever and Zama wanted to scream for help. As if he could hear her thoughts, she felt something cold against her cheek.

"We are going to do this the easy way, utter even the smallest scream and I will blow your brains out. I will bury your body in the closed mines. Don't worry no one will mourn you or search for you. Now move." Zama felt a warm wetness between her legs, she had wet herself.

"Please, I have babies. They still need their mother. I promise I won't come anywhere near Swazi again. I will disappear, anything you want." She was begging for her life and crying piteously.

"My children don't need you to poison them. They have a mother and you want her dead. Now get in the car before I shoot you." The gun was corked still against her cheek and she had no choice but to get in the car.

He handed her the car keys with the gun still pointed at her. She hesitated before putting the key into the ignition. For the first time in a long time, Zama offered a prayer that the car wouldn't start. But the engine purred to life and she had no choice except to change gears and slide out of the driveway.

The car was driving smoothly, maybe she cut wires which weren't important, she comforted herself. She reached the gate smoothly and drove out. Just as she was about to reach her car she realized there was a car following her. Zama panicked, maybe these people were coming to finish her off. She stepped on the gas and the car started flashing lights and warning her that something was wrong with her engine.

Zama tried braking, but the brakes weren't working and the car tailing her was catching up on her. The car suddenly veered off the narrow road, tires screeching as Zama tried unsuccessfully to turn the steering wheel. Then the car flew off the road, flipping over as it went down the hillside. Zama would have been flung out of the window had it not been for the seatbelt and the emergency airbags.

When the car finally came to a standstill, landing on its roof, tires in the air Zama could smell blood mingled with the smell of diesel and smoke. All the windows were smashed, and some had cut her face, but she was still breathing. She tried to take off the seatbelt, but she couldn't move.

"Help! Help!" she screamed but her cries were swallowed by the heavy darkness. She tried harder to move but her legs were stuck. Then she heard a crackling sound before the car burst into flames. Desperate now, she tried to get out of the seat, but she was trapped by the seatbelt and the airbag.

A blood curdling scream cut across the night as flames licked Zama's flesh, melting her suit against her skin. The screams continued until the smoke got too much and filled up her lungs and she was choking on her own blood and the smell of her burning flesh. No coherent thought formed in her mind as she breathed her last pain-filled breath.

CHAPTER TWENTY-FIVE

As the car comes to a standstill, nerves attack me and my hands feel clammy. I feel my hand being squeezed and I look up into a charcoal whirlpool. I draw strength from the love and pride shimmering through his eyes. I take his hand with courage and step out of the car.

"I'm dazzled by your beauty," he says seductively against my ear and it sends ripples all the way down there. He smirks when he notices my body's reaction to his proximity. Tease!

We are standing at the entrance of Mandvulo Grand Hall in the palace. His hand on the small of my back feels intimate and proprietary, turning up the heat. It doesn't help that he's dazzling in a dark grey tuxedo, his beard freshly groomed. Those supple lips puckered in concentration as he scans the room for Khanyisa.

I spot Khanyi as she rushes to us. She's a vision in a red A-line gown with a high scooped neckline. I think its demure until I get a peek of her lithe leg through the mid-thigh slit and as I accept her embrace my hands fall on her bare back. Her face beat is tastefully done; she even has a silver crown on her artfully coiled afro. Her scarlet lips part in a wide smile as she inspects me, holding me at arm's length.

"Wow cousin, you clean up really good. Is that a Balmain gown?" I smile at her gushing compliments.

I ended up settling for a proper ball gown, it's black with a sweetheart neckline and a puffed-out skirt. Because all black is forbidden in royal terrain, it has a silver belt and gemstones all over the bodice. Hlongwane picked out a beautiful grey stone necklace piece with matching drop earrings. The stylist also manipulated my unruly hair into a sophisticated coiffure.

"I had to look the part cuz," I say as she kisses me on both my cheeks.

I've had to accept that Khanyi is very affectionate and she somehow always manages to draw me from my shell. I watch as she hugs and kisses Hlongwane's cheeks. He has a soft spot for her and their easy relationship is refreshing.

□

"Don't worry you're totally going to crush it tonight!" I wish I had her overflowing enthusiasm and take life by the horns mentality. I'm still a work in progress.

The last State Banquet I went to, was the SADC one as *Babe*'s date. I was 17 then and it had felt like I had transformed into a princess. Today I am standing here as the chief of Maphalaleni and I feel *Babe*'s presence so strongly. It's like he's right next to me in a rented tux. *Stop it Swazi,* I chide myself as I feel the tears welling in my eyes. He's been gone for a little over a year now but the pain is still fresh, I wonder if it ever goes away.

"You did a great job," I say quietly to Khanyi as she links our arms together. She was the one responsible for organizing the banquet.

"Say the word and I will immediately start planning your wedding. Scratch that, I will immediately execute the plans I have for your wedding in this very room." She states in a dramatic stage whisper circling her free hand across the ball room. I can't help but laugh at her.

"Nice try, still not happening." She pouts prettily and mutters something about stubbornness that I don't quite catch.

The décor is tastefully understated with vases of red roses on the interlinked tables. The tables are lined on both sides of the red carpet which will also serve as the dance floor later. The crockery and cutlery are all gold and gleaming. Hlongwane opens a blue and gold chair for me and I sit gracefully. I don't really feel like going around the room socializing, rubbing shoulder with Swati elite before my speech.

My name is called out sooner than I expected and I find myself alone in the podium facing everyone. I smile at their polite applause.

"It has been a year since I have been bestowed the honour of serving *iNgwenyama* under Maphalaleni. In that year I turned my father's house, well technically its mine now, into a home where the misfortunate can find refuge. Girls kicked out from their homes for being pregnant, we take them in. Young brides-to-be whom we managed to rescue from child marriage. Albinos like Hlosi who are unwanted or have special needs that their families can't afford, we take them in. The shelter provides soup kitchen once a week and those hungry can come and eat even though they don't stay there." I wait for the applause to simmer down before I continue talking.

"At first, my advisors were vehemently against this move because they said it encouraged children to misbehave and fall pregnant. That families were right in disciplining their children any way they saw fit. I told them that as a mother I cannot eat and live well while one of my children is cast out and suffering. Instead of banishing them into the unknown, we take them in and have instructors who teach them skills to take care of themselves and their children. We have organizations sponsoring our home and an adoption agency which helps girls who feel they want their children to have better lives with other families. Occasionally a baby is dumped just outside our gates and we take them in.

It's still early and people are still warming up to the idea of the home, but it has done some good for those who have come to us. One of our wards is called Nomcebo. When Nomcebo first came to us she had been heavily pregnant, malnutritioned and with *sjambok* marks on her back. She didn't utter a single word until the baby was born and she asked for it to be put up for adoption. Her baby was one of the first to be adopted and she is beginning to find her voice again." I catch my breath, pleased by how everyone seems to be taking my words in.

"We all have a collective duty as leaders and influential people of eSwatini to nurture our youth and protect our children and women from abuse of any kind. Yes, we have internationally funded organizations but the main burden, the onus of protecting our subjects lies with us. May we find it in our hearts to serve them with courage, kindness and most importantly accountability. Please feel free to write out a check towards the hospital we are intending to build in Maphalaleni. Thank you." I catch my great-aunt's eye, and she nods her head at me in approval.

"Your father is so proud of you, as am I." Hlongwane says when I get back to my seat and that's all the validation I need.

……

"Khanyi tells me that you are refusing to marry that poor boy," *iNdlovukati* says and I wish Khanyi was close so that I could strangle her.

I finally got a moment alone with my great-aunt and it's an ambush. Hlongwane may have asked me to marry him a couple of times, once in front of Khanyi and I told him I wasn't ready to take that leap yet.

"It's not that I don't want to marry him, it's just that after last time and our botched lobola negotiations, I just think it's better if we stay the way we are." I wish I can look away from the wisdom and understanding in her eyes but that would be rude of me.

"My baby, you can't live in fear of the past repeating itself or things not working out. Everything works out as it should in the end and all you can do is grab each moment and live it to the fullest. That boy loves you. I may have had my doubts about him when I first met you and him, but the way he stares at you and the way he has stood by you assures me that your father chose well." She says looking over my shoulder.

I turn my head in the direction of her gaze and I find Hlongwane's eyes on me. His stare so intense that it's as if everyone else in the room doesn't exist. Those gorgeous charcoal whirlpools still create butterflies in my stomach. He maintains eye contact while he's moving from across the room until he's right in front of me.

"Sorry your majesty but may I steal this beauty for a moment." He says while bowing in front of my great-aunt.

"With my blessing, son." She responds while looking at me with eyes full of meaning.

"Let's dance," I suggest to Hlongwane and he takes my hand and leads us to the dance floor.

We've come so far and boy am I glad I ended up in hospital and had to undergo compulsory therapy. The truth is we were both drowning in our issues but we hadn't been raised to know that meant we needed to talk to someone. Had you asked me two years ago what I thought of therapy I would have told you that's a white people thing. Therapy has left us exposed and vulnerable to each other and forced us to own our truth. Some days are still bad but most days are great.

"How are you feeling on the anniversary of her death?" Hlongwane asks as he makes me lean into him and rest my head on his chest. This question has been a constant in our therapy sessions ever since Zamaswazi burnt to ashes in my car.

"I'm making peace with it. Even after everything I still longed for her approval and acceptance as my sister but I hope she's finally at peace." I tell him honestly.

Zamaswazi's death came as an unpleasant shock to all of us. Till today, no one knows why she was driving my car and yet she left hers under a tree. No one knows why she drove down the mountainside causing the car to overturn and explode. The police suspect that she might have been drunk or high on drugs. The news of her death was especially hard on Lenhle but it also brought us closer, we only have each other now.

......

I look up at Lenhle with the sun dancing on his hair and that troublesome lump lodges itself inside my throat. His shoulders are no longer stooped but broader since he took up the gym and he has never looked like *Babe* more. He takes my hand and tucks it into the croak of his arm, an action similar to when *Babe* was walking me down the aisle all those years ago.

Only this time I don't have any blinkers in my eyes or expectations of a happily ever after. Instead of the numerous people who graced my wedding, there's only a handful of people beaming at me as we walk down the sandy aisle. Makhulu, Khanyi and Nokwanda are teary while my great-aunt looks like a peacock is lodged in her chest. Ntsikelelo is looking dashing next to Mpho. While Melusi is standing next to my man. Aphi is trying to keep the notorious twins in check but now that they have Labo as well as Lenhle's two daughters and two sons in tow, they are reigning terror.

This time I wasn't sucked into a body shaper or burdened by the weight of a ball gown. I am barefoot in a flowing ivory gown. The dress clings to my girls, bringing them out in all their ebony glory. The ankle bracelet Hlongwane gave to me when I told him I was ready for us to go all the way, twinkles delicately as I move. The hairstylist managed to delicately thread in real flowers into my unruly mass of coarse hair. The golden hoops that my great-aunt gave me shimmer brightly in the sun.

I catch full-blown pictures of me during Umhlanga dance, one full-length and one close up, back when I was seventeen in banners behind the priest. I look glorious with my bare chest even though I was at my biggest then. My eyes tear up at his gesture, this man has been telling me I'm beautiful ever since we reconnected and today for the first time, I believe him. The tears fall when next to one banner there's another of *Babe* walking me down the aisle at our first wedding.

We've reached him and he wipes my tears with his thumbs before shaking Lenhle's hand and taking mine. I barely register what the priest is saying, something about wives submitting to their husbands and husbands loving their wives the same way Jesus loved the church. All I see is Hlongwane and the look of love in his face. It is now time for our vows and I go first.

"Hlongwane, Ntunjwa ka Langa, Mahamba kancane Sokodi, Mthiyane, Ndwandwe, Zikode, Mabhuqa, Ngwane," his eyes are still trained steadfastly on mine. "Thank you for being the anchor that my heart finds rest in. For the longest time I thought I hated you and that you made me hate all men. Truth is I could never hate you, hating you would be like hating a part of me. I was hurt but forgiving you is something my heart did before I acknowledged what I feel for you. I look forward to learning and seeing life through your eyes, to feel what you feel, to be your home and your lifelong companion. To bear you children and raise them with you."

"NaDlamini wami, NaNkosi, Sidlubula Dledle sika Nobamba, Lokothwayo, Ludonga luka Mavuso, Sidwaba Siluthuli, Mlangeni, Sobhuza, Mntungwa, Kunene. Every step I've taken in life no matter what direction I took, would still have led me to this moment right here with you. I'm glad I walked away when I did because I wasn't ready to love you right. I'm ready now to forsake all others for you, I'm ready to put in the work until I am worthy of your love. I am ready to love, honour and cherish you like the queen that you are."

□

He stops and just looks at me for a while until the priest clears his throat and he continues.

"I want to be the one you turn to when it gets too much, I want to be the one to wake you up and bathe you every morning. I want my nights to be filled with your soft snores and my days filled with your loud laughter. I want to give you the world NaNkosi but please be patient with me. I promise to love, honour, protect you with my life and cherish you until I take my dying breath." When he's done there is applause and cat whistles from our audience and we end up laughing. The priest finally gets to say what he should have said a long time ago.

"With the power vested in me, I now pronounce you husband and wife. You may kiss the bride."

He grins as he takes his sweet time claiming my lips. The sun is shining through his irises, twin ambers of blissful promises. My train wreck saved my life.

CHAPTER TWENTY-SIX

I've prepared a scented bath for us, in record time and she's between my legs, Zikode nestling painfully against her butt cheeks. Tonight is all about her, putting her satisfaction above mine. I wash her back while throwing tiny kisses down her spine, her shivers and the moans escaping her mouth cause Zikode to throb painfully, but I ignore my own needs and massage her girls over the lather of bubbles.

She's leaning against me giving me full access to her body and I take advantage of that and explore her body thoroughly. By the time I reach her folds, she's a shivering mess but I take my time giving more attention to her core. Swazi whimpers as I massage her Yoni and that sound shoots straight to Zikode, this is pure torture.

I cut short our bath and dry both of us before carrying her to our bed and laying her gently on the bed.

"Lie on your stomach baby and put on that blindfold," *she* looks at me questioningly, but does as I instructed without uttering a word.

I place some pillows underneath her chest and urge her to relax. I pour some coconut oil onto my palm and rub it against my palms to warm it before I massage it into her shoulder blades. "Relax for me baby," her shoulders are tied in knots. I want to worship every spot in her body until she becomes putty in my hands.

I massage her from neck to toes before coming back for a butt massage. She's completely relaxed now even purring as I continue fighting not to just have my way with her delectable behind. I can't resist spanking her generous butt and she whimpers. I flip her over and I harden even more at the sight of her breasts.

I pour more coconut oil and massage her front as thoroughly as I massaged her back adding random kisses on her neck and sucking her nipples because I just can't help myself. Her eyes are now tiny with arousal and that's what I'm all about tonight, reducing her to an ecstatic mess. She tastes like coconut oil and pineapples as I lower my head between her legs to suck and lick her like my life depends on it.

"Ntsika, baby...love..." I chuckle against her folds at the fevered way she is calling my name. I'm relentless until I feel her tensing under me and she screams something close to "I love you!" as she comes undone from my tongue.

"Ntsika!" this time she calls out my name in pain.

I tried being as gentle as I can but the moment Zikode pushed through her barrier she tenses up in pain. I try to shut it out but the picture of that girl thrashing underneath me as I clumsily thrust past her barrier floods my mind. Her screams of pain which turned into piteous cries haunt my eardrums. Her tears turn into blood.

"Hlongwane look at me Zikode. It's me, Nomaswazi. Look at me Ntsika." Her voice and her gentle touch bring me back and I'm clutching her to my chest, still inside her.

"I'm disgusting Swazi, how could you even give yourself up to me knowing what I did. She was screaming so horribly but I still got an erection. I..." Swazi puts her finger on my mouth and I can't stop shivering.

"Look at me," she commands and I look into her eyes. Instead of disgust and resentment there is so much love in her eyes.

"You have to forgive yourself now, I want this. I want you. I love you so much and you deserve all of my love." She says in-between kisses and I feel Zikode stirring back to life again.

"Let me in and only focus on me. Keep your eyes on mine. It's just you and me. Feel how my body trembles at your touch. Feel how hot I am for you." Lord! Her heat is almost my undoing.

You'd swear I'm the virgin. Only the Lord knows how many women I have slept with, I never kept count. This is different. I have longed for this woman for so long, I have had countless erotic fantasies about her that it feels like I've already been inside her. Yet being inside her is far from what I envisioned it feeling like. I feel like I will combust from her heat at just my first stroke. She opens herself up to me and I thrust in gently and carefully until Zikode is buried to the hilt inside her heat.

"Don't close your eyes, look at me." I see the fiery lust in her eyes and it burns my soul, brandishing me as hers. I slowly ease out of her and thrust into her and I see the pain that she tries to shield me from.

"*Ncesi* baby," I kiss away the tear at the corner of her eye and hold still, not taking my eyes off hers.

I thrust in again and this time I see a dart of pleasure mingling with the pain in her eyes. I thrust deeper and a soft moan of pleasure escapes her parted lips and her irises are dilating. I thrust deeper and harder and her irises are drawing me into the web of her soul. I thrust again and the slight tremor of her hips and the wanton pleasure in her eyes tip me over and I have a sudden blinding orgasm, one which sears my soul and brings tears to my eyes.

I can't remember the last time I nutted so quickly and yet I'd sworn to myself that tonight is all about her. She seems dazed and confused, I feel like such a tool. She kisses me so sweetly and I feel a bit better, we still have the whole night. I can do better.

......

I had to get Swazi out of the house early because we have one surprise stop before jetting out for our honeymoon. We left everyone at our Durban beach house, they wanted to accompany us to the airport but I declined. Nomaswazi keeps stealing glances at me, crossing and uncrossing her legs. I laugh silently, I think someone might be getting addicted to Zikode. Let's just say I more than made up for my first run and I had her screaming all the way to touchdown. Thank whoever invented soundproofing rooms.

We pull up at the studio and she looks at me expecting answers but I'm not giving her any. They are expecting us, and Swazi looks bewildered as they drag her to do her make-up. Her eyes find mine and I just smile at her. I find the director of the studio with my parcel that Sean, my assistant, dropped off.

One of the photographers is teaching me how to take pictures and the best angles to use. This is one photoshoot I must do on my own, I can't have anyone gawking over my wife. I go to give her the parcel and she takes out the pieces and eyes me suspiciously.

"I'm no longer a virgin Hlongwane," she whispers not wanting the make-up crew, who are discreetly standing a little distance from us, to hear.

"I know that *nkosatana,*" I say tilting her chin and she's already blushing, "but can you just do it for me? It will be my wedding present." I add my rare smile and I know she won't say no.

"Fine," she mumbles biting her lower lip and I have to clear my throat before informing her that she should wear a robe on top and they will bring her to the room where we are going to have the shoot.

My breath hitches thirty minutes later when she unties the robe and lets it slide to the floor. She has lost a lot of weight from when her father was sick leading up to his funeral and her depression after Zamaswazi's death. I can't wait to feed her back to her previous weight. The morning runs have toned her curves which are still visible, and her legs appear longer. My favourite breasts are still full and perky with their thick dark nipples. It's one thing to look at a portrait of her in *Indlamu* and its quite another actually looking at her in person.

Her scars have faded and look like tiny marks on her thighs, but they take nothing from the perfection of her ebony skin. The lighting in the room lends her skin a golden glow making it shine and glimmer in a rich dark chocolate colour. She's nervously covering her breasts and rubbing the scar on her wrist.

"Look at me baby, you're the most beautiful creation on this earth and I just want to capture your beauty. Trust me ok?" It's funny how bold she can be at times and at times she hides behind her timid shell.

Slowly she relaxes and even smiles when I remind her of how mean she was to me that day at the car park of Van Gogh. She's laughing and throwing her head back when I mention her throwing up all over my back as I was carrying her in that dreadful leather dress. I can tell she's also enjoying the shoot now. All this time I'm clicking away. At every angle my wife is breathtaking. I'm grateful that my father chose her for me and even though I almost blew it, she still took me back.

We manage to catch the flight from Durban to Johannesburg, where we take the almost fourteen hours' flight from O.R Tambo International Airport to Velana International Airport. The long flight is worth it when I catch sight of the aerial view of the place from our chopper ride. We are in one of the largest private islands in North Male Atoll; the breathtaking One and Only Reethi Rah Maldives. They could have been more adventurous with the name but what remains is the place is heavenly.

Then the villas spread like crow feet in the water with their thatched roofs did not prepare me for the opulence of the villas inside. The high roofs create an airy and relaxed atmosphere the moment you step in and the earth colours with a dash of white and yellow here and there in the décor give the place a warm homely feeling. The villas remind me of my Bangkok project which was a mighty huge success, it set my company up for life and made me afford this costly honeymoon.

It's worth every penny to see Nomaswazi this relaxed in a very skimpy bikini while soaking in the sun next to me. We are both looking up at the brilliant blue sky, no cloud is in sight and it's the most majestic sight. Underneath us the water moves quietly in shades of turquoise, teal and indigo and it feels like it's just the two of us in the middle of the ocean. Here we're free from our responsibilities and our demons are firmly locked away, we are free to fully love each other.

......

She's up to something, I can just tell from the nervous

energy that she's emitting. She takes a deep breath and brings out a blindfold from behind her back. I try to untie her robe but she quickly swats my hand and forces me to wear the blindfold. My curiosity is piqued but I play along. She takes my hand and leads me somewhere, I can't see a thing I can only hear her heightened breathing and thudding heartbeat. She's now standing in front of me, her lush curves mashing beautifully with my hard physique.

"Touch me," her voice is confident and commanding.

Confusion, excitement and a frisson of excitement dart through my body awakening all my senses. The satin gown has come off and all my prying fingers can feel is lace. I tentatively move my large hands straight to her breasts, my weakness. My long fingers trail the half cup bra which barely covers her excited, engorged nipples and from which her girls spilled out enticingly. I rub the lace on her nipples and the friction jolted a painful current straight to my groin.

Her breathing is noisy and her head is now resting on my shoulder and my hands are massaging and teasing the flesh barely covered by the lace. I finally let go off her girls and allow my hands to explore further downwards.

"Tell me what you are seeing in your mind," her voice has changed from commanding to breathy showing how affected she also is by my touch.

"All I see is you. Standing before me, glorious in lace. I can see your breasts straining out of the lace begging me to free them. I see your tiny waist making way for your heavenly buns. I see..." my voice falters when my hands come in contact with her exposed butt. I choke at the mental image in my mind and I can't stand the torture anymore.

I rip off the blindfold and the image I'm staring at in the full length mirror in front of us, is one that will stay in my mind forever. Nomaswazi is standing there in the Love Thyself ensemble I bought for her when we first went to Durban and it fits her perfectly. What's more striking is the confidence with which she's wearing it. We've come full circle and I realize now that we are both facilitating each other's growth. I know, sometimes it feels like Donna now resides in my head.

I wait for the guilt to kick in or the self-loathing but all I feel is hot-blooded lust. I groan and bite the sensitive skin between her shoulder blade. She shudders in pure pleasure. This is one woman I wouldn't mind pleasuring my whole life, not for atonement but because pleasuring her gives me so much satisfaction and pride.

"Like what you see?" she almost purrs and I pause my onslaught long enough to respond.

"I love what I see." Then I proceed to show her just how much I love it by worshipping every inch of her body without removing the lace. I want to brand my touch all over her body the same way her love is branded on my soul.

My heart. My Nomaswazi.

□

THE END

ACKNOWLEDGMENTS

I suck at acknowledgments because I'm always scared I may omit someone, but here goes. To my parents Jerome and Nobuhle Khumalo, thank you for always allowing me to find and go my way even when its different from what you envisioned for me.

My partner, Mthabisi Nkomo, thank you for always investing in my dreams and never trying to change me. Most importantly thank you for giving me the most adorable daughter, Kataleya Thingo. Thingo thank you for being my motivation and keeping me company while I write.

To my editorial team, Thembi Mazibuko and Dzikamani Ncube thank you for taking the time out of your busy schedules to go through the first edition of Hlongwane and Swazi's story. Thembi, thank you for making me fall in love with Hlongwane. My little brother, Ashton Ryan Mzobanzi Khumalo, thank you for allowing me to read the story out loud to you and helping me with research to make it more believable. To my cover girl, Siphiwe Hlongwane, thank you for allowing me to use your pictures, they were my inspiration.

Lynn Gasa, your honesty is what I value most in our friendship, thank you for always pushing me to be better. Khosi Nkanyezi Buthelezi, ah my guiding Star, where do I even begin. You were only supposed to proof read the story but because you always pour your heart into everything you do, you ended up as my doula through the rebirth of Nomaswazi. The marathon work you put into helping me strip down and make sense of the flow of the story, I can never thank you enough.

To my Distribution team at Protea, thank you for always going above and beyond to ensure that these books are perfect and in every imaginable shelf. Phil West I know I probably gave you a few grey hair with this book, thank you all the same. Leigh-Anne thank you for pushing this book.

To my cover designer, Steve (West Park Design) thank you for doing a stellar job and Takalani M thank you for always being so open to share information with me.

To the family I have made on Facebook, my Mo 'gels, my Harvard wives club, my BTC book club, BBB book club, the Bear family and those who follow my personal page. I'd need another book to thank each and every one of you individually. Thank you for making me believe in my craft and for giving me purpose and vision. I am nothing without your support, your shares and the daily laughs. I appreciate you.

TRANSLATION PAGE

Babe (Father)
"*nkhomo*" (cow)
Umhlanga (Reed dance)
lesibumbu sakhe sati wonke emapipi aseMbabane (she is the village bicycle)
"*Umhle NaDlamini ngkufitela inhlanhla lenhle...*" (You look beautiful NaDlamini, I wish you all the best)
Ndvodzana (Son)
mbonile umakoti wakami (Did you see my daughter-in-law)
Umakoti wakami yena?" (And my daughter-in-law?)
Skoni sawubona, unjani?" (Greetings)
Ngikhona babe, (I'm fine father)
Vosho (dance style)
Makhulu (Granny)
mfondini. (guy)
nkosatana (princess)
"*Ngiyacolisa naNkosi*." (I sincerely apologize using her clan name)
Nkhosi! (Laawd!)
Angilufuni lolusito lwakho!" (I don't want your help!)
Balance me real quick here (Help me understand)
umkhaya (Experts)
sitambu nemabhotjisi (samp and beans)
ngicela ube wami (please be mine)
Ngicela umukele lutsandvo lwami (Please accept my love)
Ng'yakuncenga (I'm begging you)
Indvuna (The Chief)
Inkhundla (Constituency)
Indlamu (traditional Swati wear)
lusiba (feather)
Akulotjolwa intfombi kulotjolwa umfati (the bride price is paid for a woman who is legally bound in marriage and not for a single woman)

Nomaswazi

Nkhosi (C Ngikudzinga eceleni kwami sonkhe sikhatsi (I need you next to me always)
Zikode wakho yakutsandza yeva? (Your man loves you, ok?)
Make(mother)
iSishwala (thick porridge)
iNdlovukati (The Queen Mother)
Inkhundla (Assembly)
I khant! (Cannot deal)
lihiya (traditional Cloth)
panga (machete)
linchitsamuti kwenu (a tree near your homestead)
Sawubona nhlitiyo yami (hello my heart)
ungumake webantfu besiSwati (you are the mother of the Swati)
Ndlovu ezidl'ekhaya ngokuswela abelusi (clan praises)
Abo Dlamini o Lokothwayo, bo Mlangeni, Sobhuza, Mntungwa, Kunene bayengibita (the Dlamini ancestors are calling me.)
Nkhosi, Dlamini, wena wekunene (the elder sings his praise names)
Hamba kahle Ndlovu ezidl'ekhaya ngokuswela abelusi, uyidlalile indzima yakho walucedza lubanga lwakho. Sengiso sekutsi siyolahla leLilangeni. (Go well, you played your part. It is time now to go and lay him to rest)
Imbongi (Poet)
iBandla lami (My council of advisors)
iNgwenyama (King)
Ncesi (Sorry)